THE

CONFLUENCE

a novel

William L. Domme

THE CONFLUENCE

© 2015 William L. Domme

Cover design by William L. Domme

ISBN 978-0692403532

Every animal has enough brain to tan its own hide.

— Godwin Merritt

confluence [kon-floo-*uh* ns][i]

noun

1. a flowing together of two or more streams, rivers, or the like: *the confluence of the Missouri and Mississippi rivers.*
2. a coming together of people or things; concourse.

1375-1425; late Middle English (< Middle French) < Late Latin confluentia

kill [kil][ii]

noun

1. a channel; creek; stream; river: used especially in place n ames: *Kill Van Kull, Catskill, Sawyerskill*
2. to deprive of life in any manner; cause the death of; slay.

1660-1670 Americanism; < Dutch kil, Middle Dutch kille channel

Chapter 1.

Up in the Sawatch Range in Colorado, Echo Cliff's rugged face dominated the ridge above the tree line and looked down on the gentle saddleback that narrowed into the gorge where Cut Creek turned to a quick running mountain stream flanked with dense stands of towering lodgepole and ponderosa pine. The cliff's sheer wall could be glassed with a little effort as far as Butte, the resurrected boomtown the Cut Creek Pass silver mine almost singlehandedly brought back to life. Godwin Merritt rode his red roan appaloosa, Creasy, down from his sprawling ranch which sat higher on up across Cut Creek from his neighbor's cozy little log cabin. Godwin watched the striped hooves as the stallion trampled the wild winterfat that had overtaken the once clear trail leading to his neighbor's. The remnant white wooly fruits of the dense winterfat shrub fell like snow after the horse and rider. Godwin looked up at the smoke wafting out his neighbor's chimney, ascending the still air that late summer evening. He rolled up his shirtsleeves and sweat peeked out beneath the dark hair on his forearms as he tied up Creasy to the corner post of his neighbor Danforth's porch. Godwin held the worn hidebound handle of his brown leather satchel filled with cash and silver totaling five thousand dollars at the doorstep of his neighbor's little house that evening waiting for Danforth Smith to answer his knock.

The old man better sell. He sighed.

The door swung open and the stooped curmudgeon waved him in. "Evening, Merritt," Danforth said.

"Lieutenant Smith, good to speak to you again. Fine summer evening, I say." Godwin stretched a borrowed grin. "Might be a bad winter coming though judging by the dogwoods around the porch here."

The old man nodded. "Yes sir. They're bleeding red into their stems a little earlier than usual." Danforth's glassy eyes hung on the satchel a little longer than he would have liked. "I appreciate you sending your boy down Monday to call on me and set up a chat. And the pie your Freda sent with him didn't sit long uneaten."

"I'll pass the word along. I think it's good we stay in touch. Much going on around the mountains we'd be wise to discuss to keep things as neighborly as they've been, Lieutenant Smith."

"I see. Come in and sit with me. I don't stand too long these days." Danforth led his neighbor inside. "I suppose the day won't be too long off that standing up will be just a memory, like being a young soldier fighting the big war."

"I hope it isn't so. I hope you get to be up and around years to come," he said. *By god, the war's been over twenty-some years, Johnny Reb.* Godwin gritted his teeth and nearly bit his tongue at the mention of the big war. There wasn't a conversation the two of them had that didn't include Danforth's mention of fighting in the Civil War. One of those conversations happened to occur when some of Smith's kin were up visiting. A great-nephew pulled Godwin aside on that occasion and informed him that the extent of his dear, great-uncle's war time soldiering had been spent guarding some western Missouri outpost that saw not a single bullet fly in engagement with the Union Army. The only shot, his great-nephew confirmed, was fired by a forty-three year old conscripted drunkard who tried to shoot the cock off a weathervane during one of the poor sot's more exuberant outings with the bottle.

Danforth was in the midst of picking at a scab on the back of his scalp and paid no mind to his neighbor pacing the knotty planks along the window on the far wall, quite away from the fire. Danforth gained purchase on the scab and with some relief pulled it through his white hair. "I suppose we have some more serious matters to tend than just the chitter chatter of pleasant folk as my blessed mother used to say it. So, come. Tell me what's itching the birds in your tree."

"You're a smart man and I didn't ride down here to pull any wool over your eyes. I'd like to purchase your property and combine it with my own. I'm ready to give you a fair price for the value of your wonderful land." Godwin patted the bulky satchel beside him and said, "As a matter of fact, I'm prepared to give you payment here and now if that's what it takes."

"My lord, what do you have in your carrying bag, son?" Twinkles struck Danforth's eyes like sunlight on a pile of silver dollars. "That is a sharp looking son of a gun."

"You know Red Eagle?"

"Sure, Red Eagle Raw Hides up McCormick from Dr. Spuss. He's Half-Ute." Danforth spit on his floor. "You ever cross paths with them?"

"Not up here," Godwin said.

"You're lucky."

"Well, he made this here for me. Hell of a process really. You familiar?"

"I think I am. He likes to get messy with it, jiggering with the brain and everything, always seemed a little crazy to me. He's a mixed-blood though, no use in trying to make sense of it." Danforth stared at Godwin. "No, he sure doesn't tan hides the regular way."

"That's right. He doesn't."

"I forget what he called it though, the process."

"Brain tanning."

"Right. Morose feller, ain't he?"

"I think it's his spiritual side. He said it keeps the act sacred, allowing the mind and body of the animal to stay interlocked." Godwin made a motion with his fingers overlaying themselves.

"Suppose I can see that," Danforth said.

"He said something else that's stuck with me ever since he made this particular satchel years ago. He was kind enough to let me sit in while he made it. Watched the whole process from kill to finish. Just about the time he handled the wolf's brain, mashed it in a bowl, and worked it over with a smooth stone ball, he commented, 'Every animal has enough brain to tan its own hide.'"

Danforth chewed on that for a long moment. "Some truth to that."

"There is, I believe. Yet, it's one of those things that I actually have a hard time pinning down precisely what it means."

"I understand you, Merritt. It's got a depth that isn't visible. Like a pond buried in fog."

"Anyway, I like to share that. I guess maybe if I say it aloud enough times the true depth of it might be revealed some day."

"Well, so what's in the beautiful bag old Red Eagle fashioned for you, Mr. Merritt?"

"I have enough silver certificates bearing the image of one Stephen Decatur and a few solid silver coins to account for every pine needle and creek pebble on your property should you choose to part ways and relocate."

Danforth Smith sat with a blank stare while he chewed a phantom lemon behind his considerable white moustache. Godwin checked the calluses on his own palms. He gently pressed the top of his leather vest as if to smooth out a crease. He would have politely done that for an hour if it took the old dog that long to respond to his proposition.

Finally, Danforth spoke. "Would you like a drink? I have some tepid coffee. It wouldn't take long to heat it beside the fire. I also have a bottle of whisky you might enjoy."

The thought of getting drunk crossed Godwin's mind but he failed to find the virtue in being roped into an hours' long palaver full of secondhand war stories. "Coffee is fine, Lieutenant Smith."

The old man made a motion to get up.

"No. Let me. You rest a minute." Godwin pointed to the metal pitcher on the big table. "This the coffee, here?" Godwin stood at the table for only a few of seconds but it was long enough to scan an aged letter creased in two folds and obviously intended to be delivered once upon a time. It appeared to be just two pages and on the first he saw it addressed in a clearly personal manner to some man named Farragut. The last page had writing halfway down and was signed "Danforth Smith." Godwin was surprised it did not include Smith's rank, proud as he was of his service in the Confederacy. "I'll just set the coffee near the fire a moment." Godwin's shirt was already stuck to his back from the heat in the old man's shack. "Actually, I don't mind my coffee lukewarm or even cool. Sometimes that can be just as refreshing."

"I prefer mine piping, Mr. Merritt. If you would, please?" Danforth pointed to the fire.

With his back turned, Godwin closed his eyes and wished the old man ill.

"Godwin, you're no spring chicken yourself now. If you don't mind my stating quite the obvious." Godwin flashed a quick grin. Danforth continued, "What would you want with all that land, yours and now mine?"

"I would like to leave my children with enough land to split and live near each other when the time comes for me and my wife. Many years from now, god willing. Look, I know your plat runs quite a ways out from the banks of Cut Creek so with my ranch and acreage up and down the other side…"

"That's fine and well. But, what about your business hauling silver out of the mountains? Don't suppose I'm sitting up here sippin' weak coffee from reused beans and eating wrinkled potatoes while a horde of silver hides underfoot?"

"I don't think that's the case, unfortunately. All the veins we're pursuing down in the mines are running south, southwest. We got one branch jumping off northwest but it appears to be drying up, in a manner, Lieutenant Smith."

"That is unfortunate, for me." Danforth glanced over to the coffee, Godwin took the hint and poured him a piping cup. The front of Godwin's shirt stuck to his stomach now and the thought of hot coffee nearly made him ill as he sat back down across from Danforth.

"Is the coffee hot now?"

Danforth nodded. "What say I call down on my brother the sheriff in Butte and have him rustle up the assayer to get the numbers coming out from your mine? Would he be inclined to tell me the same? That all your excavating is running away and not toward any property this lonely old soldier holds?"

"I can't speak for the good Sheriff down in Butte, but if he looked at the deeds and receipts I would be surprised if he came to any conclusion contrary to what I've told you. I can wait if that's something you want to do." Godwin said.

"Tell you what. It's getting on in the evening and I need to retire soon. Could you get my whisky and plunk a few gulps of it into my coffee?"

"I would but I don't see where you have it stored."

"It's just in the other room beside the wash basin where the pots are drying."

Godwin went to the other room. The bottle stood on the countertop like a big, bright knife in the back. No mistaking the label on the thing. Did the old man in the other room really not understand its significance? Godwin put his palms on the countertop and screamed silently with his jaw flexed open. He could have ripped the whole countertop off the wall.

"Could you find it, Merritt?" Danforth hollered over his shoulder.

"Yes, sir." Godwin picked up the bottle and juggled it with one hand while he considered its label. Stamped lettering with "BRR" in bold black ink stung him and a headache ripped apart his mind. Black Rock Runners. It wasn't whisky. It was Mantabawa River hooch cooked from notorious

Mattocks family stills. A sound he hadn't heard in decades burst forth, the memory rose vividly in his mind—the steam saw he operated as a sawyer's apprentice back home, spinning wild with Mattocks' blood. He heard the whap-whapping of long belts that circuited the pins and gears. He winced at the sound of the blade screeching to a stop as it jammed into a log it didn't have enough power to cut. He tore just short of a march into the room where his neighbor sat.

"Ahh, good. This whisky is just what we need to cap off our discussion," Danforth said and twisted the cork from its neck.

"I really think I must get back. I've said what I came to speak of and Freda will be getting anxious if I don't return soon," Godwin said. "You'll excuse me, won't you?"

"When a lady's concern is front and center a gentleman cannot refuse."

"A gentleman and a good soldier."

"Indeed. Thank you, Mr. Merritt. It's been a pleasure having you here. If you don't mind, I will take you up on that offer and inquire into the mine with the sheriff down in Butte."

"I wouldn't expect anything less than a thorough investigation into the matter. Good evening, Lieutenant Smith. Thank you for your hospitality," Godwin said and made his way to the door.

"A handshake? For the continuation of prosperous dealings between neighbors?" Danforth said.

"My manners. I apologize. Once my wife gets into my mind I find it hard to focus sometimes," Godwin returned with his hand stuck out like an oar.

"The confounded nature of a beautiful woman in a man's life. No need to apologize, neighbor."

Godwin couldn't help thinking the word neighbor had come out as an assurance that they would always be so and that his angling for Danforth's property would be nothing less than futile. "Just one other thing," Godwin said. "The whisky.

Where did you get it? I didn't drink any but I took a sniff when I retrieved it. It had an intoxicating aroma."

"Well, I suppose no harm telling you now. A couple of weeks ago some gentleman and his bride came to call. They were looking to do precisely what you're asking to do."

"They want to purchase your land?" Godwin bit his tongue but kept himself from cursing aloud. He could taste the blood that leaked from the puncture his tooth made.

"Indeed," Danforth said and finally grasped Godwin's outstretched hand. He shook it with the slow, firm movement of a man who wished to convey more than good tidings. "Now, I have to ask myself and it will be something I turn over many times tonight as I sip from the whisky they left me as a gift, 'what is so special about the land I've been living on for nineteen, twenty years that all of a sudden has become the object of desire for multiple parties?' Any thoughts, at all, Merritt?"

Their hands stopped shaking yet remained locked together; Godwin's slick with perspiration and Danforth's clammy with a shadow of the grave. Godwin imagined the old sot, all twisted up in his Confederate grays, three sheets stinking of gin, stumbling around his post trying to shoot the cock off a weathervane in western Missouri. He'd give him one thing though, he still had enough wits to know there was something valuable about the chunk of property he landed on after the Union victory scattered the threads of the 'stars and bars' in the wind.

* * *

That evening, when the boys had fallen asleep and Godwin had a chance to finally rest his mind a moment from the worry of how things were going to shake out with his neighbor, Freda sat down beside him at the long table in the kitchen. The wood stove was cooling finally and the blonde Labrador sat at the open door letting the breeze soothe him to sleep.

"How was Danforth?" she asked.

Godwin fought to keep his eyes open as he studied a spot on the table. She put a hand on his forearm and waited for a response. "He's got suspicions," he said.

"What happened?"

"Some folk came to call on him and see about buying his property."

"Out of nowhere they stumble on his land and think that's the spot they want to make a home?"

"He didn't say where they were from. Sounded like flatlanders looking for adventure, I suppose."

"Something's not right. People don't just stumble onto Echo Cliff out of nowhere."

Not out of nowhere. "We have any ale?" he asked.

Freda went to the pantry off the back of the kitchen and poured him a stein from their barrel. It trickled to a stop, only filling the stein a little over half way. She was able to rock the barrel in its stand. Empty.

"That's it for the barrel." She set the stein in front of him. "The others will be brewed up soon enough."

The stein was nearly cold in Godwin's hands and he held it without drinking for a while. The dog farted and the breeze carried it up to their noses. "Must have got a hold of a shithouse rat outside today," he said. "Or did he sneak into the garden and eat all our lettuce again?"

"He's been sluggish lately. Hopefully he's over whatever it is soon. I need an aspirin. You?"

He waved it off. "I don't know what to make of the other offer on Danforth's property. I'll have to get down to Butte in the morning and talk with the lawyer."

"God, do you trust him? Do you trust Mr. Jefferson?"

"I would say I do. He's done right by me and Cut Creek Pass."

"The mine brings a lot of money. I mean to say, bad guys don't always wear masks when they set out to rob."

"No. That's true. But, why wait so long to try to swindle me? He'd had plenty of opportunity over the years if that's the predicament you think I'm in."

"Who's to say? He's the one that came to you with the information about the mine and the entrance at the pass not being square on Merritt land. My question is, how did he find that out? From whom?" Freda said.

"Are you staying up?" Godwin asked.

"I am going to have to lie down in a bit. This headache is killing me."

"Is that the aspirin Dr. Spuss give you?"

"It is. I don't know. I just don't think it's working anymore. I'd hate to take more than he said but it seems that when I do the headaches dull again."

Godwin motioned her to come to him. Their embrace was true and warm. She kissed him on his clean-shaven cheek. "Goodnight, God."

"I love you, Freda."

He chewed on the notions the day brought him. The ale was gone in a gulp. Mattocks in town again. A lawyer who might be looking for a big payday. A neighbor just sober enough to ask questions. The issues stung his brain and when his clenched teeth shifted and ground across themselves he sought his wife's aspirin. The bottle Dr. Spuss gave her on a regular visit to the ranch had a plain brown label with red ink that read, "Albany Drug: Cocaine." Beneath the large type was a billowed banner, "For the afflicted brain." He took one pill and went to the porch to smoke from his pipe. Every time he closed his eyes to inhale the smoke, he saw the blood on the big saw blade and smelled the sawdust piled in heaps around the old steam saw in the mill beside Sawyerskill. The sky was clear and he counted stars to distract himself.

The old man better sell.

*   *   *

Two days' ride by coach from his jurisdiction, the Lake County Sheriff sat on the cushioned bench with his boot up on his knee. A folded copy of The Rocky was in his hand and a scrawl of ink on its top margin read, "Helmut Mattocks, 8:40 to Fort Collins." Sheriff Smith sat still and rested his forearm so as not to disturb the laceration he received in a knife fight inside the Copperhead Saloon in Butte two nights before. His head ached from the blows he took in the fracas and maybe a little more from having to shoot a man in the belly who tried to help him break up the fight between two miners down from Cut Creek Pass, the silver mine Godwin Merritt owned just up the trail from the little town which had gone bust when the gold ran out but boomed once more when Merritt came to town and happened upon a silver vein so long and true the locals nearly made him a king when he got to work setting up a fully operational mine. The locomotive chugged to a crawl with its wheels squealing to a stop. The whistle blew wide open and filled Poudre Canyon.

Helmut leaned forward to duck the roof of the train car. He towered over the rest of the riders walking the platform to the depot and Sheriff Smith watched as he ducked through the doorway into the dim depot. Helmut looked for the face he hadn't seen in years. As Sheriff Smith approached, he recognized him and his curious moustache straight away.

"What's the news on that son of a bitch, Merritt?" Helmut said. His knuckles were white around the handle of his suitcase, an old beat up thing that smelled of old smoke and whisky from where the sheriff stood.

"Helmut, how was the ride?"

"Rough. Thought the new railway here would have some updated equipment. Seems to me they're using rails and wheels they found at the bottom of a gorge beneath a busted wreck of trestle work. May as well rode a donkey cross country for all the hell it played on my back. Why don't they cast open some of these shutters and let the damn sunlight in?"

"I suppose they're just trying to keep the depot from warming up too much as the day wears on. But things are building up faster than you can imagine out here, Helmut.

Soon, we'll have all the conveniences you have back east. What's new on the Mantabawa River? Anyone take to the great beyond I should know about?"

"Been a quiet season. The Bog Bay Devils down south Michigan are keeping to themselves and the Merritt's on Sawyerskill are quiet as a possum walked in front of a feral hog. Shall we find a better place to talk?"

"There's a good hotel with big steaks where we can sit however long we need. I've got a horse for you."

"I'm going to hit the outhouse first," Helmut said.

The marble bar in the front of The Ashley Hotel was long and high. Their boots hit hard on the dark oak floors that gleamed with the reflection of the sunlight off varnish so thick it could probably stop the coffin-handled bowie knife Helmut wore on his hip. The swing door to the kitchen popped open frequently and the sounds of pots and glasses banged and jostled through the cavernous dining room. Along with that came the smell of carrion and fresh bread that turned Helmut's already hungry belly into a thoroughbred chomping and stamping at the gate. They sat to eat at a table near the window. The dining room was loud with the jocular talk of Ft. Collins' hustlers and politicians.

"Lively place, huh? Old Collins is being shaken up by new Collins. The future of this city is at stake." Sheriff Smith drank his coffee, waited to see if Helmut was interested in the wide-open possibility of setting up a franchise out west.

"Butte's about a day away on horseback, right?" Helmut asked and examined the silver fork in the light reflecting off the crystal chandelier.

"A little over."

"So in two days' time you should be able to set up the purchase of that land next to Merritt's and execute the whole deal by the end of the week and telegram the confirmation to my brother, Gunther, before I even get back home?"

"Sounds simpler than it actually might prove to be."

"But you can do it?"

Sheriff Smith nodded with a mouthful of peanuts from the dish the waiter brought them.

"Good. If the answer was no, I'd have to ride down there and kill the old bastard that sits on that land. I don't want to do that. Surely, you can convince your older brother it's in his interest to move on to greener pastures. I'm giving him the opportunity to be on top of those pastures instead of below them."

"He's a tough drunk but I know he's not an idiot. We'll get you that land and the entrance to Cut Creek."

"Thank you, Sheriff. I'm staying in Fort Collins for the week. I'll be in contact with Gunther, so if things aren't on schedule in a week's time I'll be headed down to Echo Cliff. Your brother's body will be taken up to Merritt's ranch and Godwin'll be arrested for his murder."

"By who?"

"You're the sheriff."

The lump in the sheriff's throat made it hard for him to swallow the steak he gnawed. He wanted nothing more than to spit the fatty blob of grey meat across the table and ride to his brother's house. Sure, Madame V., illustrious proprietor of Wichita's, that flourishing gentlemen's house in the center of Butte, would front him the money to convince his old brother the sale of his land was legitimate and honorable, but what would he owe her then as sheriff? Even through the river of whisky that flowed in Danforth Smith's body, he'd be able to sniff out the transaction for what it was—a boomtown hustle by a cadre of misfits trying to get in good with outsiders that came to town looking to hang the supposed savior of Butte by his neck for crimes committed decades ago and hundreds of mile away.

* * *

Two days later the door was open when Sheriff Smith arrived at his brother's little cabin east of Echo Cliff in the shadow of the Merritt Ranch. It was just before eight by his pocket watch—the one he swiped from the miner during the brawl in the Copperhead. The morning air was crisp. Fall settled in and it would be no time before the path to his brother's would be unnavigable beneath the many feet of snow sure to come. Sheriff Smith went inside with a hand on his pistol and the other carrying a bag of money.

He found his brother curled up on the knotty planks beside the woodstove. The sheriff put the bag down on the chair. He knelt down and shook his brother.

When Danforth opened his eyes, the nausea overtook him and he vomited on the floor.

"Goddamn, brother."

"What are you doing here? What time is it?"

"I've come to wake you up," Sheriff Smith said and picked up the whisky bottle on the table. This stuff must be stronger than your blithe spirit is used to."

"You bring a bag of money too? I knew you would. I've already shooed off two honeymooners and big Godwin Merritt."

"Here, drink this." He handed his brother a cup of coffee.

"I ain't drinking no cold coffee," Danforth said. "What time is it?" His voice quivered now with effort.

"I forgot you like it hot. Sorry." He set the cup on the stove and loaded some wood into the fire. "We need to talk about your future. It ain't here, not on this mountain no more. I've got all the money you could need to get on and settle up somewhere else. Maybe in town or up in Denver if you need something more thrilling. Plenty of drunks up there to keep you company."

"I don't see the trouble with an old man living or dying on the land of his choosing. This is the land of the free still, damn it."

"It's not about principles anymore, Danforth. This is about you staying alive."

A serpentine curve crossed Danforth's brow. His tongue was all sweat and slur as he eyed the BRR.

Sheriff Smith picked up the bottle of BRR. "It's these folks. Black Rock Runners. They're after Godwin Merritt and they want your land. They don't want you. Don't need you."

"So those honeymooners…"

Sheriff Smith tilted the bottle at him.

"Well, I'm not moving. They can come and try and take it from me."

"That's what they're doing. Just take the money and move on, Lieutenant."

The serpentine eyebrow appeared again. "Let me see the money." Slurs and sweat.

Sheriff Smith handed his brother the bag. "It's $100 coin notes."

"This is differenter than the money Merritt brought down."

"You look like you've seen a ghost."

"He looks young."

"Who?"

"Commander Farragut. Admiral now, I suppose. What time is it?"

"Are you okay, Danforth?"

"I just need to get to Butte today. What time is it?" Danforth looked into the portrait on the coin note again, "Gosh, he looks strong."

"Did you know him?"

"When I was on the U.S.S. Saratoga he was my commander." Danforth put his hand on his heart. "He made a name for himself protecting the Liberians and American merchant interests off the west coast of Africa in the 20's."

"1820's? You weren't serving then."

"No, I know. I was aboard 1847. We were sent out during the Mexican American war in the Gulf of Mexico. That expedition was doomed from the start. I enjoyed a shitty outbreak of yellow fever while stationed off Tuxpan. That's Mexico. Gulf Coast. What time is it?"

"15 to 9."

He examined the coin note again. "Time is a merciless bastard. Admiral Farragut's dead now. I read it in The Rocky years ago and drank myself silly that week recalling the bad boys of Farragut's sloop of war. And, how the Union Navy stabbed me in the back with a medical discharge in Pensacola, Florida. It was just a slight cold. I could've served for years and made Admiral too."

"Yellow fever isn't a slight cold, Danforth."

"It was for me. A couple of sailors died before we arrived in Florida but mine was nothing but some sniffles and a cough."

"Farragut. He was a tough one."

"You're not going to budge one inch, are you?"

Danforth shook his head.

"Well, how about a shot?" Sheriff Smith uncorked the bottle. He tipped the BRR way back and took a hard pull. He handed it over to his brother. Danforth tipped the bottom straight up and sucked down the remainder. He was gulping hard on the whisky with his eyes closed tight like in prayer. Sheriff Smith shot him in the chest point blank and the bottle fell to the floor to shatter in pieces. His brother died instantly but his eyes stayed open and Sheriff Smith couldn't stand to look at him any longer. He took to the porch and pulled the cigar from his coat, a dirty wool jacket with patches on the elbow where the knife had sliced through in the saloon. He leaned on the post and looked up to the high wall of Echo Cliff while he puffed little round smoke signals from his cigar. The stems of the dogwoods along the porch were red as the blood pooling beneath the poor sot's rocking chair.

Two riders approached out of the woods and rode across the bridge that separated the land Godwin Merritt owned from the land he wanted. One pulled up alongside Sheriff Smith's horse with his hand raised up. "Dick Mattocks."

"Christ." Sheriff Smith jammed his cigar down on the post. He waited for the other rider to say his name.

"Glenn Mattocks. You the sheriff?"

"Yes sir. I was told you men wouldn't be necessary should this matter resolve itself in due time."

"Well, Sheriff Smith, the plans have changed. Now, we know this is still fresh and you're likely a little sensitive to outsiders at the moment but we have a job to do. You don't need to be here any longer unless you just find yourself to be the helpful sort. Either way, that corpse in there is going up to Merritt's ranch."

"Let me gather a couple of things inside and I'll leave you to it. I'm not interested in helping any more than I have to."

Dick waved him on. He hollered after him, "He's fine now. No pain."

Sheriff Smith rummaged the house for some papers, anything to identify the property. It was no use. His brother had nothing but empty bottles and regrets.

"We need to get a move on, Sheriff." Dick spit a gob of wet tobacco toward the porch.

"Take it easy. Man's got a right to say his peace to the dead."

Dick and Glenn, the brothers Mattocks, spit simultaneously.

Sheriff Smith rode the trail into the woods that led back down to Butte and tried to plan his next move, arresting Godwin Merritt.

Chapter 2.

Weeks passed by the time Irvin led the Mattocks brothers on the rough trail up the mountain. On horseback through light snow flurries. The edge of the road was the edge of the mountain and the snow slickened rock gave Irvin and his two men a hell of a time. The horses' nostrils glistened and flared as their breath shot out in long gray puffs that lingered longer than the men liked it to or figured it should.

Dick Mattocks, "the brick shithouse," as Irvin referred to him most of the time on account of Dick's bullish physique, said with a shiver, "You know the sad bit is we're just in the foothills. Look up there near the fog. That's when we really start to hike."

His brother, Glenn, walked astride the makeshift sled his horse pulled. "That's no fog, Dickie. Those are the damn clouds. We might meet our maker up this way."

"Ain't got no maker except dear old ma, may she rest in peace," Dick crossed himself like the good little Catholic boy he used to be.

"Aye, and don't forget dear old Pa back home, twisting his moustache in his grave and making fool errands for us lads." Glenn pulled a tall flask embossed with BRR, the initials for the family brand of moonshine, from his pocket. "God bless, ye, Worrell Mattocks." He let the moonshine sting his lips and held it in his mouth for a moment before letting the alcohol slide all the way down to warm his chest and belly. "Can't believe little Gunther Mattocks is calling the shots now."

The horse that pulled the sled made deliberate steps and pushed his hooves into the gravel with such force he left imprints that the sled could not smooth out as it dragged along behind the mighty beast whose grey hide blended well into the surrounding environment—clouds and granite, stream and road. The brothers' arms strained to steady the crate on the sled. Down in Butte they attempted to tie the thing to the horse's back but it shifted dangerously from side to side even when the horse was on level ground so they rightly abandoned hope of making good and decent time on their adventure up the high mountain to the Godwin Merritt Ranch.

"We've carried this damn trunk high enough up this mountain," Dick said. He set his hat back low over his brow and lit the stub of a cigarillo nearly gnashed to mush after being shoved in the brim of his hat the last time they'd stopped to piss. "I'm not dragging it another foot until you tell me what's in it."

"You'll pick it up or I'll shoot you down right here in the stream," Irvin said.

"You shoot me, who's going to carry this two ton son of a shit?" Dick pounded the top of the crate with his fist. "You ain't even Mattocks. What the hell they got you in charge for anyway?"

"Shut up, Dick," Glenn said.

"No, my name's Dick Mattocks and my family's name is the one's at stake here. You, Mr. Irvin…well what's your damn last name anyhow? You ain't no right to be calling the shots in matters of the Mattocks family."

"Shut up, Dick," Glenn said.

"Ah, shut your own self up. I'm pissed off. Ain't you the least bit unnerved this outsider's telling us where and how high we ought to be hiking?" Dick took off his hat and smoothed his greasy hair back tight against his scalp.

Irvin waited for Dick's rant to stop. He watched him pull a butt and light up a little too close to the crate for his comfort.

"There'n see, Glenn? He don't got no words. He knows he's not Mattocks," Dick said.

"You don't want to smoke around that crate there, Dick," Irvin said and took a step back.

Dick studied the fear on Irvin's face a moment and tossed his lit cigarillo over the edge of the mountain road.

"Yeah, boss. I got a mind to know what'n we're getting on with in this here trunk up this here mountain. I saw you open her up last night and throw up sick something evil beside your tent. I'm starting to think Dickie's got a point."

"You both went out to Echo Cliff and collected Danforth Smith about a week ago, right?"

"About a fortnight now, would you say, Dick?"

"And where did you take the body?" Irvin asked.

"Red Eagle."

"Starting to put the pieces together?" Irvin asked.

"Oh, hell no. That ain't Smith in the crate now." Dick put his hand on his gun.

Irvin drew on him. "It doesn't matter what happens to him now. He's got a new role to play in this tale."

"I don't mind shooting sons of bitches and I don't mind making it messy to drive home a point. But, this...I ain't...I don't..." Glenn paced a circle beside his grey paint looking for the words to finish his thought but it disappeared just like his horse amongst the identical looking heavens and earth.

"It's how I told you when we set off yesterday morning and I can't tell you fellas any more than that. We've got to deliver the contents of that trunk to the man that lives on up the mountain without him seeing any of the three of us. That's the stipulations put down on the payoff. So you want your big silver payday and barge full of whisky you couldn't drink in a year each, you'll shut up about knowing what's in what and who's waiting where."

"You can put your pistol away, boss. We didn't mean to rile you. It's just a mighty bitch getting along up the steps to the heavens here with a load we knew nothing about," Dick said.

"It's all for the reward, fellas. We've got one goal. Now let's take this mountain, not be seen, and slide back down to Butte where we can work out the knots this hike is sure to tie into us all," Irvin said.

"There's a long-legged blond back at Wichita's I'd like to get reacquainted with just as soon as we get back to town," Dick said.

"Forget about her. Get this crate up the mountain or none of us get paid." Irvin led the horses on foot and his subordinates struggled on with their once mysterious cargo. They were only a quarter of the way up the mountain.

"I don't need this money. I can go back to the Mantabawa and work the stills and not have to put up with this suicidal trek," Glenn said.

"Yeah, go back home. Go right back to Gunther Mattocks and tell him to stick it. I don't care if he is your blood. He won't abide a repudiation on such a scale. No, you can trust me as sure as the blizzard about to come bury these mountains, if you go back and haven't done this job, you'll be lucky to just be exiled," Irvin said. "There's a reason you boys are out here and not charged with running the business back home in any meaningful capacity. I don't know if it's punishment deserved but it is what it is and it ain't what it isn't. Let's suck it up and do this right."

They approached a curve that hid what lay beyond; any danger could lie in wait or just the continuance of their treacherous ascent. Irvin made the bend on the mountain road first and decided right there they'd have to pick that spot to make a camp and settle for the night. The road fell upon a wide plateau where the stream cut across from another slope. Tall pines hard in the icy air pointed off the plateau at every angle making a patchwork of ramparts—a natural fortification that Irvin knew they'd be hard pressed to find further along up the mountain.

"Well, if we're gonna make camp, let's get the camp made. It's going to get dark sooner mooner," Dick's pleasant tone caught Irvin off guard. He watched him closer now.

"Sooner mooner!" Glenn said. "Haven't heard that since we was boys."

"Get the crate in the first tent. I don't want to take any chances of it being seen." Irvin cracked the whip so to speak and took to drawing out a pit into which he could make a fire. "I'll get the fire cooking. Let's hope to hell the snow don't come down tonight."

"Irvin, who do you think might see the world's worst coffin, a bear?" Dick said.

"Just get the fucking crate in the goddamn tent. Jesus H.F. Christ." Irvin struck his flint with feverish strokes, the spark ignited the wad of cloth he'd placed for lack of kindling beneath the branches, and a sneer broke his frustrated expression.

The brothers didn't speak to be heard for most of the night. The constant grumblings from Irvin did little to shore up their confidence in the success of their mission. Glenn and Dick played the quietest game of poker in the history of the west as Irvin sat mumbling the lines of a packet of documents he kept always inside his vest. He read with the faltering syntax of a pupil called out in the back of the schoolhouse and forced to read aloud and although he was barely literate it still put him at the head of the class regarding the Mattocks brothers grunting and spitting over their card game on the other side of the fire. Dick and Glenn glanced over at Irvin often and surreptitiously so as not to aggravate their mysterious boss.

* * *

Beyond the weak circumference of the campfire light and well into the darkness of the plateau that extended out into a serene winter valley, thin branches of new pines, grown up after the fire that scorched the region two summers ago, cracked and gave way to a horse whose rider had likewise come to call on the Godwin Merritt Ranch. Jack Hanshaw made his way in wide circles from Butte to where he now roamed. He kept a camp in the entrance of Cut Creek Pass. The mine closed for winter because the trails became inaccessible for the men and the silver they would need to haul. This made it a wise place for Jack to hideout, which he did, often from lawyers, gangsters, and sheriffs depending on what kind of racket and swindle he'd undertaken in the region. If times were too tough for Jack, he'd run all the way down to Four Corners near Coronado.

He saw the light glowing on the near horizon in the maze of trees and false cliffs that crisscrossed the darkness. He got as near as he should without his horse being heard and tied her to a tree trunk. He stalked the fire in his heavy furs seeming like a jumbled hybrid of bear, fox, wolf, and man. Jack found a ledge overlooking the camp where three men sat passing the night. If it were Jack's call, he'd just shoot the men where they slept.

* * *

Sheriff Smith kicked his boots up on the corner of the table and made himself at home in the Copperhead Saloon in Butte, Colorado. It was half past nine in the morning and he'd had it with nursing the cold that was making his occupation more of a headache than it usually was. The bartender brought him a half-empty bottle of Farrar whisky, a direct import from the state of Tennessee and the sheriff's drink of choice inside and outside of the Copperhead.

"Forgetting something, Zeke?"

"Right, Sheriff." the bartender retrieved the latest issue of the Rocky and slapped it down on the table beside the sheriff's boots. "Just got the paper in an hour ago."

"Thank you, Zeke." Sheriff Smith knew, full well, it was not the bartender's name.

"Sheriff," he saluted and returned to the alcoholics at the bar.

Sheriff Smith drank a glass of his Farrar whisky and immediately poured it half full. The whisky aired out while he read the paper. "Holy cow, Zeke!"

"Sheriff?"

"That fire that burned down half of Chicago last week is gonna cost them big time. Says here they're already counting over one hundred fifty million in damage and rising." Sheriff Smith chuckled.

"What's funny about that?" The bartender stacked glasses on the bar near to where the sheriff sat so he could hear him. Last week an outlaw pulled a gun on a local conman and shot him dead over by the window. Fired the gun right by the bartender's head. He hasn't heard a thing out of his left ear since.

"Says in here a cow kicked over a lantern and caused the whole conflagration. Can you believe it? One-hundred fifty million."

"What's the point? Why rebuild that glorified stockade? Hell, my pa lived there as a kid and said he wished the whole town would've burnded to the ground. He's up in Denver now. Drinking himself to the devil, I suppose." That was Slim. Sheriff only knew him as Greasy Slim, was something of an apprentice to the bartender.

One of two anonymous drunks seated at the bar interrupted, "Well, I'd say he damn near got his wish then. They ain't got nothing on Jimtown, here."

"We don't call it Jimtown anymore, thank you," Sheriff Smith said without removing the newspaper from in front of his face.

"You can put lipstick on a hog…," the drunk started to say.

"But that don't mean she ain't a whore," the drunk beside him said.

"Gentlemen, the town charter has been revised and approved by all city fathers to rename our bustling town, Butte. Please, show some respect," Sheriff Smith said.

"You changed it from Jimtown to Butt?" the first drunk said and giggled himself sideways on his stool.

The sheriff was on his feet and behind the drunk with a raised pistol before he even realized his predicament. Sheriff Smith hit the butt of his gun on the man's thigh and jumped back as he fell from his stool. He grabbed the man by his coat collar and hauled him out into the street. Deputy Morrison stood out beside a post that supported the balcony above the Copperhead sidewalk. "Morrison!" Sheriff Smith shouted.

Deputy Morrison hurried to help and they carried the drunk to the Butte jail, which was behind the businesses on the other side of the street. "These are the times I hate we're a two street town," Deputy Morrison lamented.

"This town is going to be the pride of Colorado one day, by hook or crook, I promise you that, young Deputy," the sheriff said.

"I'd love to see the day."

"Let's lock this guy up for a night or so and see if he finds any respect for our fair city as the fog clears from his pig sty of a brain," Sheriff Smith said.

They left the bum locked in the big cell. He was unconscious from a nasty blow he'd suffered when Sheriff Smith "accidentally" lost grip of his shoulders. His head hit the ground a little harder than it might've if he'd fallen off his barstool which is exactly what the sheriff was going to tell him when he saw him the next day. "I'm going back to the Copperhead to finish my paper," he said.

"You mind if I head over to see Dr. Spuss? I've got a hitch in my belly that ain't settled for days," Deputy Morrison said.

"Get a shot of whisky. That'll fix you up."

"I tried that."

"No you ain't. Not mine. You need a little Farrar from the muddy creeks of Tennesse. Trust me, you haven't had anything like it." Sheriff Smith slapped him on the back.

"All the same, I'd really like the doctor to get a read on it. I appreciate the offer, sir." Deputy Morrison made his way down to the corner where Dr. Spuss kept an office as well as his private quarters above in the last building on the north side of McCormick Street.

Dr. Spuss heard the bell ding on the back door. He heard the boots hit each step on the stairs and his heart went quicker in his chest as he hurried round his room tidying up the place. He tucked in his shirt and laughed as he wondered why.

Knuckles softly rapped behind his door and he flew to answer it.

Downstairs in Dr. Spuss' lobby, Deputy Morrison sat on high-back cedar chair.

"Dr. Spuss, I need some of the medicine you give to Madame V.," the young boy said. "I'm sorry to bother you."

"I was just not expecting you. Anyone. I was expecting no one," he said. "Is she okay?" He motioned for the young boy to come in.

"She just said she's in need."

"I'd prefer she come to me herself. This is serious medication, not child's play. Promise me you'll give this to her straight away with no funny business."

"I have no use for the stuff. It's all snake oil to me," the boy said.

"Well, just as well. Be off though and please don't mess around with it," Dr. Spuss handed him the small jar, about the size of a thimble, with the white powder inside and the Albany Drug label outside. Dr. Spuss had become a friend to many with his willingness to provide cocaine so very often and for such a variety of disorders.

The boy slid away out of the back door again and flew to his mother's business, Wichita's, in the center of McCormick Street. He tucked the cocaine into a little wooden box on his mother's desk and returned to his post in the basement hallway where a sleazy attorney as dirty as he was fat snuck in some nights for clandestine romps with the less fortunate prostitutes in Madame V.'s employ.

Chapter 3.

A man chewing on a plug of tobacco concealed himself in the umbrage of the pine stand just beyond the rolling prado of the Merritt Ranch. A snowflake fell and landed in silence upon his grey woolen lapel and his tattered sleeves hung frayed upon his decaying hands. He spit a thick gob and a muddy stream of saliva run through with the thin fibers of tobacco and a little blood from his rotten gums clung to his chin and stretched toward the dark soil of the sparsely covered understory. Lieutenant Smith wiped his chin with his forearm and his hands fell to his shined buckle, which read MOCS— Missouri Confederate States. Energy like a thought left his mind and flew across the ranch right up to the distant house where Godwin worked on the roof.

Godwin dug his knees into the slope of the roof as he hammered the last shingle. The hammer struck the nail down and down, each blow louder as the noise ricocheted between the mountains. With the sun falling more and more out of range, the purpling vault had a weight about it, the kind it gets when heavy snow is but an hour away.

"God? Are you going to come down? Dinner is ready and the children are waiting," Freda called up to him.

He laid his hammer in his toolbox—a long wooden rectangle with a straight rod of wood for a handle. He looked across his roof one last time to make sure he got the patches down and done. "I'll be in," he hollered down to her. The door banged shut underneath the porch roof where he stood. He took his bone-handled pipe from his coat pocket and smoked a very small wad of tobacco. From the roof he looked down on his land, his buildings, his woods, and across toward the mountains.

In the quiet of the shadow of Echo Cliff, he felt the stirring of his darkened history in the gashes that scarred his mind. He experienced in sharp detail the sounds and smells of his time spent in the lumber mill on Sawyerskill when he was seventeen. He learned from his foreman that kill was a Dutch word for stream. He was just an apprentice sawyer then and the memories of that summer forged themselves into his mind and became its very tissues. The whap-whapping of the thick belts that ran around the pulleys and cogs of the steam-powered circular saw beat between his ears then as he stood on his roof. The smell of warm sawdust filled his nose and when he looked down expecting to find his roof beneath his feet, he saw nothing but the lumber mill's dirt floor and the sawdust spattered with blood violently thrown off the screeching saw. He swooned with a mind numbed by shock that cut off communication with his feet and he tumbled toward the edge of the roof.

He woke up a few moments later flat on his back, looking up to the sky from the grass. A face moved into the white sky. Godwin's mind strained to understand. It was Lieutenant Smith in confederate gray and with a bottle of BRR swinging from his left hand. With his right hand, Lieutenant Smith raised his revolver. *Trying to shoot the cock off a weathervane.*

"Godwin, are you okay? Can you get up?" His wife was on her knees beside him with a cup of water ready if he wanted it.

He grumbled curses, got onto his hands and knees, and searched for the strength to stand up. He found it after chasing his tail for a few moments and leaned on her all the way to the porch. "Let me stay out a bit. The air feels good."

"You certain, love?"

He nodded with his hand flat on his chest.

She went in to eat with the children.

He concentrated on his breath. Tried to calm it. A dull ivory woolpack enveloped Echo Cliff. The clouds stalled over the range. Thunder barreled down the mountains. Snow was not too long off Godwin supposed. Once it started to fall, it would be a while before they could make outside contact.

He held his bone-handled pipe up to his mouth. Aloft, in front of his face he noted the slanted notches that marked off the length of the pipe from the bowl to a point just beyond halfway toward the mouthpiece. The notches were small, near to a fingernail clipping. The notches were aged, darkened by sooty residue. They were permanent shadows that marched toward the fire when he inhaled and the wad of tobacco glowed incarnadine in a tangle of black veins. The notches were there to count…back in the years of Godwin's life when keeping count was important to him. He always fixated on the first notch—near the base of the bowl where the fire would glow and wan as he inhaled and pulled it from his mouth. That notch belonged to the Mattocks cousin who attacked him when he was seventeen and got run through the steam saw like any old log piled up along Sawyerskill. Now the notches could scatter like thorns in a storm and leave his pipe clean of account to trigger in Godwin's mind a fugue—a snow-globe with flakes aflutter in a blinding blizzard leaving him bewildered in a new, wonderful amnesia that would make him just as content as a bullet in a gun.

Godwin waited on the man from Cut Creek Pass, Jack Hanshaw, his brother in law. If he didn't make it by the time those clouds rolled over the mountain he might not make it alive. Jack's telegram said he'd be there, "…nothing to worry about." However, the man hiding out down Cut Creek Pass was known to be given to lies and false maneuvers. After all, there was a reason he'd holed up down Coronado, near Four Corners, months on end.

Godwin stood on the porch, puffs of white smoke from his pipe sharp smelling in the cold mountain air drifted up to dissipate and be gone. The stillness troubled him. Nary a gust or whisp of a breeze. Just a stillness that settled in with the big clouds.

He descended the steps and took a sweeping survey of his front yard. He squinted into the woods that lay too far beyond his porch to make out anything of real detail. Godwin went inside and shook the cold off his face.

The man in the woods turned and went off down the trail. A bottle in one hand. A gun in the other.

* * *

The next afternoon they had settled into a card game, Godwin and his two older boys.

A cry from the crib startled his wife in her rocker. Their infant, Erwin, had a fever that started two nights before. It worried her immensely. The only sleep she'd stolen were quick naps in the wooden rocker that creaked the floorboards sometimes waking her or Erwin.

Godwin stood in the door to the bedroom where Freda sat with the baby. "Is he hot?"

She rocked the baby in her arms holding his head to her chest. She didn't need to say yes. The fear of losing Erwin, of not being able to get help, of waiting for his fever to break sat on Godwin's heart like a boulder. The baby they'd buried before their oldest, Edwin, was born never left his mind. A decade and a half ago, he'd been down Cut Creek Pass keeping camp, waiting for the Mattocks bastards. Up all night, up all day. Taking turns with Jack who's down there now, or on his way up to Godwin Merritt's ranch. Seemed to Godwin a regular schedule his old enemies kept that every spring a ragtag group would try up the mountain and be put down with ease by Jack and a few gunmen working for Godwin at his mine. He thought they might have given up finally as the years had passed with uneasy peace and quiet. It'd been a few years then that the last push by the old Mattocks clan was made on his ranch.

"Tell Elwin to build the fire," she instructed her husband. "It's too cold. Especially with that drafty window."

"I'll get the boy."

"God?"

"Yes?" He walked to her and kneeled beside them putting his hand to their infant's little back.

"You need to pray that this boy gets well again." She started to sob.

He kissed her earlobe. "I love you always, Freda Hanshaw." He struggled to his feet as his hand tried to support his own weight.

"No sign of my little brother yet?"

Godwin stood in the doorway dazed. The stress of the day took a toll he tried hard to shake.

"Are you still taking the medicine Dr. Spuss gives you?"

"Yes. Times. Sometimes it doesn't help." His knuckles were white while he held the doorframe. "I'll take some tonight if'n the boys get to sleep with no fight."

Godwin walked out of the house and found Elwin building a toy wagon with the hand tools outside the horse barn. "Boy, the fire needs to be built in the baby's room. Get that wood up there and set the fire for your ma and brother."

"Yes, sir." Elwin put the saw down on the barrelhead he was using as a makeshift workbench.

"If you see Edwin in the house, tell him to come out here and help me hitch the plow up to Merlin. And put the tools away. You won't have time to play around before it gets dark."

Elwin hurried off toward the woodpile on the south side of the home. The Labrador with hair as blond as any wheat field east of the mountains got up with great effort and charged after Edwin.

A blur out of the corner of Godwin's eye. A fox running out of the coop. A chicken cold in its teeth. Godwin drew his revolver and fired twice at the fox. The shots echoed between the mountains where Godwin's ranch sat. Too fast. *The son of a bitch startled though.* The fox bit clean through the chicken's neck. The head fell to the dirt and the fox made off with the rest.

"Did you get him, God?" Edwin, the eldest son asked. He stood off a ways with the big wrench that could have doubled as a horse femur.

"No, boy. Just missed the son of a bitch again. Bring the wrench. We need to get the plow on Merlin. Those clouds aren't gonna sit on that range forever."

"Don't think Merlin has enough left in her for the beating we're about to take out here," Edwin said. "Don't get me wrong. I know she's a strong mare and all but, her best days might be gone."

His father ignored him; hated doubt. More than that, he hated when his sons doubted him. He was Goddamned Godwin Merritt and no force of nature was a match for him. His rage alone would melt whatever this coming blizzard might dump on his ranch.

"Make me a promise, son."

"Yes, God."

"Promise me, when you're out in this world on your own, you'll take that damn Irish doubt and self-loathing and wring it like that fox did to that chicken. The last thing a man needs in this world is to have his insides working against him. Plenty of people will be there to do it for you."

Edwin leaned the big wrench up against the steel wall of the barn. Godwin slid the big barn door that was nearly twice as tall as the Merritt men were and its wheels ground across the rail with a roaring tumble.

"Get over here and help me latch this door open," Godwin said.

Inside the house, Elwin was just setting the fire in the baby and ma's room. "Ma, you think we'll see Uncle Jack before the snow settles in?"

"I suppose we should. He'd surely wait out the storm better up here than down there in the mine. He said he'd be here."

"Did you ever go to Sawyerskill?"

"That's where your father and his brothers grew up back east and I grew up not too many miles away."

"Have you ever been there?"

"The mine?"

"No. Sawyerskill."

"Once upon a time, when your father and I were newly acquainted we spent many days together walking the banks of that stream, talking about our future."

"What was it like?" Elwin was a sober boy. Dry of humor and not given to anger quite as quick as Edwin. For this, his ma and pa were eternally grateful. On the other hand, his lethargy, bordering on depression, did cause some apprehension in the Merritts as they tried to bring levity into the young man's life.

"God! Damn it!" Godwin boomed and his voice came through the window's cracked single pane.

Elwin looked at his Ma.

"Pa must have lost his grip again," Ma said.

"Why do you reckon?"

"The plow is down on one end and Pa's wringing his hand."

"Think they need my help?"

"I think it would be a good thing. Go on down there and get that plow on with Edwin. I'll finish setting the fire."

"Will Erwin pull through? He looks sick awful." Elwin looked on as the baby slept fitfully rubbing his button nose with a balled up fist.

"He'll be fine. It's just taking our little man here a couple of days and a hundred prayers to break this fever. Go on, now. I'll finish the fire. You're a good son, Elwin."

His heart bloomed as he made his way out of the house.

But, then Edwin yelled, "Well, what took you so long, you sad sack of sobbing beans? Pa's breaking his back out here and you're off doing who knows what."

"Mind your business, boy," Godwin said. "Elwin was building a fire for your sick baby brother. It's not his fault the doctor ain't fixed my hands yet. Sides. Ain't nothing you're doing right now to help matters. So just hold up your end of the plow and keep your 'pinions to yourself. Maybe, instead of cursing you could say a prayer to the Almighty your brother's fever breaks."

"I got it, Pa," Elwin said and took the other end of the plow in his hands. "Just get us centered over the jig."

A rifle shot coiled in echoes from the distance.

"Impossible to tell where it came from," Edwin said.

"Uncle Jack?" Elwin guessed.

"I wouldn't be so sure. Edwin, you have your Colt holstered?"

"Always, pa."

"Good, son."

"Probably just Uncle Jack, maybe shot a buck or something on his way up the pass," Elwin hoped.

"Stop calling him Uncle Jack for Pete's sake," Edwin scolded.

"Let him be, boy."

"Yes, God," Edwin said.

"Let's get this plow up by the house. Edwin, walk Merlin up with the plow. Come on, Elwin, we'll wait on the porch and see what we see," Godwin said.

They sat for an hour. Godwin and Edwin sipped coffee and smoked tobacco. Godwin from his bone-handled pipe and Edwin from a little wooden one he carved over the course of the summer fishing at Sheep's Head. Elwin stared out from the porch. He was vigilant, leaning on his tip-toes, and wanted not a little to impress his father should he see whatever it was that caused the lone rifle shot so near it must surely have been fired on the grounds of the Godwin Merritt Ranch.

Upstairs the restless baby returned to sleep. Freda was down in the kitchen warming the kettle and finishing off a glass of ale from the first barrel of the batch they'd fermented in late September. The running stock of the ranch, inventoried fastidiously by Freda, constant in her accounting of their boys and their pantry, never fell to the meager quantities she had known growing up in her poor parents' shack. It was as certain as sunrise in the morning that three barrels of beer stood on hand as more fermented in the cool stone pantry on the backside of the house.

She poured another glass of ale and sat thinking of the baby they'd lost before Edwin was born; the one they called Jack.

*   *   *

The pines at the entrance of Cut Creek Pass stood like sentinels with straight backs stiffened by some anxiety. Down near the gulch, where the stream flowed, a gust of wind would whip a spasm into their crowns. The stillness would return and straighten them. Waiting. Listening. Watching.

Cut Creek Pass had been a madhouse of paranoia in its heyday. The silver came out amongst armed guards under cover of night. In dark hoods they rode their take high to the Godwin Merritt Ranch where it was stored in cold vaults beneath the misty mountain surface. The horsemen, the quickest mode up the range, were well paid, well fed, and well laid when they went back into town, into Butte. They rarely asked for more. The ones who did were never again seen.

Behind the pines at the entrance of Cut Creek Pass, a man sat bleeding on a rock. The man they called Jack. He'd dodged the bullet. Made sure of that. Checked five or six times. All the same, the stone that broke his fall also busted his leg. He had crawled under a bush unseen by the rifleman, surely one of the posse that'd been whipped up by the scheming sheriff back Butte way that he'd seen by the campfire. Jack wished he hadn't told Godwin to call off the hired guns to lend him a hand with the lookout this season.

Chapter 4.

Almost a quarter century back on the banks of the Mantabawa, the Black Rock Runners busied themselves growing their distribution networks for the moonshine that would keep their family name in the consciousness of the region for centuries to come.

Gunther Mattocks was just about thirteen years old when he began helping his third cousin, Ollie, run the stills that the Black Rock Runners kept hid around the woods up and down the Mantabawa. Gunther's twin, Helmut, had an ailment that kept him from the work all that year.

One morning, Ollie arrived at Gunther's house with a cousin just about the same age who would become something of a hero and martyr to the twin Mattocks boys. Ollie introduced their newly arrived kin. "This is your cousin, Anthony, from way down the Mississippi. He's made a healthy trip up here to help us out a piece. You guys have a lot in common and I know you'll get on with no quarrel." Ollie focused in on Gunther. "Right, Gunny?"

Gunther Mattocks nodded.

They rode the trail through paper birch with blistering bark and white ash trees on horseback to the stills they'd left to the care of the continually drunk, Albert Huncell. He wasn't real Mattocks, Ollie liked to say, but he admired their standing on the Mantabawa and wanted much to be one himself. The banks were muddy and the short limestone ledge striated with dolomite and shale and laced with wild fronds of maidenhair ferns led them to a horseshoe clearing where the still sat hidden.

On the ride, Gunther quizzed Anthony. "So, how'd you get up this way? Horse? Train?"

"A bit of both?" Anthony said.

"A horse-drawn train?" Gunther joked.

"No, a train-drawn horse," Anthony said. Ollie smiled and let a belch of a laugh that went unheard by the two cousins behind him.

"That would be a fine sight. What's the town called around your home?" Gunther said.

"N'awlins," Anthony said.

"The New Orleans?"

"The very one," Anthony said.

"I hear that's damn near the other side of the world," Gunther said.

"It's quite a shift from your neck of the woods, cousin Gunny."

Gunther looked back at him with a grimace.

"You don't mind if I call you Gunny?"

"No trouble, cousin."

They were considerably silent the rest of the ride. They showed Anthony the stills they were working with. Mostly the same, they had a few gimmicks inside and out that were different enough from the type they were using down the bayou that a day of instruction would be helpful should Anthony find himself out working on his own sometimes.

"I'm impressed, Ollie. We haven't seen tricks like this down home. And you don't get no heat from the law in these woods?" Anthony said.

"Not so much, these days. We got them pretty well taken care of so they leave us be and hassle the dogs that run the poison hooch a little west of here, near to Sawyerskill. Mantabawa though? That's ours."

"Ours up to and including Sawyerskill," Gunther boasted.

The first still they came to was set up and running just the way it should be and Ollie looked around the near vicinity to see if Huncell was around. "Maybe he's taking a shit or something," Ollie said.

"We can wait a bit and see if he stumbles back, the poor bum," Gunther said.

"He the best you got?" Anthony joked.

"He's loyal," Ollie said. "He's as loyal as they come outside of blood."

"Well, how long you reckon we give him?" Anthony said.

"Have a chew and enjoy the scenery," Gunther said and passed him a little pouch of tobacco he'd taken from his belt.

"Here y'all got varmints up here to trap that still pull big money, that true?" The massive bulge of tobacco between his gums and lips softened Anthony's consonants.

"Well, they damn near killed off all the badgers around our way and those used to go for real shiny nickels. Too bad really, 'cause if they keep on going that way pretty soon all your socialites and debutantes back east are gonna be wearing rat shawls and possum coats if that's all that's left wild out here," Ollie said.

"That'd be a sight," Gunther said.

"What's a sosha light?" Anthony said.

"Social-ite," Ollie corrected.

"Oh," Anthony said as if that explained it thoroughly.

"We should probably head on out to the next one. I suppose Old Huncell may be somewhere further along the way," Ollie said.

They rode for half an hour to a spot beneath the canopy of timbers beside the Mantabawa where a minor rapid swirled around the bend. The smoke from the fire at the still didn't rise much through the humidity and peppered the air beneath the canopy with its aroma.

Ollie led them on horseback into the area. As they made their way around the brush and boulders, Ollie stopped his horse with a sharp tug of the reins. He pulled his pistol and levelled it toward the boy talking to Huncell. "Get back, there, Gunny. Back up and out of here," he hollered.

"Who is it?" Gunther said.

"Merritt. I said get on out of here, now," Ollie said.

Huncell threw up his arms shouting, "No, no, no. Just wait a moment and listen. He don't want a fight. And he's just a boy."

"He's just a bastard. I don't give a damn what he wants. He's got no right to be standing on Mattocks land. Step aside, Huncell."

"No. You need to listen to this boy. He's got a proposal."

"And he brought it to you. No offense, Al, but you're not a businessman in any sense of the word."

"Mr. Mattocks, I don't want nothing but to end this mess," the boy said from the log he'd been sitting talking to Huncell on. "I want to see if my idea will make your family put all this violence behind us."

Ollie dismounted and held the gun in his hand as he approached the boy. He stood on the other side of the fire from him. "You're Darwin's boy. What are you drinking that gave you the nerve to set foot on my land? I know it wasn't our shine."

"I do apologize for my intrusion. I'm here to say I want to stop this fighting between my old man and your family. I think you can do your business and we can do ours and not have any more people get hurt because of it. My ma is up for days with shattered nerves, talking to the moon, and sleeping through the day. I don't want this battle for my life either."

"Well, boy, that's a talk you're gonna have to have with your pa. He's done blown up, dumped out, or otherwise destroyed valuable inventories we can't get back. Cost us a damn fortune with his antics," Ollie said.

"I can't talk to him any easier than I'm talking to you right now."

"You got stones, I'll give you that. Come over here facing down certain death to share some dream your little fool heart has about peace in our time. Why shouldn't I shoot you down right here and float your little corpse down the Mantabawa and send a telegram to your pa to let him know he can recover his boy at the confluence?" Ollie said.

"The deal is this," he began, lips quivering, knees shaking, "Mattocks, here and everywhere, can run all the moonshine they want and yes, even up and down Sawyerskill,"

In the distance Anthony whispered to Gunther, "I thought you said y'all ran Sawyerskill?"

"More or less." Gunther waived him off.

Darwin's boy continued, "…and I'll get my father to go along with it."

"You can't promise anything close to that. Your pa says he fights with God's own sword. He's not gonna give in just because his little boy wants to live to see old age."

"He's not as up on God as you all think him. He just throws that around to spook you. If you and yours can let Merritts run our business, which has nothing to do with running moonshine, then we can open up the whole west Sawyerskill region with no intervention. That, I can deliver."

They sat a long, silent moment and finally Ollie spoke up, "I'll take this back to my uncle. He's the last word on this. Meet me back here in a fortnight. You need anything for reassurance?"

"Some shine?"

"Albert," he hollered.

Albert was fidgeting with the still, checking this and that, trying to avoid the tension.

"Albert, you deaf old man!"

Albert perked up and listened with a cupped hand behind his ear.

"Get the boy a jug."

"It's not for me," the boy said.

"Don't even tell me your old man is drinking our juice."

The boy nodded.

Gunther shouted from the distance, "What's your name, Merritt?"

"Godwin."

"How old is you?"

"Just seventeen."

"Brash kid, ain't you?" Anthony said.

"No disrespect, Mattocks," Godwin said and took the jug from Huncell who stretched a tiny curve of a smile and hoped the Merritt boy would hurry up and get the hell on out of there before he got hurt.

Godwin mounted his own horse, lit out across the Mantabawa, and disappeared into the timber that led to Sawyerskill.

Ollie walked over to Huncell and backhanded him across the cheek. "You son of a bitch."

"Well, if you didn't want him on site why didn't you just shoot him."

Ollie fired once between Huncell's eyes. "Because, you dumb bastard. That would have started a war that would kill us all." Ollie dragged Huncell's body away from the still. Anthony ran over to lend a hand and Ollie looked at him.

"It's okay. We do this quite a lot down N'awlins," Anthony said.

After they'd buried Huncell in the woods Ollie gave Gunther and Anthony their new orders. "The stills are yours. I know you can work these, Gunny, and you can show Anthony everything we do to make Black Rock. This will be your responsibility for the foreseeable future. Maybe when Helmut rehabilitates he'll help you two out. But that will rest on Uncle to decide."

"It's a big job, Anthony. You gon' be okay to do it?" Gunther said.

"I'm up here to help out, cousin."

"Let the education begin, then. Come on over to the still 'cause we don't have any time to waste." Gunther showed him the details of the set up. He looked down and saw the blood dried on Anthony's hands. "Go wash in the river before we go on."

Anthony looked at his hands and shrugged.

Gunther nodded to the river.

Over his shoulder, Anthony hollered, "I'm with Huncell on this one. Why didn't you just shoot the dumb kid? Pretty disrespectful him traipsing on Mattocks land. I know down our way he wouldn't have got word one out his mouth."

"His time's coming. But, it ain't for me to say when that it is. That's for Uncle to decide. Him and Darwin's got a lot of history and Merritt men don't die until he says so. You gotta trust me. It ain't our place to decide."

"Yeah, but…"

"No. Let it be."

* * *

A week later Anthony walked the edge of Sawyerskill. His footsteps were quiet on the wet leaves as he followed Godwin. The sawmill was desolate as the darkness settled over The Confluence. Godwin's lantern light cast golden light and Anthony followed it from a safe distance. He watched Godwin enter the lumber mill and saw the building light up through the windows with the bouncy flames of other lanterns. Anthony stood up with his back against the outside of the mill listening to the paddlewheel dip and rise in the waters of Sawyerskill. His palms were slick with perspiration and his breath came in short bursts.

Anthony mounted the steps toward the light in the mill as quiet as he could in his roughed up alligator-skin boots.

Chapter 5.

Sheriff Smith sent Irvin and his men out from an office above the center of town weeks ago to extract payment of one type or another from Godwin Merritt. The boss told him, there in that high office, "God owes us a payment. We can take it in cash or we can take it in blood. Now, I and my partners prefer to take it in cash but if the matter cannot be resolved then the next logical step is to take our blood."

Irvin had no idea what this debt applied to; he was a simple man, averse to contracts and fiduciary minutiae. All he wanted was a job and his payday.

The big one, Dick Mattocks, did most of the talking in the office downtown. "What you're asking us to do in the middle of a blizzard, that takes money, provisions. We can't do it for less than 20."

"Dick, listen to me," Sheriff Smith said, "the price is set. We're talking with others. The job is up for bid. Make a smart choice here."

"A true free-marketeer. Putting the job up like some kind of construction contract. Well, we can do it for twenty. But, it will have to wait until the blizzard passes. We're not about to go rushing up a mountain like a bunch of arrow-slingers into gunfire." Dick put his hat back on and went to the door as if he were the last word on the matter.

"Then you might as well get the hell out of my office 'cause you're only wasting my time. We've got a deadline here, Sir, the weather be damned. Now are you in or out?" Sheriff Smith took his rifle up from beside his desk and plugged a couple of shells into it. The other men stood up. "I've got to go arrest some bums trying to shut down Wichita's. Worked up parochial conservative types, you know, trying to put an end to all the sinning from here to California."

Irvin had not taken his eyes off the black clouds rolling over the range. "Getting dark up there, boss. Maybe too dark."

Dick said, "That's his way of saying he's not keen on the job."

"You've got twelve hours to decide. Be here at six-hundred with an answer. Six-o-one and the job goes to the other guys. Now get the hell out." Smith followed them out the door and escorted them to the street.

Irvin and his men took to their horses and rode down McCormick while Sheriff Smith blasted his rifle into the air and yelled at the crowd in front of Wichita's. "This is an illegal assembly. Disperse at once or face a night in Butte's cheapest hotel. There's plenty a room for all of you in the cell over yonder." He motioned with the barrel of his rifle over his shoulder.

One of the few men in the midst of the protesting group approached Sheriff Smith with a pamphlet, "Sheriff, these women are being abused…a.a.abused verbally, physically, and s.s.s…"

"Sexually," a woman beside him scolded with narrowed eyes behind wire-rim glasses under a starched black bonnet.

"These women are all gainfully employed and free to pursue other employment anytime they choose. You all move on out of here or face arrest. Why don't you all head over to the Copperhead and have a frothy ale and consider the sights our growing town offers."

"Sheriff, I don't see how a man in good conscience, such as yourself…" the lady began to say.

"I said move it." He motioned to Deputy Morrison who stood on the other side of the crowd and had been watching since they gathered.

"Alright, gentleman, come with me. You get to spend some time in the cage. Your friends here can bail you as they see fit." Deputy Morrison pushed them on across McCormick.

"Got your flock good and ruffled now, I suppose," Smith said to the woman.

"This town is an abomination. You're an abomination."

"That's just the way we like it." He tipped his cap to her and went into Wichita's.

Chapter 6.

Smack in the middle of Butte stood the Copperhead Saloon, its sidewalk planks grey as tombstones. The most trafficked business in the little mining town reluctantly opened its brass frame doors to any patron with the nerve to step in and see what waited behind those big glass windows that let on little to nothing behind the hard reflecting sun in the daytime.

"I dig graves." Jack Hanshaw smiled and waited for the barman to respond.

"I pour drinks. Need one?" He finally said.

Jack waved him off with the flick of his wrist. He turned to the guy next to him. "What's his problem?"

"That's Suds. He don't talk. Don't want to talk. He blew up on a guy come in here about a year ago started telling him his life story. Almost beat the man senseless. He just doesn't want to talk. Hard to get rid of him though."

"Oh? Why would that be?"

"He's my son." He waited for the embarrassment to wash off this strange new face. Then he stuck his hand out. "Frank Miller."

"Jack."

Frank waited for him to finish.

"Just Jack," Jack said.

"Okay, Just Jack. Nice to meet you. Go easy on the boy. And he'll go easy on us all." He tapped the side of his head with his finger to suggest the wise thing.

Jack felt sorry for Frank. What a lot. Own a nice saloon and have a shithead for a son beating the clientele. Then again, maybe the poor bastard had it coming. Doesn't do to not know when to keep quiet.

"So, how long you had this place, Frank?"

"Been in the family thirty years. My pa gave it to me. Settled here just about the time the gold ran out."

"That long? Picked a good spot then."

"Things really took off when they started finding silver ribbons all up and down the mountains. Rough crowd in the beginning but things settled evenly. Eventually, it always does."

"I believe truer words were never spoken."

"What about you? Where you from, Just Jack?"

"Jack Hanshaw. From down around San Luis. Small New Mexico town. Just south of Albuquerque. You know Albuquerque?"

"Yeah, I have spent some time down there. We go down every year or two to see my wife's family. May she rest in peace," Frank said and crossed himself.

"Sorry to hear that Frank. She deceased long?"

"One day is too long, friend. Yeah, she met the Lord ten years back. Doctors said she had cancer. They said it was so thick and run amok there was little but to watch it finish her off."

"Hear more and more of it every day, seems. Don't know what they're putting in the water these days but it just don't seem right, rivers and wells all seem to have something fishy about 'em the more you look around." Jack tried to console this man he'd just met and then began to wonder what got in him to make him so concerned. Usually he'd feign a little sympathy just to move the conversation along and get to somewhere a little more useful but something about this old codger with the mealy mouthed shithead of a son took hold of him.

"Suppose there might be something to that what with the way the world seems to be gathering steam and falling all over itself to get bigger and faster. What happened to just picking a spot and making a decent life and passing it on when the time come? Everybody got to be a tycoon these days. Get rich, step on the next guy, die in an ivory tower somewhere surrounded by servants glad to see you go." He took a drink of his water. "Sorry, Jack. We only just met. Not my place to go laying all my woes out like they matter or concern."

"Not at all, Frank. You look like you and the missus built up a nice life around here for your own. More folks ought to take a cue." He stood and pulled his wallet from his coat pocket and pulled out his money. "But I better get on down the road. Got business waiting for me."

Frank stuck out his hand. "Good to meet you, partner. I hope that we'll see you when you come back this way. Just remember, we don't keep hours after midnight."

Jack shook his hand. "That's great. Hope we can pick up where we left off."

"Oh, uh, where you going to? Iffen you don't mind my prying."

"No trouble, friend. Heading north to Grey Head, Wyoming. Family friend found a little oil up there in that flatland. Gonna see if I can lend a hand."

"Best of luck then, Jack."

The sun poked through a heap of billowy clouds just after noon, Jack Hanshaw cut eastward across town toward his business, toward the lawyer.

Bernard Jefferson, "A lie-yer of no standing," he'd recalled Freda Merritt as once having said, demanded a meeting at his office situated above an apothecary and damned if it wasn't the last building on the main street of Butte right across from Dr. Spuss.

Jack Hanshaw was a troubled man paralyzed before a fork in the road. Down one path, he would aid the man who could make him king of the confluence, Helmut Mattocks himself. Down the other path, he could keep his family.

* * *

One year back, in San Luis, under the pink glow of the dry summer morning, Mr. Bernard Jefferson Esq. came to call on Jack Hanshaw in his dilapidated shack near Four Corners.

"I can offer you coffee or stream water?" Jack said.

"Coffee is fine."

"What is it you want, then?" Jack heated an iron pot on a single burner stove on the porch of his shack.

"I have a piece of news that might make someone on this porch a rather rich man. Hell, young man, it might make both of the someone's on your porch rather rich men." Bernard squealed a high pig whistle of a laugh and felt the buttons on his trousers pinch a mash of belly hair coiled in the under flub of his round abdomen. "But, as with all propositions there is a substantial hazard."

"What size of reward are you talking?" Jack said.

Bernard pursed his lips and held his open hands apart about shoulder wide. He looked down and then spread them apart to double the width of his corpulent waistline.

"What kind of risk?" Jack cocked his eyebrow.

Bernard frowned just slightly and pinched his fingers nearly together.

"Seems too good to be true." Jack handed him a jag of coffee and picked up a cup of whisky he'd been drinking the night before, but if he were to be honest with himself he'd really been drinking even at dawn that morning. He was only about an hour into sleep when Bernard woke him up on the flat bench beneath the glassless window on the front of his shack.

Bernard got to looking at Jack real sharp and figured he might just be drunk enough to side with him and his partners in stripping the Merritt mine clean of all its future revenues. The only question, he supposed standing there in the already hot air in the tiny shade of that worn out shack, would Jack stick to his decision if and supposing when he sobered up? It'd be profitable, more than stealing the hand of Midas, he presumed, if he were to hire a man to see to it that Jack Hanshaw's throat never went dry of whisky or beer until the deed was done.

"So how do you plan to get the goods out of Godwin's hands?" Jack said.

"Well, without going into the who and the what of the details, let me just assure you that while God may not be on our side, we do have the next best thing." Bernard rocked on his heels and smugged up his face with a smirk as crooked as a sidewinder.

"And what would that be?" The stale piss wind of whisky breath floated from his mouth.

"The law, Jack." Bernard fanned the air in front of his nose.

Jack kicked sand across his plank porch. He squinted tight enough to reveal the jagged line of teeth behind his sunburned lips. He smacked his lips a few times and spit gobs of saliva over the porch railing. "I don't know, Bernard Jefferson. You're asking a lot of a man who don't got a lot."

"That's why we've come to you. For all the gold his silver's bought him, your brother in law still lets you sweat it out down here in San Luis. Hell, you're just about one step above a beggar," Bernard said and stepped nearer to Jack. He clenched his fist in front of Jack's chest, "What I'm offering you here, now, is a chance to make things right, make things right…legally and personally."

"I hear you. I'll need a day or so to sleep on it."

"Understood. I want you to ride up to Butte in two days. Come to my office on McCormick. No matter what you decide, come. Tell me what your decision is." Bernard stepped down from the porch. "Just come to Butte and talk to me about what you decide."

"Bernard?"

Bernard turned around and stood in the San Luis sun, a hot morning sure to make a fat man sweat like a pig on a spit.

"You have an ace up your sleeve?"

"Beg your pardon, Jack?" Bernard said.

"You better have more than the law on your side if you're going up against God Merritt."

Bernard half-saluted Jack with two fingers off his brow. The desert swallowed him up in the distance as he made his way north.

*   *   *

Bernard's office was a mess of papers shuffled across a wide maple desk supported under one corner with a dense volume of the recently revised Colorado legal code.

When his secretary came in and told him, lo and behold, who was in the outer office, the heaping mass of human greed nearly waltzed off the floor. "Bring him in. Bring him now."

"You look well, my friend. Smell like coffee? Can it be that you've found your way back on the wagon?" Bernard said.

"Maybe. And, maybe not," Jack said.

"Speaking of wagons. See this horse, here?" Bernard pointed to a portrait of a beast of a brown horse on the wall beside the door. A black quarter horse bred for racing.

Jack glanced at it.

"No, really look at 'er."

"I know what a horse looks like."

"Right. I bought 'er when I quit the booze. Well, a year and a half later, but…"

"I'm not in the mood, Mr. Jefferson."

"Alright, Hanshaw. I know we're both busy men and time is of the essence to my partners. Here's what I know and what I, *we*, would like to have done: a spot of trouble and a few miscalculations in the deed to the silver mine that had made Godwin Merritt a fortune revealed that the entrance to Cut Creek Pass has actually been standing on his neighbor's property from day one. That would render, legally speaking, all of the wealth that had been extracted from Cut Creek Pass over the years to the possession and right ownership of the name on the neighbor's plat, a man no one's seen or heard from in anyone's recent memory, Lieutenant Danforth Y. Smith. The old bastard could be dead for all anyone around here knows."

"I'm sure Godwin knows if Lieutenant Smith is alive and kicking," Jack said.

"That may be. The interesting thing about that is the man who would be required to certify such facts before a judge who wouldn't come within two hundred miles of here is the Sheriff, his brother. He's under contract to an interested party who shall remain anonymous."

Jack stood up and leaned on the corner of Bernard's maple desk. "This cheap little swindle won't stand up to any scrutiny. Hell, the ignorant wretch that cleans the linens at Wichita's could tell you that. If this is all you got, then…" Jack pushed on the desk. The book supporting the desk slid and gave under the jostle and his desk pounded the floor causing a cascade of papers to tumble over the edge.

"Damn it, Jack. It's going to take my secretary three days to sort through this mess. What the hell's your problem?"

"You call me up here with the promise of wealth beyond imagining and suggest it's all but in the bag and then lay out a hustle cheaper than Soapy Smith ever conjured down in Leadville? The flimsiest con ever devised west of the Mississippi as your cause for premature celebration? Cork the champagne, you son of a bitch, because Godwin won't be brought down with a two-bit hustle."

"Jack, you're naïve." Bernard pounded his fist on his desk causing more papers to slide to the floor. He pulled the burning cigar from his greasy lips. "This country was built on two-bit hustles. Not only are we going to do it, we're going to run him out on a rail and take his silver to boot."

Jack was at the open door. "You come to me with a plan, not a child's daydream, and we can discuss this again. If you don't come up with something better, you can bet the Sheriff will be out of a job and you'll be lucky to still be above ground." He slammed the door and the black race horse fell to the ground.

Chapter 7.

The garden leaned with the landscape as if always poised to slide off the ranch to the near horizon. The garden was a two hundred square yard plot on the west side of the house. If the snow was as bad as Godwin thought it could be, the spinach, rye, and other greens wouldn't make it. They spent the early light of morning spreading hay and laying long planks to hold it down.

"After lunch we'll set the oil pans around the walks. We can light them when the snow begins to accumulate. Should help keep some of it low enough to get out of the house to the outbuildings. I don't want to walk through five feet of snow to get the eggs out of the henhouse and keep the horses fed." Godwin said.

"Won't the snow put out the fires?" Elwin asked.

"Eventually. But for a while the ground will stay warm and reduce the load."

"Unless the wind whips up drifts," Edwin said.

Godwin ignored his son's pessimism. *Damn Irish doubt.*

Freida sat in a hot bath and the sound of Godwin's pistol rang. One shot. She knew it was his. She closed her eyes and sunk her chin back below the surface. Erwin screamed in the crib in the next room. "Please, God Almighty, help my son."

She changed his dirty cloth diaper quickly, cold in her towel and wet at the shoulders; her red hair half damp and stuck to her neck. She smelled lilac and poop.

She nursed Erwin at her breast until he fell asleep again and rocked him beside the big window in the great room watching Godwin and the other two boys set the pans with oil along the front walk and down the trail at least to the hill where the mountain began its descent and the trail began to wind. If they'd gone any farther she didn't know.

In fact, they stopped at the hill to smoke. Godwin from his bone-handled pipe and Edwin from his wooden one. They let Elwin drag off Edwin's once.

"Come spring I'm taking you along back to Sawyerskill, Edwin," he said.

"How far is that, God?"

"I suppose it's about a thousand miles from here where your grandfather lived."

Edwin sat up and the smoke that irritated his eyelids now sharpened his thinking. "I'd like to see the town for sure."

"It's a healthy ride from here. Still more than a couple days, suppose, on the train."

Elwin knew better than to ask if he could go along with them. He didn't know why. But, he knew it wasn't his journey.

"You're quite the smoker now aren't you, Edwin?"

"Is it okay?" The oldest son averted his eyes, uncertain of his father's opinion.

"It's good to smoke. You're a fine son and deserve maybe a couple of glasses of ale tonight." Godwin said after much consideration, "For all the help today."

"Can I have a glass too, God?" Elwin said.

"No. In good time, the pastimes of men shall be yours for the taking. Be a boy, as much as you can now." Godwin put his arm across Elwin's shoulders. The strength of his father's arm weighed down on him and he knew he trusted his father until the very end of time.

"Can you tell me anything about Sawyerskill? How big of a town is it? What did Grandfather Merritt do for his livelihood?" Edwin inquired.

Godwin looked to Echo Cliff and his eyes fixed on the sheer face. The whap-whapping of the belts filled Godwin's head. He smelled the warm sawdust fresh off of the big hot circular saw…and the blood. He raised his pipe to his lips and gracefully filled his lungs and his eyes fixed on the notch at the base of the bowl on his pipe.

"Pa?" Edwin said.

"Was grandfather Darwin's house nice?" Elwin said.

Edwin nudged his brother's elbow and shook his head.

Godwin tapped his pipe bowl upside down on the fencepost he leant up against and shifted his hat low over his brow. With his pinky finger he wiped out the bowl with more torque than Edwin supposed was necessary. Anyhow, it served to let Elwin know that this was not the time to be resting over a talk with the old man.

Edwin stood discomfited. "What else is on the list to make ready for the storm?"

"I want the bales built up in the barn. Make stalls for the horses to keep warm in. Gather the eggs, Elwin, as you go. You'll go out tomorrow too, if she hasn't bore down on us yet. Edwin and I will chop up the firewood and you can carry it in the house. Fill up the hearths, upstairs and down. Tonight, when the work is near as done as we can get it, we'll sit down and have our ale and wait for the storm to come down from its high place."

"Are you expecting Uncle Jack will make it up here this evening finally?" Elwin said.

"Jack's a gambler. He might waltz up here smack in the middle of the worst of it," Godwin said.

They were inside the house when the coyote wandered through the yard. He had a spot of blood on his haunches that matted his pale hair like as not the cause of his strained gait. Carefully, Godwin made his way to the porch with the rifle up to his shoulder. He could kill the coyote and they could butcher it up and cook it tomorrow.

From the window in the kitchen, Edwin announced, "God's gonna put that lame dog out of his misery."

Freda was mending Godwin's fishing vest at the table. "Why don't you start making the cornbread your girlfriend, Dolly, taught you to make while you're just standing there watching your father shoot that poor thing?"

"Dolly's not my girlfriend, Ma."

"Yes she is," Elwin said. "You told me she was this summer."

"Ma, when you're done with God's vest can I use your threadin' kit?" Edwin said.

"No." Freda ran the needle through the fabric and pulled it straight up until her arm stretched as high as it would and she brought the needle back down and repeated until the hem on the sleeveless vest was secure. "Don't threaten violence against your brother." She placed the needle between her teeth and checked her work and tasted the metal of the needle on her tongue.

"I'm not threating violence. I was just going to help him keep his mouth shut."

"You don't back talk me like that. You might be growing into manhood but you still have no cause to back talk your mother."

"Sorry, Ma." Edwin watched her and waited for her to look at him but she didn't.

"Now are we going to be getting that cornbread you know how to make for supper tonight or are you going to refuse a mother's wish?"

"You really know how to lay on the guilt." Edwin turned and went around the kitchen and got a bowl to mix in and gathered the ingredients.

"Have your brother help you. It doesn't hurt to have more than a couple of cooks in the house," she said.

"I'm supposed to go check the horses one more time and load up the hearths." Elwin said.

"Do as your father says then, son."

Elwin walked through the front room and caught Godwin on the porch with the rifle hoisted to his shoulder and pointed out into the yard. Elwin slowly moved to the other side of the window and saw his father's target.

The rifle shot ripped between the mountains on the edges of Godwin Merritt's ranch. The coyote was dead before the echo of the shot finally fell silent. They'd have more work tonight than Godwin had originally planned, but it'd be a sin to let that coyote wander off to die useless as a bear fart.

He leaned the rifle up against the porch steps and tugged his gloves on. When he was home on his ranch, his hands rarely saw the light of day, always in a pair of thick pigskin gloves. He genuflected beside the dead coyote. "There, friend. All's better. No pain. Thank you for this gift. Better to be useful than selfish." He grabbed the front legs. The teeth snapped shut and the coyote snorted air. Godwin dropped the legs and fell on his butt. "Just a death spasm. You got me good, friend." He grabbed the beast's front legs again and stood to drag the coyote to the out shed.

Elwin entered the shed just as Godwin finished hanging the coyote by his hind legs. It was an abattoir. A stone rut in the floor let blood run out beneath the one-by slats and a half dozen hooks hung from the low beam that ran the width of the shed. Godwin designed and built the knife rack that hung on the wall. He used magnets to let the knives seem to float in front of the wall. The rut in the floor was stained dark with old blood. Sometimes when the boys got into trouble it was their punishment to get the scrub irons that were near the size of blackboard erasers and work the blood off the stone rut.

"What's that smell?" Elwin asked.

"The animal."

"No, God. The smell from your pipe? It's foul."

"It's medicine. It's from Doctor Spuss," Godwin assured.

"What's it for? Your hands or your back?"

"My mind, child. It's medicine for my head."

"I don't think I want to watch you butcher the coyote. I'll go finish the hearths," Elwin said.

"That's alright. It's a foul chore sometimes puts food on the table." The boy was gone when Godwin cut the throat and let the blood spill out. The trench in the floor was bright red now and the smell of fresh blood hit him sharp in contrast to the cannabis that he smoked.

He thought of Jack. He took the knife and stuck it in the animal's abdomen. He gutted it. He still worried about Jack.

Every animal has enough brain to tan its own hide.

Should he sneak down tonight? Creep into Cut Creek Pass without a sound? See if "Uncle Jack" was handling his business? No, he promised Edwin they would sit and drink ale. Still, the snow soon to fall, pressed on his nerves and agitated the paranoia bred into his blood by Darwin and the insane feud he just wanted to keep from his ranch.

Godwin had his knife in the coyote's flank, stripping the hide.

"That what that half-Ute Red Eagle showed you?" The voice was neighborly, right down to the gentle timbre Godwin recalled Lieutenant Smith issuing forth with down in his log cabin at the end of summer.

It couldn't be though. He'd seen the blood beneath the old man's rocker and knowed it was true as the night following day he'd been murdered though no one claimed clapping eyes on him since he was last visited by God Merritt himself.

He stopped and looked at the man in the shed.

"It is a foul chore. Yet, you seem to derive some pleasure from it." Danforth Smith removed his cap with a brass C.S.S. pin stuck in it and smoothed back his slick sandy blond hair. Death had been kind and restored some years to the once salty curmudgeon.

Godwin put the knife down and wiped his bloody hands on a rag. He rubbed his eyes and looked again, the blood not fully wiped from his hands left soft crimson rings around his bloodshot eyes.

"You look sick, Merritt. I just came up for a chitter chatter, you know, between pleasant folk."

"You can't be here. Not really."

"I am. You could ask me to leave but…"

"Leave me." Godwin slammed the butt of his fist on the butchering table.

"But, I don't think you know what you're up against."

"I've taken too much medicine. That's all."

"No, that's not it. Tell you what. You put the money you promised me for my land in my house and I'll help you win this feud with those half-wit bootleggers from the confluence you can't seem to shake on your own."

"How can you know a thing about my family? I don't believe any of them would talk to you. What business is it to you?"

"Keep cleaning the beast. I want to see what Red Eagle showed you while I tell you a simple tale."

Godwin stared at the apparition in his gray military dress, the lieutenant holding the handle of his scabbard in such a cocksure manner as though he were about to call for a charge on an unseen enemy phalanx.

"Go on. Clean the beast while I speak."

Godwin took another knife from the magnetic rack and began to strip the hide from the body.

Lieutenant Smith slipped into his story, "Years before I took my rank in the Confederacy I was a sailor in the United States Navy. I served aboard The Experiment with a man named Farragut who later became the commander of the U.S.S. Saratoga, the sloop of war I served aboard shortly thereafter. In the early days, we were part of the Mosquito Fleet and it was our job to eradicate the pirates wreaking havoc on the Caribbean and Gulf of Mexico. Are you familiar with those regions?"

Godwin nodded as he worked the hide off the coyote, wrenching and cutting the heavy skin off.

"When we were chasing the pirates we would often take prisoners and on one such excursion we captured a few men who looted merchant ships up and down the Gulf of Mexico with a notorious Cuban they called Diabolito. I was in charge of watching these prisoners. One of them, Hernan, spoke enough English to tell me of their conquests. He said many things that sounded too good to be true but I believed him just the same. The look of awe on his comrades' faces when he spoke of some of the things Diabolito showed them convinced me of their virtue. He told of a ritual performed on Diabolito by a medicine man on the Mexican coast that gave him an ability to see what no one can, the future.

"I was spellbound by his tale and went to Hernan many times on that expedition aboard The Experiment to hear more and learn where it was that this ritual took place. This pirate was doing business the entire time. He said without money he couldn't give up the information. I had no money but I knew Farragut well and he'd carelessly let me see the stash he carried on ship. I stole a hundred from him that night. The pirate smiled when I gave him the notes. He told me the location, the tribe, and the name of the one who performed the ritual. I grew desperate to learn this and gain the power it was quite evident their Diabolito possessed with the way he eluded capture on so many close calls.

"It wasn't until many years after that I had a chance to pursue this quest. Once again, I found myself under the command of David Farragut. This time aboard the U.S.S. Saratoga. We were running a blockade off Tuxpan on the Mexican Coast; the location where the tribe lived was not far off. In the long days we were stationed there I contrived by low means to gain access to the money Farragut held in his Commander's Quarters. This would be the second time I stole from Commander Farragut. I snuck off and made contact using the information Diabolito's men gave me and paid the money they told me it would require."

"You found the medicine man?"

Lieutenant Smith nodded. "I found the power. There was no time to waste to get back to the Saratoga. I hastened through what felt like a physical hell or influenza. Aboard ship, I found that many of the crew had come down with Yellow Fever. My own ailment brought on by the ritual intoxicants their man gave me resembled the fever so much they put me along with the others off at the base when we finally landed in Pensacola. It was January 6, 1848. I'll never forget it. I couldn't talk my way out of the medical discharge even though, true to the pirate's assurances, I would see it coming. I begged Commander Farragut to keep me on. As much as I tried to assure him my symptoms were benign and that I could be of utmost value in the future, he declined and put me off at Pensacola."

"You see the future, but can't do anything about it? Doesn't sound like any power I'd want." Godwin nearly had the animal stripped.

"Sometimes the future is what it should be. Mine, for instance. I was old. Too old to move on."

"I don't think so. I think you're just crazy."

"Who's talking to a ghost while they clean the skin off a coyote, Merritt?"

Godwin rubbed his temples with tight fists and shook them at his neighbor with the knife in one.

"Put the money in the oak barrel beside my fireplace and I'll help you win the war with your old enemies."

Godwin threw the knife toward Lieutenant Smith but he was gone. It stuck in the wall. Godwin punched the skinned breast of the coyote and the animal swung on the creaking hook like a pendulum.

Chapter 8.

The barrel in the pantry stayed cool all year round. Built of stone and sealed with a wooden door on iron hinges, the pantry kept cool as a cellar in any weather.

Godwin came out with two glass steins and set them on the farm table in the room off the kitchen. The cold mountain air slipped in through a sliver where the wall joined the window. He was relieved to be resting after the hard work chopping a half cord of wood.

"It's starting," Edwin said. "The snow is starting to fall."

Godwin sat at the farm table, drank half of his glass, and watched the first flakes fall slowly outside the window. The logs crackled bright red in the next room, broke, and settled into a strong fire.

Edwin sat on the bench beside the window, looking out, wondering what it was his father was looking for in the snow. It was his own reflection that kept his father still. What creases time had whittled into the skin of the man in his chair. What worries whitened his temples and beard; furrowed his brow and made smiles rare. His footsteps in the sawdust were quiet the way footsteps in snow are and the whap-whapping of the belts made their distant echoes. Times he wondered were the lumber mill still standing beside the sometimes roiling Sawyerskill.

Upstairs the baby was restless and crying. Freda lay in bed beside Erwin, rubbing his tiny back. "You're doing better, Sweet." She hummed a lullaby her grandmother taught her, one her grandmother heard as a girl in Bavaria. The words' meaning now lost to Freda.

She began to pray the rosary. She thumbed the beads through her palm as she slowly gave in to the comfort of the bed and the warmth of the fire and the silence of the snow, halfway into the Glorious Mystery.

Into his second stein, he decided that this snow was a good moment to let Elwin drink his first glass of family ale. "Come to the pantry, Elwin. You too, son," he said to Edwin.

The pantry was dank and dim. Candlelight from the sconces in the kitchen and fire in the iron stove made their shadows dance like puppets on the walls of the half-dark pantry. He pulled a stein down from the shelf and handed it to Elwin. "Pour your first draught. Tonight you get only one. Enjoy it slowly, son."

"Thank you, God," Elwin said. He took the stein and put his nose to the brew—smelled it deeply. It was dark amber below the foam top. Foam that a nickel could float on he guessed. Edwin was first to hold his stein out. Then Godwin and Elwin stuck theirs out. They made a silent toast. "The hard day done. The fires lit."

The snow fell quicker.

"God, why didn't Uncle Jack make it up by now?" Elwin asked. "I thought I heard you say to Ma that he was supposed to come up from Cut Creek Pass."

"Jack could have been cut off by the storm anywhere west of Cut Creek. He may have decided not to come at all." They left the pantry, left the big barrel there in the candlelight. In shadows, it stood like an ox behind the door.

They returned to the great room where the window had grown a thin beard of frost. The front porch rail creaked long moans in the night wind and blowing snow. "I'm going to go out on the porch a minute, God. I want to see the snow," Edwin said.

"Put your gear on. We don't need any more illness in this house," Godwin said. As Edwin wrapped his blue wool scarf around his face Godwin continued, "And don't be out there long enough so your nose drips."

Edwin took a drink of ale and set his stein on the wide windowsill. He picked up his pipe and packed a fresh bowl of tobacco. He checked his pocket for the box of small wooden matches and said, "Be back in a few moments. Need anything when I'm out?"

"Funny, Ed," Elwin said. A dark tone slipped into his voice that he'd not expected.

Edwin looked at him sideways a moment and then waved him off as he walked out of the room. Godwin sat in the room alone with his young son sharing the family ale. He preferred quiet to the casual chatter where spaces of clumsy apprehension could be relied upon to let slither in the poisonous snakes of gossip and rumor. He preferred his thoughts to the amusement of others. However, the obligation of making for Elwin a memorable night of his first drink of ale brought to his lips an unusual effluence of idle talk.

"Have you met Edwin's girlfriend? I thought you had gone along with him this summer to the girl's family home. Good people, aren't they?" Godwin said.

Elwin, sat up straight. Excited to engage with his father in what was casual and manly conversation he assumed, conversation between hard-working men with a belly full of ale and an atmosphere of pipe smoke. He eyed Godwin's pipe desirous to know what it was to smoke and drink but knew that his ale in hand, even though just a single stein, was a major rite of passage and his father made certain he accepted its boundary. *One stein and enjoy it slowly*, he'd commanded. His brother had disgraced the privilege one evening two summers ago. He'd drunk himself oblivious and Freda found him before dawn, naked on the porch swing with a broken stein at the bottom of the steps. He wasn't allowed into the pantry until this spring. The lock finally removed from the big wood door hung from a nail overhead as a reminder against drunkenness.

"The Spretlezbuns are a very good family, God. Mrs. Spretlezbun made honey rolls with caramel glaze for us while we were visiting. She said we could take some with us but Edwin politely declined, saying the trip home would take too long and the rolls wouldn't last the journey with two hungry boys excited by summer adventures." He sat back and shrugged. He was unsure of how his excitement would rub his somber father. He didn't want his father to suspect him drunk but the ale was beginning to get hold of his better nature.

"I believe it's time you got yourself to bed, son. Finish up the ale and get along."

"Yes, God."

"Son?"

"Yes, God?"

"I enjoyed talking with you just now. I want you to know."

"Thank you, Pa."

"Goodnight, son."

"Night, dad." He stopped in the doorway to the kitchen, backlit by the tall candles and the earnest fire in the iron stove. He saw Edwin through the window smoking his pipe and looking up to the heavens through the falling snow. Elwin put his stein in the dish tub and went up the stairs in the back of the house. He washed his face over the wide bowl on his dresser, brushed his teeth with the baking powder, and rinsed with the water in the pitcher. In the morning he would take the bowl of dirty water outside to the spot behind the house where they dumped their waste water. He lay in his bed thinking the soft intoxicated half-dreams that his stein of ale had let him have before he finally fell asleep.

Outside, Edwin was thinking of the girl, Delia. Not the one his mother had called his girlfriend earlier today. Not of Dolly. He was thinking of her sister, Delia. Her older, taller sister. Her makeup. Her legs. Her breasts, he'd been caught looking at. "Little man," the older sister had quietly said, "mind your manners, little man. That is what ladies desire." He had never been more embarrassed.

The ale called him and he was about to go inside to get another round when the hinges squeaked and Godwin stepped out onto the porch. "Evening, God," Edwin said. "Pretty nice out here, cold as it is."

"The silence is beautiful," Godwin admitted. It was so, at that moment, that the torment of the steam saw and what happened there in his adolescence was muted. He harkened to it as if lost without it but savored the silent snow for the time being.

Thunder boomed just then and bounced between the mountains in an echoing jest. "Mostly silent. Elwin go to bed?" Edwin asked.

"I sent him off to bed. He was beginning to get romantic about the summer. You ought to be getting inside as well. Just the same, help me light the oil in the pans. I think it's really going to hit its stride while we're all asleep tonight. Got plenty of matches?"

"Yes, God. Got a mostly full carton here. Got your gun? In case another coyote comes round out of the blue. That was a heck of a shot you made off the porch today."

"Nothing to it. Was as close as I'm likely to see in my lifetime. Besides. The poor mutt was already lame when he stumbled on up to our ranch. No, with the snow coming down as it is we'd be lucky to see a coyote before it was right on top of us tonight."

They began the slough into the yard. The first pan was hard to light for both of them; Edwin on the south side of the lane and Godwin on the north side. The wind wasn't fierce but it did reduce visibility to a couple dozen feet and made it difficult to keep a match lighted long enough to ignite the oil pan.

Three men sat on horseback behind the tree line in a stand of pines. They'd silently watched the figure on the Godwin Merritt Ranch smoke on the porch. They could not figure if it was only a boy or Godwin himself. Irvin watched intently, looking for definition in the silhouette that stood still in the night. When Godwin had finally stepped onto the porch to join the figure Irvin was glad they had waited to make a move. Yet, now they watched the men do something peculiar in the yard crouching over something they could not make out from the tree line. He wondered what it was and held his men back.

Finally, Godwin got the first one lit. He crushed footsteps along to the next one and got it lit just as Edwin lit his first one. Now the race was on. Though they didn't say so explicitly, they began a race with their torches. A bouncing glow lit the rolling yard. If there was any smoke it became invisible in the snowstorm. They'd find their way in with no problem though. The oil burned well. The snow was not quick enough to put the damper on. These pans became burning breadcrumbs to light their way back home. An owl called from the woods in the hidden distance. Godwin looked toward it but saw only snow. He'd taken a few steps farther when the keeper of the night flew but a yard or two in front of him, knee level and straight as an arrow. He saw something freed from the shallow snow, defying gravity under the barn owl's graceful ascent. They were near to the hill now where the last pans were set. There was no time to rest for a smoke now. Godwin felt the pain coming on from the cold as his knuckles slowly made to lock up in his wet pigskin gloves.

Edwin took a cue from his father and they ran up through the fiery lane to the warmth of the great room. "One more stein?" Edwin suggested.

"No. Too cold for that. Come on. Let's sit in the kitchen where the stove is hot." They removed their outer gear in alternating shivers and huffs. Edwin cleared his nose from a new cold. He felt it in his chest already. Standing by the stove and rubbing his hands near the grill on the door where you could see the progress of the fire he wondered where God had gone to.

The pantry door opened and Godwin stepped out with an unmarked bottle. "Something Jack gave me last year. Ale is useless at this point. Whisky will keep us warm."

The men in the trees retreated down to their camp. There would be no contact tonight. The fires on the lane had sent a chill into Irvin's spine. The Godwin Merritt Ranch became an ominous fortress in the veil of snow and the glow of fires.

Chapter 9.

"Have you ever seen anything like it, Sheriff?" Deputy Morrison asked. He drank a sip of whisky from the two ounce shot glass the bartender brought him. The bottle was open and stood in a sharp shaft of sunlight piercing the wooden shutters behind them. The Copperhead was empty and wouldn't open for another hour or so.

Sheriff Smith moved away, his frantic feet clapped the soles of his spotless boots atop the brick floor. His dark glasses hid his bloodshot eyes. "Not since we fought those savages down near the border."

The deputy didn't say anything. It hadn't been him that was by Sheriff Smith's side as he fought in the canyon for weeks with a group of cavalry boys against some Mexicans who thought they were going to take back the southwest. It had been Robert Morrison, his father. Shot in the head by god knows whom. They closed the case on it before his old man was covered over in the grave. The deputy had his doubts, expressed by his mother before her own death. She'd mentioned the Sheriff, who was a deputy himself at the time, had grand ambitions to be a U.S. Senator and thought a surefire way to get there was to be a Sheriff in a bustling metropolitan territory in the new states. She was certain there was more to Robert's death and that Smith was responsible for the cover up if not his actual murder.

Sheriff Smith had seen a body before and more to the point, he'd seen a dead body without its head. What he hadn't seen was so much evidence left behind implicating the guilty.

If they found the trail of the guilty, they'd find the man who'd given the order. As it was, that man was looking at Sheriff Smith in the mirror in the bathroom at the saloon. He punched the mirror and cussed the men in spit-riddled curses. The headless Mr. Jefferson was loaded down with identification, notes of who he'd met and intended to meet that day, and a pair of red cotton women's underwear Sheriff Smith was just certain belonged to the silly gal that did the number on his leg and left him with his now signature hobble. "A hitch in your get along," he now heard his father's voice say in his head every time the ache in his leg got to be so much that the respite and shade of his cocaine became inadequate. He took another sniff. The room began to shake and he felt weak in his limbs and tried to grasp for something to hold onto. He lost his grip and passed out.

A while later, Sheriff Smith found himself coming to in a chair in the Copperhead. The ducked heads were sunken into shoulders like vultures on a ridge, sitting at the bar; hunting memories with ounces and pints and quarts of alcohol, trying to kill whatever doom lurked over themselves usually self-inflicted by misguided wisdom and dumb ideas and dreams of quick cash and perfect crimes.

The bartender took his order, poured him a neat whisky, and set a folded up newspaper in front of the sheriff. He took the drink and the paper to a table against the back wall beside the bathroom door.

He downed his whisky before he even got to the table. When he sat down the bartender saw he was empty. He brought the bottle, "We just got our shipment in last Thursday," the bar man said. Tennessee bourbon whisky— direct from Alexander Farrar himself. Corn whisky distilled in shouting distance from Duck River in Noah, Tennessee."

"Proud of your whisky, I see."

"I just know you like a good whisky, Sheriff."

Sheriff Smith handed him five dollars and that was that.

The glint in his eyes blinded him to the stranger at the bar; the one loser who didn't fit in.

In the bright light beside the picture window at the other end of the bar was a true outsider. The long coat, the white handle of the Colt sticking just outside the coat, and the small boots that nervously tapped the brass rail beneath the bar. The stubble that barely hid soft features and pinched nose and the curly hair that hung down just beneath some straight hair at the earlobes. The bartender nervously eyed the stranger he'd just served. Finally, a drinker beside the man said, "You ain't local, is you?"

The other man just shook his head and walked out the door.

"Hey, what's with that guy?" he asked the bartender.

"Never seen him before. Something not right though," the bartender said.

"I'll say. Smelled like cigarettes and perfume."

"Don't worry, pal. Maybe he actually got some action instead of losing like us."

"Speak for yourself, man. I get mine regular." He took a drink of beer and after he barely swallowed his gulp he finished his thought, "Like the 5:50 out of Denver."

"I bet, man. Yours has five fingers with hairy knuckles and is attached to your wrist."

A shoving match broke out and the Sheriff ruffled his papers in front of his face. A shoving match always broke out in the Copperhead around that time and that time just happened to be whenever the bartender unlocked the door and started serving booze to guys with nothing to lose and barely anything to pay.

This time was different.

This time the guy who started it had been shoved too far and he pulled out a little dagger and drove it into the other guy's hand. He stuck it clean into the bar. The man screamed like a stuck pig and pulled the handle as hard as he could. He couldn't get the knife out of the bar and started throwing bottles and glasses as hard as he could with his left hand. Being a righty, his throws were off the mark of his moving target. Then he did the only sensible thing and drew his pistol. He shot the bartender and shot the man who stabbed him. The bartender would live but the stabber would not.

The bartender crawled to the fourteen-inch thunder stick he kept under the sink and shot the man who shot him—dead in the chest.

Sheriff Smith threw his paper down on the floor and chucked his empty glass across the room. It hit the wall and shattered. "Goddamn it! I can't even have a drink in this shit-box saloon without everything going to hell."

The bartender tried to speak but he was gripping his arm in pain.

"I'm going to have to confiscate that blunderbuss now, chief," Sheriff Smith said.

"Rightly so. But, you saw what happened. I was only defending myself."

"You're lucky you got that shipment of Farrar in, Zeke."

The bartender nodded trying to tie a dirty towel around his arm.

"You might want to pour a little of the cheaper stuff on that wound before you tie it up with that dirty rag," The Sheriff spent the night cleaning up the mess. He hadn't seen a thing and didn't care. He believed the man who poured his drinks and wrote it off as settled and over. He'd never pay for a drink again in the Copperhead.

Back at the county lock up, the deputy said, "You seem to find death easily."

"I find it easily forgettable," Sheriff Smith said.

"I believe it. After this night, I'd be looking to forget some things too."

Smith knew the Morrison family had suspicions about Robert's death and hell, maybe those suspicions even implicated himself as the murderer. Nonetheless, who was this scumbag to cast a suspicious eye his way? "Deputy, Bernard Jefferson, respected as he was in Butte and Lake County for being a mad dog in the court room was far from innocent."

"Still no cause to cut off his goddamned head. What kind of stone cold maniac cuts off another person's head? I don't know what kind of world we're living in. Seems like Book of Revelations stuff there."

"Ain't no reason to be had but the thing to keep in mind is Bernard Jefferson had cultivated an impressive list of enemies in his day. Don't read too much into it lest you lose your own head, so to speak." The sheriff fell into his chair and kicked his boots up on his desk. "Why don't you go on home and get some sleep. Have a drink or stop by Wichita's and get some tail."

"I'll just go home and sleep it off. I don't know how you do it, Sheriff."

"Nothing to it after a while."

Deputy Morrison left and quietly sauntered down to Dr. Spuss'. The door opened and Dr. Spuss embraced his friend. "You look terrible."

"I've seen some awful shit today."

Dr. Spuss kissed his friend and they collapsed into bed together to forget the troubles and ease the terrors sure to haunt Deputy Morrison for a time to come.

Chapter 10.

Erwin's fever broke that morning. Freda was reading Moby Dick in the great room and Erwin was bundled in a blanket in his bassinet just a few feet in front of the fireplace. She'd been up since three in the morning and wished she'd slept longer but Erwin's restless cries as he struggled to get comfortable kept her mind and body tossing and turning.

When she noticed it had broken she wept. She ran in to tell Godwin. She woke him from some deep snoring sleep but he was happy she did.

Godwin glided out of bed and ran to the baby. He scooped Erwin in his arms and kissed him in a long silence. Freda's belly fluttered and she smiled wide as the sunrise.

Godwin returned Erwin to his mother's arms. He kissed her and felt the spark between them that had dulled over time.

"I'm going to run the chores. I have a suspicion the boys will not be up for some time," he told her.

"I'll see you in the kitchen for breakfast then," she said barely able to hold her eyes open.

Hours passed before dawn. He worked diligently in a contented relief that he saw no end to. As the sun whitened the range, Godwin worked toward a stopping point and made his way back to the house.

He stood then at the kitchen window. Dressed in denim overalls and thick boots; his pigskin gloves were shoved in his back pocket. His mind raced trying to come up with some quick chore to get done.

"The fires stay lit, God?" Edwin said. He was leaned up against the doorway—puffy eyes and mussed hair.

"You slept late," Godwin said.

"I forgot to set the alarm."

"The cows didn't forget."

"I'll get my coat and go milk them."

He was already down the hall to the mudroom when Godwin boomed, "No need. I got them before dawn." Godwin felt his own voice bang within his chest. It was the kind of baritone that echoed inside like a fence post swept round and round a fifty-five gallon barrel.

Edwin dropped his shoulders out of sight of Godwin. He stiffened up, "Sorry, God. Thank you, sir." He rounded the corner back into the kitchen knowing what was next.

"Maybe next time you'll save that last glass of ale for another time."

"You're right, God. But, I don't think it was the ale."

Godwin recalled then, the whisky he'd poured for them after setting the oil pans alight. "Fair enough, Edwin."

"Think we can get down to the stream this afternoon or does it look too deep out there?" Edwin said.

"I don't know. May have to just try and see how far we get. I don't think Elwin should go. Something were to happen, he needs to be able to take care of the house."

"He'll be upset," Edwin said.

"Who'll be upset?" Elwin asked as he came into the kitchen fully dressed and ready for the day.

"You. When you can't go along to the stream this afternoon. Might be too deep out there."

"I'd say it is. Look at it. It's still coming down real strong. I'd rather stay in just the same. I can give Ma a break. She said Erwin's fever broke this morning."

"You got up and at 'em early, Elwin. Proud of you, son. Up and around like a man." He didn't even glance at Edwin.

"Freda!"

"Yes, God."

"What's the breakfast menu going to be?"

"Bacon, biscuits, and eggs."

Godwin went to her. He sat on the couch. Erwin lay on the floor between their feet. "Do you mind if I get breakfast cooking? I want to get a start on down to the stream to see if we can snag some fish. It will break up the eating good if we can add some fish to the table."

"I don't mind at all, God. Just don't burn the bacon. Do you mind if I read here a little while longer then?"

"Take a rest." He looked at Erwin. "You did a great job getting him through his fever. I love you, Freda."

She squeezed his hand and returned to her Melville hardback and he took his oldest to go get their own fish.

Godwin was at the back door when his legs went loose forcing him to brace against the doorjamb. The old belts of the sawmill and the steam whistle shot through his mind. The face filled his closed eyelids like a painting on black canvas. He'd only blinked but the face was as clear as the day he'd seen it. Two eyes bulged and swollen lips tenderized by repeated blows with an iron hammer that Godwin seemed to have clasped in his hand right there in the doorway of his ranch all those years later.

Edwin was ahead of him in the mudroom, "You alright, Pa?"

Godwin swallowed hard and flexed his entire face. He spit into the pan beside the door, "Let's go before it's too deep," he said.

"Ah, alright," Edwin said.

They disappeared down the lane as Elwin watched from the window.

Chapter 11.

Sheriff Smith dozed off while she stimulated him orally in the room at the end of the basement hallway at Madame V.'s. He opened his eyes and realized where he was precisely. "See, the older I get, the darker my dreams get."

Her eyes remained closed and the movement of her hair suggested she nodded in agreement.

His eyes closed and he fell back asleep. He'd been taking small doses of heroin lately to ease the back pain triggered by the remaining buckshot the doctor out on the territory had been unable to remove. The flare-ups were intense. Anymore though he didn't know what was worse. The pain? Or the cure?

She tucked him back in when she was through and buttoned him up knowing he wouldn't recall the conclusion of their transaction or demand proof or a refund. He was content to do exactly as they'd just done. It wasn't her job to ensure he be conscious. It was more her job to drive him mad.

"I must stop talking so much. Your lips open my own somehow and all the shadows that haunt me come spilling out like a child's confession of a simple offense."

"You're not the only one who opens up to me. Our business easily tricks the foolish heart as men's hearts have always been."

"A philosopher and a whore! What a deadly combination."

"A lot of things pop into your head when you perform fellatio." She certainly smiled when she said it.

So did he.

He left the basement through a hidden door into a tunnel that lead the opposite direction from the one Mr. Jefferson had regularly used. His deputy waited at the other end of the tunnel reading a book. When Sheriff Smith knocked the deputy opened the door and they went on up to the street level behind the saloon.

They walked the street in the blowing snow, voices muffled behind their heavy collars pulled up tight over their noses. The deputy boomed, "Mr. Jefferson should be on his way up to the mountain. They came and got him last night when he left Madame V.'s."

"He's gone then?"

"If you believe their word, he's done gone," the deputy said.

The sheriff's collar hid the sneer.

He knew the men well. They were relation from a generation back. His father, the sheriff before him, had introduced the organization to the town a quarter century ago. The Black Rock Runners taught a clan of misfits how to run the still and skim the till. They'd set up one of the first franchises in the region. It seemed a prodigious effort was expended by the Black Rock Runners to stay close to their enemies. Black Rock moonshine popped up in more than one town along the way. They set up stills, made cash, sent a share back home and used the rest to maintain their rudimentary surveillance on anyone who tried to put one over on them and get away. Word never got around that they were up to this backwoods mercenary work.

Sheriff Smith and the deputy stepped inside a small smithy storefront and warmed their hands beside a wood stove in the front corner. "Sheriff Smith, looks like a cold son-of-a out there," Yeats, the blacksmith, said.

"It's colder than it looks, brother," Sheriff Smith said. They shook hands heavily with all four hands piled into each other. They had other business to tend than horseshoes and hand held blades. He put his hand back to let the deputy know he should stay put. "Be back in a moment, Deputy Morrison."

"Sir," Deputy Morrison said and turned back to the fire. He heard them mumble on their way through the door to the back where the storefront ballooned into a working blacksmith workshop.

Under a pile of burlap and broken tools Yeats had a massive Wacker safe; top of the line, impenetrable by modern warfare, and heavier than a mountain. Wacker ads in papers across the country boasted, "Wacker safes never crack or your money back." Yeats stroked his beard that ran down to his belly in a V of tangled red, blonde, and white hairs. He was not a clean man, covered in black coal dust and soot, stinking of sweat and piss and whisky. He was a busy man cause he was a reliable smith but no one stuck around the storefront to chitchat and that's how he preferred it if you ever stifled the gag reflex long enough to ask him so.

"They left the cash yesterday morning, just after sunrise. It scared the shit out of me. I was passed out on the counter out front. The big one, Irvin, was banging on the glass with the butt of his pistol. Well, I'd never seen the guys before. I thought I was up shit creek way those guys looked."

"Hell of a deal," Sheriff Smith said taking the envelope of cash. Don't know just how to thank you, Yeats. Sorry for the little scare they gave you."

"No skin off my chin, Smith. I don't like to get my nose in where it don't belong but, everything work out alright? Seemed like a raw band of professionals those three."

"Yeah, well, they like to pass themselves off as professionals," Smith said walking back to the front of the shop. "But they forgot a very big part of their job." He pulled a gun from his pocket and shot Yeats straight in the forehead. The dumb shock froze on his blackened forehead and he fell straight back, stiff as a hammer into the dirt floor of his work area.

Sheriff Smith tossed the gun to Yeats' body and then pulled his own gun out.

Deputy Morrison rushed into the back of the shop with his gun up. "What's happened?" he said out of breath and looking everywhere.

"He pulled a gun on me. I'm sure he was out of his mind on that white lightning over there," Sheriff Smith said pointing to the empty bottles of hooch staggered around his bench. Definitely jars bought from the local branch of the Black Rock Runners.

"Why would he draw a gun on you though, Sheriff?" the baffled Morrison said.

"I can't really say. You know how these alkies get. He probably had no idea what the hell he was doing, but I wasn't going to stand here with my piece in my hand while he figured it out."

"It don't add up. You two were being cordial and good fellas just a minute ago."

"He was back here accusing me of all kinds of lies just a moment before he pulled that pistol on me."

"That's not so. He was talking about some guys who came in last morning and dropped some cash in here for you. Now I don't care what business you got but don't lie to me about Yeats. He was a decent man. A drunk man, but still decent as the day is long."

"Well, Morrison. The days are getting shorter," Sheriff Smith shot Morrison in the belly before he finished his thought. "...so Yeats wasn't that decent, I'd conclude."

Deputy Morrison was on his butt when the sheriff shot him again. The bullet split his head open before the echo of the shot even filled the room.

Sheriff Smith adjusted the bodies and replaced the guns so that the whole scene wrote the lie he was crafting. "No need, really. I'm the goddamn law here," he huffed as he moved the bodies a little this way and a little more that way.

He lit a cigarette off a red hot iron that had been stuck in the coals.

He went to the storefront and watched the big show snowstorm that somebody's god was putting on. He noticed some faces in windows across the street looking for the scene of the commotion. He stood far enough back that they probably couldn't see him. He stubbed out the cigarette on the plank floor in the front of the building and ran out the front door to the druggist. He rushed into the shop screaming, "Doc, Doc!" He was out of breath, "Morrison's shot. I need help. Yeats' shot him. Come on!"

The doctor, rounded the corner. Doctor Spuss; an athletic man in his late thirties serving time in the backwater town doing community service for some trumped up charge back in the capital that he was distributing a demon plant that caused well-mannered Christian men to lose their minds with lust and commit all sorts of deviant and heinous sexual acts. He'd denied selling cannabis sativa but the drug had been planted quite literally all over his property in the center of town. So there he was chasing after Sheriff Smith to help the already dead Deputy Morrison; a man he'd met on his first day in town and immediately fell in love with. The doctor and the deputy had been in the throes of their illicit affair for more than two years when Doctor Spuss slid on his knees to the side of Deputy Morrison's corpse. He lifted his head in his hands, half gone but recognizable from the nose down. Doctor Spuss screamed for the whole world to hear. He screamed for the love they never spoke about to anyone. He collapsed over the empty skull whose brain was now in many places at once.

"What happened?" he helplessly sobbed and spit snot off his lips. "How did this happen?"

"I don't know. I..." Sheriff Smith trailed off through squinted eyes beginning to see pieces of Morrison's life he'd not seen yet. Some portrait was taking form before his eyes.

Things he'd sensed through a deep fog of Deputy Morrison's general ambivalence.

"Did you really think there's something I could do to help him? Half of his head is blown apart." He wailed, "Your beautiful head." Doctor Spuss went silent. He froze with a dark shadow suddenly inside him. A foreboding. Three men enter, he puzzled. Two are dead. One is calm. Words like *foul, malice, and corrupt* swirled in his brain. He didn't know but he felt he'd already solved the crime. But, whatever Sheriff Smith said the truth was that is what the truth would be. For the time being. He picked up his sobbing in camouflage and rubbed his bloody hands on his white shirt. Wiped his bloody hands on his pants. He stood up and edged to the front. "Forgive me, Sheriff Smith. The deputy and I developed a good friendship over the years. He and his wife and I got along when I didn't know anyone else in town. Who's going to tell her?"

"It's my fault. I got him in this situation. I'm his boss. And I'm responsible to tell her of his death."

"I don't even know how she'll go on," Doctor Spuss lamented.

"The way we all do, Doctor." Sheriff Smith put his hand on the doctor's shoulder and escorted him to the storefront. The open door let in a biting cold wind and snow was swirling on the floor. "Before you go," Sheriff Smith said, "I'll be needing some more heroin for my pain."

"Certainly, Abraham," Dr. Spuss said. He'd stripped all posturing from his mind. This addict with his sheriff costume made his skin crawl.

"I'm sorry about your friend. He was a good deputy," Sheriff Smith said.

"He was a better man." Dr. Spuss regarded the shop turned abattoir behind Sheriff Smith, "Neither of them deserved that end."

The sheriff nodded. He considered the doctor was suspicious. He watched him lurch back to the druggist. He knew the doctor didn't have a hand to play and decided then to let him be.

The town would have a rough go without Yeats, for sure. His job, though, became infinitely easier without Deputy Dipshit as he called him behind his back.

The undertaker would be a bit busier this week, he mused as he sat at his desk back at the courthouse. He fingered the thick bar of cash in his hands and felt nothing but relief.

Chapter 12

"This powder is deep enough to cover Taft," Edwin said.

The snow was up to the middle of their thighs. That's how they found the banks of the stream and they were lucky not to have fallen into the icy water. A tree branch cracked and broke as they approached with their poles, nets, and tackle. The branch fell mightily through the snow and into the water. It freed up a mass of snow, which began to drift downstream. The stream was visible then from that point down. "A sign from the Almighty, I'd say," Edwin said.

Godwin held his silence. He caught sight of a moose, thin and knobby at the legs and wearing a frump of a mane to the shoulders. "Wish we'd brought the rifles." He spit. "For another day, I guess." The tension hadn't left his face ever since they lit out from the ranch.

"He's not much, there. Reckon?" Edwin said.

"Enough to have a feast of dried jerky, boy."

A wolf howled through the frozen woods. It ricocheted on down the stream through the canopy of empty limbs that looked to Godwin like countless gnarled knuckles. His own knuckles. Reminded him of pain.

"We should get our hooks in the stream if we're going to try," Edwin said.

"It is getting colder as the morning goes on." Godwin took the hook and put some fatty pig meat on it. "Think we'll catch anything with this unusual bait?"

"Maybe a cold." Edwin took a small chunk of the hog meat and threw his line into the stream.

"Maybe death." Godwin actually chuckled and Edwin followed suit.

"Hope not, God. I've got a whole world to see yet."

"Fair point, son."

They sat with their hooks in the stream. "I could go gather some branches and build a fire, if'n you think we'll be down here long."

"No use. The snow's deep and the branches are all wet." Godwin stared at the calm stream, looking for any sign of a meal.

"I guess we didn't bring a hatchet anyway. No way to break them off or chop them up."

Needless to say, the fishing expedition was a bust. Edwin was able to mend his father's opinion of him and in that way they would be able to work together through the mounting blizzard. As they ascended the hill for the push home, they noted the craters in the snow that marked the driveway. The oil pans had done their job and made it easy to find the path up. They smiled and laughed and Godwin did hit his son with a snowball square in the neck. They chased each other; leapfrogging snowball throws to the porch. Freda heard their laughter when they were still halfway down the drive. She poured hot coffee with a dash of whisky and heavy cream.

Elwin came rushing into the kitchen with Erwin in his arms. He was anxious to see if there would be fish for supper. "It smells good in here, Ma. Should we share the pie with the fishermen or keep it for ourselves."

"Well Elwin, if you want to keep it all to ourselves I'll let you explain the mess of flour, raw crust, and cinnamon all over the farm table."

The back door flew open and Edwin hoisted his head into the air. He sucked in the smell of hot apples and cinnamon, fresh coffee. He rounded the corner nearly tripping on the small stoop that separated the mudroom from the kitchen.

"Glorious apple pie!" Edwin shouted.

"Shhhh! Erwin is sleeping," Freda said.

"Oh. Sorry, Ma."

"Coffee?" Godwin said.

"With a little kick to warm you gentlemen up," she said.

Godwin held her sides and kissed her hair. She turned and kissed his mouth. "You better warm those lips up."

He took his coffee by the iron stove. Edwin joined him there.

"How'd you make out? Any fish?" she asked.

"No luck. But worth the try," Godwin said.

"We should try tomorrow. Take some firewood down too. Really go to catch," Edwin said. "Elwin could help haul wood."

"I don't think we're going anywhere tomorrow. The craters are beginning to fill in fast," Godwin said. Outside the world had become a white wall of blowing snow. It went on and on. They were awestruck at once. Up 'til then it had only tried to come down.

"You boys go out again you might freeze your little butts off," Freda said. And she froze.

Her eyes didn't move. They remained open and fixed.

A tremor in her bottom lip.

Godwin stared. Waited for a cue.

Thud.

Freda collapsed to the hard kitchen floor.

Godwin dropped his coffee on the stove and rushed down to her.

He held her head in his hands and looked at her eyes. "Free! Free! Say something. Say something, Freda!" He looked back and yelled at his sons, "Get some water. Get the couch set up with pillows. Go, goddammit! Do something."

They rushed to help.

Edwin got the couch. Elwin got the water.

Godwin got under her and picked her up across his arms. He carried her through to the great room and laid her on the couch. She was convulsing. Her eyes closing and opening, the pupils rolled like the mill wheel into Sawyerskill. Godwin held her tight and put his ear on her breast to listen for what, he didn't know. Her eyes stopped rolling after a minute.

However, she didn't move. She laid there fixed on the ceiling with her arms and legs motionless. Godwin began to sob. He didn't move. He didn't make a sound. He kept his head on her chest and hoped for a miracle.

Shallow breaths shot from everyone in the room. Shallower still were the ones that worked from Freda's lungs.

Edwin picked up Erwin from the floor. Erwin looked wide-eyed around the room as he sucked his thumb. As he scanned the room, he caught sight of his mom and reached toward her. Edwin carried him into the kitchen.

Not sure of himself, Elwin knelt beside his mother and began to pray softly. Her hand squeezed Godwin's ever so lightly and let go. She moaned with no definition and a flat cadence, "—ove. Uhhhv. Oooh"

Her eyes closed. She took shallow breaths. Godwin put his hand on Elwin's back and felt the breathing of his son as Elwin prayed the rosary. He leaned his head into his father's shoulder.

They sat that way for an hour.

Time stood still inside the Godwin Merritt Ranch even though the shadows of the mountains grew long upon the deepening snow.

She took her last breath and the moan of her final exhale shook Elwin to tears.

Godwin put the boys to bed after hours of assurances and promises.

*　*　*

Snow fell upside down when Godwin opened his eyes. He was on the bed in his room with his head beneath the window. The wall was cold when he felt around for bearing.

He watched the snow at its strange angle and felt the bottom drop out when his light-headed paroxysm triggered a shiver. Freda's bottle of aspirin was open beside his half-empty whisky bottle. He sat up on the edge of his bed and lit his pipe with a leftover pack of the cannabis Dr. Spuss prescribed him. The edges softened in the room. The candlelight expanded and he saw the embers roasting in the fireplace. He put a fist to his temple. "Freda." He moaned quietly and then began to pace. The draft that came through the window frame tickled the leaves of paper resting on the bureau across the room. He saw them flutter and seized upon them.

The letter to Farragut from Lieutenant Smith. He ran his fingers over the signature. On his desk beneath the only other window in the room was an envelope with a tricky document that would have made the sale of Lieutenant Smith's land to Godwin Merritt legally binding. He walked across the room with the Farragut letter and noticed every knot in the floorboards and every snowflake in the window. His perception slowed space and time and the distance between his bureau and desk became expansive. He removed the document from its envelope and laid it side by side with the letter. His eyes narrowed and the wrinkles up his face deepened as he strained to see the words on the paper. *Bring the candle.*

Godwin got up and retrieved the candle from the ten-gallon barrel with the iron bands. Her copy of Moby Dick sat upon the barrel lid and he brushed it with his fingertips. She told him it was great but he had no interest in reading it. He enjoyed listening to her tell him about the books she read. His hands clenched and he took the candle to the desk. He sat and stared at his reflection in the window. The snow fell hard behind the face he stared at that waved with each flicker of the flame. He took a blank page from the journal she got him for his birthday to use keeping track of inventory on the ranch. It was leather bound. Inside the cover was a photograph of Godwin with the first dog they ever had on the ranch. The dog's name was Sawyer and when he died from old age, Freda took his body to Red Eagle and asked him to make something useful for Godwin. He returned the beautiful journal to her just before Godwin's birthday.

He slowly tore out a blank page with intense pressure and focus he recreated the signature of his neighbor. He examined the first pass closely. He was certain it would not do.

He'd go down to his neighbor's little house at once. *Put a gun to his head. Make him sign it or else.*

He shuddered. Someone was behind his reflection. He turned. "Just the draft on the flame."

Godwin was halfway down the trail in deep snow getting heavier as the night went on. The little house of Lieutenant Smith's was dark and when he got closer he saw the door open and no glow from a fire at all. Godwin drew his gun at the doorstep and went in carefully. Snow drifted well inside the door and fanned out like a doormat. The lantern he rode down with showed everything clearly. The blood in the rocker and on the floor below. The smear of blood in a trail from the rocker to the door. How long had it been? When did this happen? He searched the house but the only clue was the broken bottle of whisky beside the rocker. Something moved in the other room. Godwin pulled his pistol up and went to the sound of banging doors. Nothing. Another bottle of whisky was on the kitchen counter. No label. He picked it up and uncorked it. The smell was invigorating and he took a long drink from it. The satisfied sigh that came out of his mouth startled him. The light of his lantern showed something in the night on the doorstep straight across from where he stood. A silhouette. Godwin corked the bottle and went to the door with his pistol straight out from his arm, the bottle in the other. There was nothing but snow and Creasy. Godwin put the bottle in the boot that was lashed to the saddle. He hopped up on Creasy and turned her toward home. On the edge of the wood just past the bridge that separated Godwin's land from the land he wished to own he saw the silhouette of a man again standing in snow up to his shins. Creasy galloped when the heels went into her flanks.

He was dead drunk when he sat back down at his desk. He scribbled Danforth Smith a hundred times, his hand flying across the page with each new signature. They all looked different than the one before and he knew it would never work. Then something occurred to him. *Who would there ever be to confirm it was a forgery?*

The bottle of whisky he brought from the little house sat half empty on the desk beside the candle. He took up the quill once more. A presence in the room guided his hand and steadied the once sloppy strokes the whisky brought on. Halfway through the f in Lieutenant Smith's given name, Godwin became aware of the lightness of his hand. He glanced to the window where his reflection showed in the candlelight with the falling snow as a scrim. Leaning over him, with his hand on Godwin's hand was Lieutenant Smith in his Confederate grays and wide brim hat. He was younger than Godwin had known him. Their hands still writing, Lieutenant Smith grinned. They wrote the final letter of Smith and the draft from the window extinguished the candle. Godwin was alone in the dark and drinking the rest of the bottle he pilfered from his neighbor.

Chapter 13.

"Jack Hanshaw? Never heard of him," Mr. Jefferson said.

"Well, he's standing outside staring a hole into your oversized painting of President McKinley," Jamie said.

Mr. Jefferson said, "If he persists tell him to kindly wait. Pop in once and I'll wire the sheriff from in here."

She said, "I understand, Mr. Jefferson." She walked back out to the waiting area and took a seat at her desk.

On the other side of the door, Jack was shaking. His fists were turning white and purple. Mr. Jefferson's secretary was unable to speak.

"Mr. Jefferson will see me then?" Jack said.

"Not just yet. He's finishing up a meeting. He will see you, but he respectfully asks for you to wait and allow him to tie up his meeting."

Jack huffed and looked at the door and back to her. "Respectfully. Okay." He sat on the chaise lounge near the door to the hallway. He sat with his boot up on his knee. The secretary couldn't help but look at the emblem stamped into the tan leather sole of his pointy boots. She half disbelieved he wasn't wearing spurs.

"Coffee, sir?"

"No."

She didn't say anything.

"No, thank you."

"Water? Honey roasted peanuts? He keeps them for visitors."

"He's a big nut, isn't he? Sorry, don't answer that."

She feigned working on some ledger and he worked out the grimace on his face. He thought her a cute gal and wouldn't mind wine and dinner but would prefer dancing and waking up next to her.

She quietly pushed the button that zapped a buzzer under Mr. Jefferson's desk in his office and kicked the wastebasket under her own desk to hide the noise from this dangerous stranger who didn't mind getting rude on the first encounter. Anywhere but here and she might flirt back with him, but he seemed to be looking for a fight and she wasn't about to lose her job even if the greasy s.o.b. in the office behind her treated her like dog meat.

"Hanshaw. In my lobby. Looking for trouble." That was the message over the wire. Sheriff Smith received it himself.

Bernard Jefferson stood at the clock on the wall beside the door. He'd opened the panel behind the weights and looked into his lobby. He watched Jack. "He hasn't done anything yet to speak of except show up and be nosing in my business. He looks to mean harm though and I don't want my poor secretary, Jamie, to have to testify to anything that would make her not want to work for me anymore."

"We'll be over. Is he armed?" The message came back to Jefferson's desk.

"Yes," Bernard replied. He started to grumble loudly near the door behind his desk, the one across the room that opened into the public receiving lobby. He threw his voice and grabbed the door handle. He opened it and then slammed it shut.

The other door flew open.

"I sent Jamie out for coffee. Nice meeting, horse's ass."

He slapped his desk with a meaty palm. The sting in his hand steeled his nerve and he stood up and started shouting at Jack.

Jack marched over to him and stuck his finger in the doughy flesh of Jefferson's chest. He pushed him back and pinned him in front of the stout oak desk with the winding pedestals carved and polished from the limbs of the tree that used to shade his boyhood home. He was a rich man, sure. Nonetheless, the spine in his back tended to give when the truth of his bullshit was beginning to get squeezed. And Jack had a rage ratcheting down like a vice. The clear lead in this dance was the man who brought the boots.

"What are you going to do? Beat me up? Like a petulant schoolhouse bully? Sheriff Smith is on his way. I'm sure he'll be more than understanding when he finds out you're a wanted man. How old was that girl in Racine? That's right, sixteen. He's going to like you for that and like you for the theft of the Mill Run bank robbery."

"You don't even know who you're dealing with, do you? This isn't about me and you. This is about the man on the mountain. With him you got no law on your side. He is town law, state law, and federal law. He's god as far as your little ghost town is concerned. The minute they started haulin' the silver out of Cut Creek you were a fart in the wind and about as useful as a turd in a beer barrel."

"Colorful banter for a bank robbing, rapist."

"Don't kid yourself. You know as well as me that your phony accusations wouldn't stick. But go ahead and try. Sheriff Sissy might have me in stir for a day or two, hell maybe a week. But, when God comes down from his mountain…the earth will shake." Jack made for the door. "We'll just see who's left standing when he does. You've got some cleaning up to do." Jack knocked a painting of Jefferson's boyhood home, the one his sister painted for him, off the wall. He hid out in a stairwell for a moment or two gauging an escape should the sheriff have been more than an idle threat.

She came back with a cup of coffee and a disappointed frown. "What happened?"

Mr. Jefferson was standing at his door. Sheriff Smith had just walked past him. "He's gone." He slammed the door shut and she spilled a spot of coffee on her desk. She sat on the chaise lounge, the one the gruff stranger with the crisp whiskers on his upper lip had been stewing on before he asked for the coffee from the shop in the lobby down on the first floor. He'd changed the smell of the room. She wasn't sure if she liked it. But a hot bath can change a lot of things.

In his office they talked plainly and loudly.

"Say this drifter poked a kitty in the knickers and she was under the marrying age? And that's in what county, again?" Sheriff Smith said.

"Grenwol. A town in east Minnesota," Mr. Jefferson said. The gap between his front teeth just wide enough for the lie to slip through with ease.

"And he held up a bank?"

"Yes, Sheriff. Held it up like the Dalton Gang."

"And this bank was in the same jurisdiction as the farmer's daughter?"

Mr. Jefferson lit a cigar the better to blow smoke, "No, sir. That bank, he said, was east of Topeka, little burg began with an E. Can't recall the name. Sounded like a lady's name. Edna, maybe."

"Edna, Kansas?"

"Maybe, not gin on that." Mr. Jefferson sucked his fat cigar.

"Not gin?" Sheriff Smith said.

"100 proof." He coughed, "A hundred percent. Not a hundred percent."

"I see."

"Well. What else?"

"What else? What do you mean?"

"Well, I can't do what I think you're asking me to do based on these testimonies." He stood up and paced the office.

"What can you do with that?"

"I can arrest him and call the law in these towns. But I suspect you're wanting a little more decisive action."

"You see right through me, Smitty."

Sheriff Smith tapped his badge on his proud chest. "Right, pardon me."

"Let me see what I can do with these. I'll find your man in the mean."

"He's in with God," Mr. Jefferson threw out in desperation.

Sheriff Smith's boot heels struck half-moon divots in the maple floor. "Mhmm." He sat down in the client chair across from Mr. Jefferson. Their voices dropped. And Jamie, who'd had an ear fixed to the door, strained to hear the new direction their palaver had taken.

Chapter 14.

Crackling fire battled the chopped wood in the fireplace; a little cave carved out of stone where the bouncing glow of heat—life and death danced to ashes. The silence beyond barely hid the sobs of Godwin. His sons were upstairs in Erwin's and Ma's room. They were quiet as mice under ten feet of snow. Godwin sat beside her body. Holding her hand. All he thought became question marks marching off to the fire. Holding her hand.

"If we could've have made it down the road, off the mountain, we'd have got you to Doctor Spuss. I'm so sorry, Freda." Godwin stared and burned a hole in the universe. Elwin watched from the doorway.

"Come here, son."

Elwin collapsed beside his father on the couch, into his arm.

"We have to lay her to rest ourselves. We won't get down the mountain for days, likely longer with this weather. It won't be proper. But it will be with respect."

"I know, father," Elwin struggled to say. "We can do no wrong with love, that's what she said."

"She did. She'd said it just that way."

So, the next morning the Merritt men rose early and groggy after a considerable amount of ale the night before. A shot of whiskey, maybe a couple more were shared on top of the abundant ale. They'd lost much and were much lost. Godwin wanted to make a whole breakfast for his boys, show them he would lead them through this empty moment. Edwin stood at the stove scrambling eggs. He'd beaten God to the punch. "I felt pretty good when I woke up. Thought I could make breakfast for us. Not bad, considering the amount of ale."

"I understand. What time did *you* go to bed?" Godwin said.

"Don't know," Edwin said.

"All the same. Let's not pour any drinks tonight. Okay?" Godwin said.

"Agreed." Edwin hugged Godwin. The metal spatula in his hand had a chunk of eggs hanging off and it fell to the floor.

"Let's get this food on the table. Elwin's sure to be hungry."

At the table they sat in the fog of the ale. They talked little and laughed less. Godwin laid out the plan once the road was manageable. They'd go into town and inform the doctor and then the sheriff. A death must always be reported he told them. They were surprised by that.

For the time being, she was at peace—cold and covered in the outbuilding.

The whap-whapping of the belts, the screeching whine of the sawblade sticking in the thick log of an off center cut, and the tenderized lips of the Mattocks youth he'd killed that day in the mill all made their presence known in Godwin's head. His whole face was tense in flex and his teeth near to the breaking point as he clenched his jaw. The Mattocks youth who'd snuck up on him that day trying to make a name for himself, surely, was placed lifeless on the road to the homes of his kin.

The boys occupied themselves all afternoon in the great room. Godwin snuck glasses of ale in the pantry. He thought to smoke and went to the counter for his bone-handled pipe. It wasn't there. He checked the pantry. Not there. Now the casual search was on. Without rousing the boys who were keeping to themselves, he quietly made his way through the house. High and low. Dark rooms lighted. He couldn't recall where it had been last: maybe out in the building? Maybe beside his wife wrapped in the cloth and covered in the outbuilding? No. Surely not.

The minute he stepped onto the porch he'd wished he hadn't. The bear he saw was sitting in the yard unknowing the owner of the Godwin Merritt Ranch was just about cross-eyed from drink and too scared to move—an easy meal. He'd have to make a play, but what?

The door silently opened behind him just wide enough by Elwin's hand on the bottom panel. Edwin advanced the rifle just enough for Godwin to see it peripherally. Was this the play? He considered. The ale said yes. His bones said otherwise. He reached behind for the rifle without moving his feet for fear of crunching the drift that the wind had borne into the porch. He leveled the rifle and stiffened his shaking arms.

The bear rose on its massive hind legs. His colossal brown body broke up the monotonous beauty of the gray and white panorama. He stood up to full height, certainly nine feet tall. "Look at you, then," Godwin whispered, his breath visible in the cold. All he had to do was pull the trigger. His sons watched through the window. He was aware of them. If the bear turned, he would drop him. If not, he would not take advantage of such an easy kill. Besides, there would be nothing to do with the bear dead. The big thing scratched at its nose. It lowered mightily and ran toward the horizon. What it was after, Godwin would never be able to say. He lowered the rifle to his side and listened to the fading steps in the crusty snow. New snow was coming down fast now. They would be up to their eyeballs in it by the morning.

"Elwin bet you wouldn't shoot him, God," Edwin said.

"Never bet unless it's a sure thing, Elwin. If that bear turned to me he would have been dead before he hit the ground," Godwin said.

"I just knew he'd leave on his own, that's all, Pa," Elwin said.

"When do you think the snow will stop, God?" Edwin asked.

Godwin didn't answer 'cause he couldn't say. Could be today, could be tomorrow. The road would eventually show itself and they would take to digging Freda a final resting place. Way it looked though; the ground would be frozen solid for weeks. They'd have to rely on help, possibly take her down and buy a plot in town. A long time ago they'd agreed to be buried beside each other on the ranch. She'd said, "Why would we ever want to leave here? This place will be beautiful forever and I'd like to stay here with you forever." He was starting to recall conversations like these; the good ones, the tender ones.

*   *   *

They found Elwin late into the night. A lantern light flickered shadows in the window of the outbuilding where her body lay. They looked at each other inside the kitchen window. The pantry door was wide open but neither of them had been drinking ale or eating a midnight snack. "Stay here with Erwin," Godwin said. "Get him some milk warmed up. Remember, not too warm."

"Yes, sir."

"Have you seen my pipe around?" Godwin asked as he loaded on his coat, hat, scarf, and gloves. He groaned with each boot he put on and grunted as he tightened the laces from his toes to his shins, weaving back and forth over brass studs like ivy up a wall.

"No, God, can't say I've seen it around," Edwin said. "Would you like to borrow mine for the walk out there?"

"No, no, I was just curious."

"Here, take mine. It's cold out there in the outbuilding."

"Thank you, son."

"You're welcome, pa."

How the wind whistled across the frosty snowpack. It stung his cheeks, the little of them that were bare above his heavy beard. He followed Elwin's tracks from the porch to the outbuilding. He'd damn near cut a canyon in the snow to walk out there. It was waist deep in spots and not so easy to get out of. The craters where the oil pans had been lit were just barely visible out on the ground. Elwin had dug out the entrance to the outbuilding. Godwin knocked on the door, as gently as he could with his hands in thick, woolen gloves and the high energy that tweaks nerves in the frigid winter night.

He didn't answer. The lantern light danced on the snow outside the window which cast a shadow of a cross.

He went inside and shut the door to keep out as much winter as he could. There sat Elwin beside his mother wrapped in sheets. The boy was silent but had been crying absolutely. The wailing is what had stirred Godwin from his sleep and, in turn, woke Edwin to investigate the matter.

"Son."

Silence. Elwin rubbed his eyes hard and didn't open them when he pulled his fists down.

"Son. She loves you. If she were here, she would want you to go inside and talk by the fire. It's too cold out here. Son?"

"I just want to talk to her. I heard her voice in the dream I was having. She said something was important. I couldn't remember when I woke up. I came out here to ask Ma," Elwin said. He fell into a blustery sob where words became nonsense and his voice broke into hyperventilation.

Godwin sat beside him. They didn't say anything for a long while. It was okay to be mourning. But he wanted his son to be able to say goodbye and leave her rest. Elwin didn't seem to breathe as Godwin held his arm around his son's shoulders.

"Come on, son. It's time to go back in."

"I can't. I don't want to."

"We must. In due time we'll have a proper service. For now, we are held captive by the elements and the unfortunate hand of god. We will stay up and sit by the fire. You can talk or not as long as you want. I'll be right with you; awake and here."

Slow as mud down a well, Elwin got up and moved toward the door. Godwin grabbed the lantern his son had brought out. He snuffed the flame at the door and latched the door behind him. The moon was so full and the sky so clear they made their way as silhouettes in the silvery night. They cut back through the waist deep canyon. "Dad?"

"Yes, Elwin."

"I miss her already."

"I know, son. I do too. We'll be together through this. Never doubt that," Godwin said.

Edwin had built a fire so crackle roaring hot that they could feel its warmth from the door. Edwin had set out two big steins of ale but had gone to the baby's room to sleep or just be out of the way. Godwin motioned to Elwin that they should drink by the fire. Elwin furtively went to a chair and sipped his ale. Godwin downed his in one massive expression of masculine gluttony. "I'll just be a moment. He went to the pantry to retrieve another fill. He drank that one standing at the barrel just as fast as the first one. Then he poured a third and went back out to the fire. "Do you remember when we crossed the mountains two years ago and swam in the ocean, Elwin? The clowns on the beach, dancing and having some kind of party? They made your mother laugh so hard. I mean to say, they made her genuinely joyful."

"I remember the trip through the mountains. I remember swimming in the ocean. I don't remember the clowns though."

Godwin's eyes began to gloss. His head felt as if it was bobbling a little but he knew he wasn't. He knew this second barrel of ale might be a touch more potent than the previous one that trickled to an end this morning just after sunrise. "The clowns, there were at least twenty of them. Jumping and dancing and just having a gas, until the Arcadia County

Sherriff showed up and demanded they gather up their things and remove themselves. He threatened an obscenity charge. That's what one of the clowns told your mother when she approached them and asked what they were celebrating. Do you know what they told her?"

"No. This is the first time I've heard this story. I don't think I was out there that day."

"You might have been back at the cabin with Edwin." Godwin swung his empty stein and contemplated a lot of space between the outbuilding and himself. "Anyway, the clowns told your mother they were celebrating life. Simply celebrating life. Well, she had a high, hard laugh at that. She told me that night that she thought that was the best answer to the best question that she had ever had the joy of being party to and that from then on she would be celebrating life however she could. Come to the kitchen."

In the kitchen on high stools around the farm table, they sat and continued their ale. Godwin said, "See son, that day on the beach talking to those clowns who had been threatened with municipal charges, she found her joy. She found the concept of bliss and it was a seed that she nurtured across the breadth of her life. I've got to say, at this moment, I believe she is in the heaven she so seriously believed in. That she held onto that bliss no matter what the weather and is now experiencing the fruit of her life."

Elwin stared into his drink and understood further what it was to be a man having a grown up conversation. He stared and said nothing. Stared as if peering over a stone ledge in a mossy forest. Over the stone ledge and into the well where a black pool rippled as he dropped wish after wish from a place he would never be able to return to. A place with no map that distorted time and set compasses to spin in their glass capped cylinders.

Chapter 15.

Sheriff Smith was high up in a hotel room in the heart of the mountain town. A dozen buildings stood above a crowd of wind-up people bobbling to and fro whatever useless tasks they must perform. He looked down on them from the window on the top floor of the Larimer, a prestigious hotel of opulent décor and classical design, supported on marble and awash in gold.

"Are you getting cold by the window?" Jamie asked Sheriff Smith.

"No. I love to look on Butte this way," he said. "Ain't seen a blizzard like this in a few years maybe more."

"I can see that," she said admiring his reflection in the glass. She lit a cigarette and laid her bouncy brown hair on her arm atop the stack of pillows that had survived their thrashing about. The marks on his back were only partly her fault she noticed. He had scars of buckshot across his shoulders and a long sliver down the back left side. She almost asked about them last night but she found herself speechless for a good portion of the evening. He had done a lot of admiring of his own, mostly with his eyes closed in her bouncy brown hair.

She wasn't sure who'd seduced who outside of Mr. Jefferson's office but they had so evidently had something the other one wanted that there was no way to extinguish the sparks however transient they may have been.

"You've been with Mr. Jefferson for a few years now, haven't you?" he said. He was still naked and facing the window. The grin between his cheeks was wrinkled, spotted with soft gray hairs. His butt was firm for a man his age but still the sag of time could not be defied and it kind of made Jamie chuckle in her head.

"I have worked for him four years, yes. We're not together though." She smiled when he turned to look at her.

"I didn't mean that. I meant work."

"I know."

"You're a genuine coquette," he said.

"You don't mind do you?" she asked and fluttered her eyelashes.

"Not at all," he said and suggested with his eyes that she find the proof near his navel.

"I see. Why don't you come back to bed and warm me up some more?" she said.

"You're warm, baby. You're positively overheating." He jumped into the sack. "I'm surprised the windows aren't fogging up."

"Sheriff, where are your cuffs?" she said.

He stiffened. Smiled. "Bad, bad, bad." He got up and picked his cuffs off his denim trousers. "I'm going to have to lock you up and throw away the key." He grinned a lascivious and lusting sneer.

"Not me. You."

"Me, what?" he said.

"I want to lock you up." She fluttered her lashes again. She pulled him to herself. He found it hard to disagree. She took the cuffs without looking, without taking her other hand off him and without unlocking her lips from his. She cuffed one hand. He moaned and bucked in her hand. She guided him further up the bed. He moved without hesitating to be in her hand. She latched the other cuff around the headboard frame. He continued to buck. She guided him onto his back and rode him like a trick rider in the Lake County Rodeo. She put on his tan Stetson and made a hell of a show for him.

She made sure he was out. He didn't move. Didn't even politely snore the way he had after their previous night came to its conclusion.

He was still cuffed to the headboard when she got out of the water closet. He was no longer asleep though. And that was fine. She wasn't trying to escape. She would have done gone had she wanted out. She wanted answers. And she let him know. She pulled a wooden chair out from the table and swung it around to the foot of the bed. She sat spread legged and leaning on the back of the chair. "I want answers," she said.

He laughed anxious little chuckles.

"What?" she said. "Why are you giggling?"

"You." He smiled. "Playing at being a law dog. Interrogating a suspect?"

"Stop laughing." She hit him on the shin with a plate that'd had been host to a midnight snack delivered by room service just after midnight. It had hardened icing and made a thick hollow thud when it struck his shin and opened up a little skin. A line of blood rolled down his leg a little slower than she'd have thought.

"You bitch. You know you won't just walk away from this. Get me out of this cuff before you buy yourself an unmarked grave."

She tossed the plate on the narrow table beneath the window and watched the snow fall hard. The horizon was just behind the buildings on the other side of McCormick. On a clear day you could see the edge of town, not so that day.

"You'll be fine, Sheriff Stiff. I just want a few questions answered." Jamie drew her finger down his chest and over his abdomen. She flicked his belly with a thump. "You may even get a reward if I get the answers I'm looking for. That is, on top of all the amazing things we've already accomplished here in your swanky hideaway."

"Alright. Alright, you silly broad. What do you think you're going to get out of me?" He was arrogant to a fault. He knew she couldn't touch him but the cuff on his wrist rubbed him the wrong way. He'd already made up his mind about what to do with her when he was free.

"Mr. Jefferson had business with a man named Merritt. It was to do with a silver mine operated in his son's name. A son named Edwin. There was much discussion, a lot of talk, some determination that Edwin must be out of the picture. Only---"

"Stop right there, secretary. You have no idea, in that feeble little mind, what you're talking about. What you think you know and what is real are two very different though lucrative things." He pointed to his cigarettes.

"These things will kill you." She held a match under the cigarette she put in his mouth. "If I don't first."

"You won't hurt me. You need me."

"I've met men like you all over. All thinking the hapless dame can't do without a big, strong man." She was sitting astride the chair again looking at him. "I see you're still excited to see me."

"I find strong women attractive." He smirked.

"Somehow I'm certain the opposite is true. You want a mincy little kitty who's gonna curl up in your lap and gaze up at you adoringly. One that won't mind if you leave her out in the rain when good company comes by. No, Sheriff Stiffy, a strong woman would drive you mad."

"Get to your point. I've got a list of shit to do and you're not on it," he said. "Anymore."

"I know and you know that Mr. Jefferson isn't the type of man who can keep a secret. Try as he might he just can't say no to black stockings," she said, in fact, as she was rolling back up her black stockings. She clapped her hands on her thighs when they were all the way up. "There, now, what I want to know from you is who Jack Hanshaw is and why he brings Mr. Jefferson packages of silver. And not little bracelets with imitation gems," she said and shook her wrist, the little gift he'd given her over dinner in the restaurant on the street level of The Larimer Hotel, rattling silver links and dyed glass stones.

"Well, it's like my daddy always said, 'Cheap whores, cheap gifts.'"

"So, you come from a long line of dickheads then?"

"I'll smack that smirk off your little cocksucker when I get out of these cuffs."

"That's what I was afraid you'd say." She got up from the chair. In her stockings and underwear and tiny silk corset she picked up his loaded gun. "Now the nature of our little talk has changed." She lovingly pointed the gun at him. "You have proven yourself to be a poor gamesman."

"You can kill me if you like. But you'll never not be a cheap whore."

She crushed his foot with the butt of his gun. His scream was deep and native.

Chapter 16.

Sunlight at dawn drove unobstructed into Godwin's bedroom and bleached the wall relieving it of its dismal soot dusted complexion. Flecks of snow blown off branches by the swirl of currents of a soft mountain wind glinted like a million diamonds in the whitewashed panorama. The trails were laden with the tonnage the blizzard dumped. It was colder in the morning than it had been when it was snowing. The drifts were freezing. "Will we ever get off this mountain?" Godwin stood at the window of his bedroom. He was smoking out of his father's pewter pipe. In the absence of his bone-handled pipe, this would be the replacement. He thought of his father's birthdate, the only time he smoked out of the snub pewter pipe. The thick bowl and the stubbed pipe were hard to hold onto and he decided this morning that the medicine his doctor had sold to him when last they met was a necessity. Cabin fever required this. His doctor had called it cannabis sativa but it had a common name he couldn't pronounce or rightly recall. Something that he assumed was Mexican. He stayed in his room for a while. His eyes got heavy and his mouth dried out. In bed he turned himself into the calm fold of sleep in a heavy blanket Freda made when they were newly married.

On the porch, Edwin smoked his own pipe, full of tobacco that Freda had bought for him in town the last time she'd gone to the market and butcher. He had a mug with some whisky in it, about three fingers. He was definitely using the railing to support himself when Elwin opened the door a crack to tell him the beans and ham were ready to eat.

"How about the biscuits?" Edwin asked.

"I don't know how to make biscuits. That's your thing, remember?" Elwin said. "I need help with the baby."

"No you don't. You're a man. Act like it."

Elwin glared at him and shut the door. Edwin puffed his pipe again. The whitewashed earth began to make him sick. He closed his eyes and tried to feel what little warmth the sun was bouncing off the snowpack. When he opened them he saw a shadow at the hill where the trail began its descent of the mountain. It was a man and he was definitely moving toward the house.

Edwin bolted inside and ran up the stairs, "Father! God! Godwin!"

Godwin's bedroom door opened and he came out loading his revolver and marched down to the front door. He debated for an instant on whether to greet the stranger outside or let him knock. He didn't waste time opening the front door and made it clear he had a loaded firearm in hand. People don't just show up in a blizzard like the one they just sat through. He watched the man struggle through the high snow. The dark figure in the distance fell twice and Godwin wondered if he was even going to make it to the yard. "Get some water on the stove, Elwin! Edwin, get the shotgun." The door shut behind him. He heard Erwin bawling in the great room.

"God!" the stranger howled. "God, help me."

The agony in the voice couldn't distort his identity enough for Godwin to fail to recognize him. "Jack," he said in his cannabis stupor.

Inside the kitchen, Elwin looked out and wondered how long it would be before his father realized he didn't have a shirt on in the freezing cold morning. The front door banged again.

Elwin saw Edwin go to the bottom of the porch steps with the shotgun across his hands at the ready. Godwin held his hand over the barrel and pushed it down gently. The stranger was not so strange to The Godwin Merritt Ranch. A sharp pain made Godwin drop his revolver. It discharged with a king hell blast that could have woken the dead and it echoed around the ranch. The figure out in the snow, Jack, fell into the high pack. Edwin ran to help him.

"Edwin," he moaned. "I'm okay. I just thought he was shooting at me."

"No, Jack. He dropped his Colt. I don't know what he was thinking," Edwin said trying to get leverage under Jack to raise him to his feet.

"Sorry, Jack. Didn't mean to fire her off. You look like hell," Godwin said.

"You're not wearing a shirt," Jack said.

"You better get in by the fire," Edwin said. "Both of you. Lord, you two are a pair."

They struggled to help Jack who was having a hell of a time getting his legs to walk for himself. They banged his leg as they went sideways through the open oak door. "Ahhhhck, damn!" Jack grunted.

"Sorry. Sorry, Uncle Jack," Edwin said. His father glared at him over the slumping Jack. Edwin chewed his lips in; a silent apology.

"UNCLE JACK!" Elwin ran into the great room. Erwin stirred but didn't wake in his bassinet.

"Hi, little Elwin. I'm a little banged up. And your father shot at me. But, all's not lost," he tried to joke. "Where's Freda?"

The Merritt men went mute. Edwin went to the kitchen to make the hot tea. Elwin sat on the couch next to Godwin.

"What is it, God?"

Godwin struggled to speak. His glassy red eyes itched.

"God, what happened? Is she sick? She upstairs, sick?"

"She passed." His lips quivered. He stiffened and continued, "A couple a mornings back, she collapsed and gave in a few hours later. She's been stuck up here on the mountain for her god's damned blizzard."

"My god. I can't say anything." He struggled to a chair beside the fire. His wet clothes were cold on his skin. The only sound in the room was the crackling of wood burning beside Jack.

"Erwin had just broken a fever he'd been suffering through over a week. She'd stayed close to him and got him through it. Me and the boys were getting the ranch ready for this snow and now we're stuck. But how'd you get up here? That leg looks terrible."

"I don't even know. I had a bit of trouble down Cut Creek."

"Let's get tea before we move along any farther down that road, Jack," Godwin said.

Jack looked at Elwin and motioned for him to go ahead to the kitchen.

In the great room, with the baby sleeping still, Jack took out a book from the pack he'd set at his feet. He handed it over, "The devil's in the details, God. They can't hide what's in there."

"You are worth your weight in gold, Jack Hanshaw," Godwin said.

"If it were only true. I probably wouldn't have this busted up leg."

Godwin put the tall green ledger on the high shelf beside the mantel. "Tea, it's the best we've had. Come on, friend." He did a double take. He thought he saw his old neighbor sitting across from him. A headache split his mind and he heard the whap-whapping of belts and smelled warm sawdust. The blade spun wild.

They call it brain tanning.

* * *

It was a dream. Jack crawling toward the house with his busted leg and promise of the ledger was only a phantom in Godwin's cannabis fogged mind. He rocked in the rocker beside the fireplace in the great room with Erwin snug in his arms. He watched Edwin walk from one side of the hall to the other. He grew curious as to what the boy was up to. He stood up to investigate and realized it was dark outside. The entire day must have drifted by as he went in and out of his stupor. He stood in the doorway and watched him walk to the stairs and then to the kitchen door; to the stairs and then to the kitchen door. He hadn't recognized it at first and then it hit him. His father used to do this. Darwin Merritt, dead and buried thirty years now. Darwin, the sleepwalking father who wandered the ranch like a ghost when the lights were out.

Erwin screamed. He screamed until his face couldn't stretch further and his skin couldn't turn redder. Edwin turned and went upstairs at the same lethargic pace. Godwin heard his bed creak when he lay down. The baby continued to scream. Godwin hurried on stiff legs to the kitchen to give Erwin a bottle of milk. He wet the nipple in a glass of whisky and fed the bottle to Erwin. For himself, he poured a stein from the barrel. They would run out of ale if Godwin kept up his recent appetite for it.

Godwin drank to drunkenness. He sang to himself in the kitchen in a low but melodic voice. The songs came freely. Some were songs he'd heard before and some were things he was making up on the fly. The night passed with him looking out windows to the outbuilding, looking in on Erwin in the great room, and topping off his stein before it was ever half-empty. At the end of his solitary night journey, he put Erwin to bed in the bassinet in the room Freda had nursed him back to health in.

He woke up the next morning in the closet under her clothes—hanging, ready to wear. It was noticeably warm in the house. This would be the beginning of the clearing. If they got busy, he thought, they might be able to clear a path and get down the mountain in a day's time. Whatever the next few days brought it would be imperative to make a decision on Freda's remains. With a lot of work they could bury her on the ranch and inform the authorities as soon as possible. On the other hand, they could manage a dangerous excursion down the mountain in the present conditions possibly risking everyone's survival. It wasn't much of a choice, he supposed. They would begin the massive undertaking after breakfast.

"See if you can dig out the plow after we eat," Godwin told his sons.

"What's the plan, God?" Edwin asked.

"We will bury your mother within the week. I want to make a spot for her on the ranch," he told them.

"I thought we had to tell the law or something," Elwin said.

"We still do. But as the temperature rises outside, her remains will begin to turn. We must act now."

Less than an hour after breakfast, Edwin and Elwin were outside digging out the plow as fast as they could. Their noses were runny with snot. Their backs burned and felt like stone. Their arms were tight as ropes between the men and their carts that used to work the mine. It took two hours to dig out the back end of the plow, not including the yoke. Now they could start the thing shunting at least; if it was going to budge at all, remained to be seen.

It took them three more hours to dig out the front side. The chains were frozen stiff. They were back inside warming by the stove in the kitchen and drinking hard coffee with crunchy cookies that were past their prime. Godwin said, "You two really hammered down on that plow. I'm proud and grateful for you." He was flexing his fist open and closed, "I know I couldn't do it myself right now."

"How's your hand, God?"

"It's alright son, just a little arthritis, I suppose."

"Well, the chains are froze on her. We'll either have to light a fire beside her or wait 'til tomorrow and see if the direct sunlight will loosen 'em up." Edwin said, and he used a tone to indicate he'd prefer to let the sun do the work.

"We won't waste the time. The sun should warm the plow enough tomorrow. After you get warmed up a little I want you to get the eggs and milk. The animals must be wondering what happened to us by now." Godwin was sobering and the headache it had borne threatened to put him down. Maybe a small cup of ale, he thought. Just to soften the edge.

Elwin came into the kitchen and heard the ale falling into the stein. When Godwin exited the pantry Elwin said, "God, do you think the ale is making Edwin mad?"

"Mad?"

"Yes, sir. He gets angry easy. He pushes me out of the way. Sometimes. Even before Ma died."

"I'm sorry, Elwin." But Godwin became distracted by thoughts of Freda. We have to get her buried before it really warms up even a little more, he thought. His bone-handled pipe filled his mind with smoky pictures of memories when she'd given it to him. The week Edwin turned one year old. He'd been down at Cut Creek Pass overseeing a major excavation through a fresh line of silver. That day they sent a man out on a stretcher and bouncing down the mountain road in the back of a flatbed. The man, Davis Egg, survived though not whole. The bone out of his wrist never left Godwin's memory. But it wasn't a major impediment in the course of that day. Before Davis Egg even cleared the mine opening work resumed on the new shaft following the silver line. Had Davis Egg died that day he would have become the first tiny notch on the shaft of that bone handled pipe. That distinction would fall to another man; Roger Lawrence.

"I bet we could make it down to the stream good enough now, God," Elwin suggested. He looked to see if Godwin's eyes brightened even a little at the thought of fishing. There was no break in his stare. "Do you think we could try the stream today? Fish for dinner tonight would be good."

He saw Godwin's eyelids droop and rise. Droop and rise. Elwin left the room to read a book. The hours passed slowly before he heard his father's voice again.

"Let's get some gear together and go try the stream. You and Edwin go down and I'll mind Erwin up here," Godwin said.

"Thank you, God. We'll try to bring back a feast," Elwin said.

"Just be careful of the animals. These are desperate times for the meat eaters out there. Look for signs; tracks and branches. Take some matches to make a fire. The leather wood flap should get you enough to get one going and then you can chop a limb down and dry it out beside your fire."

"We know, God. We know. We'll look out for each other," Edwin said.

About a quarter past noon they set off from the ranch. Elwin enthusiastically hauled the leather flap that bundled the small wood together. He carried the poles as well. Edwin had a hand ax holstered on his hip. A .22 pistol sat on his other hip. He carried bait and hooks on his hat. A half pound of bacon cooked down to the crisp and a handkerchief wrapped around some biscuits sat in the bag he carried across his chest.

They descended the small hill at the edge of the horizon from where Godwin watched on the porch. Edwin said, "If they don't bite too quick I snuck some whisky out. It warms up your throat and chest."

Elwin feigned astonishment but smiled from the other corner of his mouth. He was growing up a man like Edwin and Pa, he considered.

"You can't say a word to God about it. Understand?"

"I know. I'd be in hot water right beside you if I did," Elwin said.

"I bet we catch six fish," Edwin guessed.

"I bet I catch six fish," Elwin said. "I bet you catch a cold."

Edwin shoved his brother in the arm. Elwin lost balance and tumbled to his butt making a pocket in the deep snow. Edwin gripped his brother's hand and helped him up. "Sorry, little brother. Thought you were a little more sturdy."

Elwin would wait for his revenge—maybe on the way back up the ranch.

"Ma won't clean the fish tonight. Does Pa know how to cook them?" Elwin said.

"Maybe not. But he'll find a way."

"She never wrote any of that down. Every recipe was kept in her mind."

"Yep. And now they're all gone," Edwin said and felt the immensity of his words. A light flurry danced down from the darkening sky. The clouds were pushing across the sky. The young men looked concerned but not deterred. They wanted to return with fish not just to eat something different that night. They wanted to prove their ability. Nearing the stream, Edwin noticed the broken branch. But it was small. And the weather had made things brittle. He brushed it off as nothing. They moved intently toward their stream. Then he caught the musk smell of smoldering wet wood, the type surely to have thick moss on its hardened bark. He put his arm out to stop Elwin in his tracks. Now that they were under the canopy of old evergreens and a myriad weave of bare limbs the flurries did not reach them. The silence was blunt upon their nerves. Edwin spotted a ribbon of evergreen branches dangling shoulder level. His eyes dug into the snow in search of tracks sure to be there. Elwin heard a soft thrush of snow way on ahead. He pointed to his ear and then pointed forward. Edwin nodded he'd also heard.

They squatted onto the deep snow. It struck cold into their legs. They looked like they'd been buried up to their necks in it. They inched forward trying against the inevitable crunch each forward inch brought. Soon, they heard the lapping water of the icy stream. And sooner still, they saw smoke.

Two men with long rifles sat on a stone before a fire. The Merritt men moved a little to their left and saw their horses, three horses. Had to be a third man somewhere. Edwin and Elwin were crouched behind a drift out of sight when Edwin smelled the burning hand rolled cigarette. He put his index finger up to his mouth to make it imperative that Elwin not make a sound. Their eyeballs were exposed as much as they could be. The fear beat like drums in their chests. They heard footsteps in sifted snow. They were quick steps and they heard them come and they heard them go. Whoever the third man was he didn't know they were there. They finally heard the men's distant voices but they were too far away to make out the words. One of the horses stamped hooves and brayed and snorted.

Elwin shivered from the cold. His teeth chattered until Edwin grabbed his brother's hand and stuck it in his mouth. He bugged his eyes at him—a silent scream to let him know he needed to keep it together. He motioned away from the campfire. They slowly moved down toward the stream, ducking behind the long cresting drift that ran atop a sloping ledge. All of a sudden there was a commotion when the men got on their horses; yelling, charging off away from the fire.

Edwin motioned to stop. He slowly peered over the drift. They were all gone, horses and men, and the snow that led off up and away from the Merritt boys had been seriously disturbed by their exiting.

"Alright, I'm going to go check their camp a minute. I'll be back here before they get back there. Wait here, Elwin." He started to walk toward the exposed stone to climb the ground. "If I don't get back before them run as hard as you can to home."

"Okay. Be careful. Got the gun ready? Just in case." Edwin nodded.

Chapter 17.

Edwin stood in the camp where the three men had left their fire burning. It was warm but only when he walked near to the fire. They had a tent up, a green canvas kind that could easily cover the three of them. A fourth grown man would have been pushing it. He walked silently with flat feet up to the tent and waited, trying to slow his quickened breathing. He could hear his heartbeat in his ears. He felt it in his lobes.

He could see Elwin watching him from just above the ledge. A branch of evergreen covered him. Edwin got up to the opening in the tent and quietly pulled it back. No telling if there'd be someone or something waiting in there. All that breathed in there was a brass oil lamp on a small crate. He looked back one more time to Elwin before ducking inside the tent. He could still see his breath in the tent but it was a little warmer without the wind rushing the ground. The place was loaded with treasure. Silver and gold. Leather goods. Some oversized tools, and to his shock, recognizable with the Cut Creek Pass emblem forged into them. He'd never seen the men who just high tailed out of their camp but he'd know those markings from the other side of the stream. He felt light in the head. His arms began to tremble. "This is dangerous, Ed. Might want to get out of here," he mumbled to himself.

He poked around in furtive little mouse steps in the bouncing lamp light; under sleepsacks, under pillows, and riffling through bags. They'd been camping there at least a few days and it was still quite a haul to the Cut Creek mouth if pirating from the mine was their crime. It didn't make sense to

Edwin who'd been told by his father many times that keeping a silver mine safe from bandits and thieves was a twenty four hour a day job. But if Jack were down there surely these men would have no access to the silver and tools inside.

He was just about to leave the tent. Unable to find any definite evidence other than the old tools that could have been hocked in town by anyone, even God himself, he stood baffled. The lamp. More importantly the crate beneath it. He moved the lamp down on the ground and examined the crate it had been resting on. It was nailed shut. It had a foul odor he'd barely noticed before and had attributed it to the dirty old sleep sacks along the tent walls. The large chisel with the Cut Creek brand would do good to pry the crate apart but what then? If the men came back and he was jacking into their crate he'd surely be tossed into the stream with a few new holes in his head.

If they came and saw their camp had been looted of nothing but the crate they'd surely move up to the Merritt Ranch and cause trouble with God. The play here was dangerous. He wasn't sure what to do. Where the men had rode off to in a thundering thrush of hooves in deep snow he could only guess. They could be on a chase that would keep them away for hours or days. Or they could have their prey and be just around the corner. Time was unknown and that made hesitation his enemy. He took the Cut Creek Pass chisel firm in hand and wriggled it into a crease. The boards creaked like hanging limbs in a windstorm. Whatever was inside rolled back and forth hitting the boards with thuds. The smell grew and drove him away. The chisel was not built for the pry job. Whatever nails they'd struck into the crate were holding deep. He stood against the entrance to the big green canvas tent and cursed the stench. Then he heard them. Thundering thrush of hooves in the deep snow. He turned on his heels to run and kicked over the oil lamp. The fire spread with pyro-maniacal gusto in the ransacked tent.

Edwin's feet barely hit the ground.

Elwin saw the tent go up. He took off toward the Merritt Ranch, toward home knowing his brother was just steps behind him. He didn't look back. Didn't yell or even let his panting breath make a sound. He still had their fishing gear in hand when Edwin took it from him in the most warped of relays. Edwin chucked it over the edge of the pass they were bolting up the mountain on. The gear would never be found.

The men didn't reach camp in time to save a thing from the fire that engulfed their tent. The burning pile of debris was fully consumed beside the stream and the burning campfire they'd left sat calmly ablaze like a sad imitation.

A pile of swearing that flew out of their big beards could have built a mountain of curses no man could summit.

"We shouldn't have left that goddamn fire burning," Thing 1 said.

Thing 2, who clearly had issues grasping social cues, jested, "Don't lose your head about it, Thing 1."

"Thing 3 punched Thing 2's calf with the butt of his rifle. It caused Thing 2 to kick his foot out of the stirrup and against the groin of his horse. The horse reared and took off straight to the stream. It bucked and tossed Thing 2 head first into the stream. He lay there in the shallow pool formed by the rocks inside. He couldn't move. Thing 1 could see it was a lame man that had come to rest in the stream. He rode his horse up to the stream and pulled his pistol. Thing 2's head was driven under by the shot. The blood swam in the current on down the stream.

Edwin and Erwin ran for their lives surrounded in the echo of the gunshot that rose up from the canyon. The smoke stood like a beam bent by the wind. They could see it from where they'd stopped to catch their breath. They might get away. But these men would surely cross their path again.

They reached the porch. Panting. Sweating. Overheated. Their pale winter faces were bright red. Their necks showed blood pumping in big veins. Elwin doubled over and held his forehead against the railing. Edwin, held his hands over his head and paced the porch. He stretched a cramp out of his side as he struggled to calm his breathing. Godwin was on the back side of the house carrying in eggs he'd pulled from the hens. The boys began to settle down enough to talk quietly on the porch.

"What do we tell, God?" Elwin said.

"I'd think we ought to tell him the truth."

"What's the truth, Edwin?" Elwin was sitting on a stool that had been chopped from a log. "What was in the tent?"

"I'm not sure."

"Not sure? How do you mean, 'Not sure,'?"

"I saw sleeping gear and crates of gold and silver. Leather bags of old mine tools with Cut Creek Pass stamped into the iron. There was a few maps, maybe of the area, not with the ranch though. And a crate that was nailed shut." Edwin pulled out his wooden pipe and smoked. "I mean, really nailed down to the goddamn heads. I tried to pry it open with one of the old mining chisels but the nails were stuck tight. I don't know. Maybe they glued them too. And it smelled awful."

"The tent smelled awful?" Elwin asked.

"No. The crate. Once I started prying at it the smell filled the tent. It was like rotting meat or something. Whatever was in there was rolling around while I was trying at it. Made hard thumps against the crate." Edwin smoked hard as if he couldn't breathe without it.

"Well what caused the fire, Ed?" Elwin said.

"The oil lamp. I think I kicked it over. I heard the horses running in the snow," Edwin said and had terror paring back his face, exposing more of his eyes than usual.

"They came back fast. I wonder what spooked them to ride off in the first place."

"Who knows. We're lucky to get back," Edwin said. "I'm wondering what the gunshot went through."

"It sounded like they were still down by the stream. They may not know anyone was there."

"Don't be foolish. We left enough tracks in the snow to lead a blind man right up here."

Elwin shrugged. "So what do we tell God?"

Edwin took his pipe in hand and tapped it hard over the porch railing. "I still say the truth. We didn't go looking for trouble. It was just there," Edwin said as he repacked his pipe with a small wad of tobacco. He passed his wooden pipe to Elwin.

Elwin judged the smoke, his brother, and his father. "No."

"Sure?"

"No, thanks, Edwin." He walked into the house empty of hand and shrugged of shoulder. He heard Godwin in the kitchen tinking with the iron stove. It would be suppertime whenever Godwin got the meal done. The set eating times he'd known were gone; cold in the outbuilding.

"Hello, Elwin." Godwin was working at some meat and filling pockets of dough with it. "You look empty handed there. No bites at the stream?"

"No, God." He sat at the farm table and rested his head on his arms flat on the table. He didn't want to make eye contact with his father—didn't know what to tell him.

"Tired?"

"Yes, sir."

Edwin walked into the room with strong proud steps. He seemed to have business to conduct. He sighed when he saw his brother, face down and beleaguered at the table. "Godwin, we have to talk."

"Shoot, Edwin."

"I stumbled onto some rough men down by the stream. Three of them on horseback. They didn't see us. But I'm sure they have figured out someone was in their camp and that the tracks in the snow just to the west of their own would lead straight to their intruder."

"What are we talking about, son?" Godwin looked to his younger son still face down on the table. He slowly rose to attend the conversation. "What camp?"

"They'd set up a tent, big canvas thing, beside the stream. It was full of crazy stuff; maps of the area around Cut Creek Pass, hard gold and silver—unrefined, old tools with Cut Creek stamped on them."

"Tell him about the other thing," Elwin said.

Edwin paused.

Godwin sat down, "Well, what other thing, Edwin?"

"I don't know what it was. They had an oil lamp lit on a crate in the middle of the tent and I went to pry it open. But I got scared when I heard the men coming back on their horses. When I ran out of the tent I must've kicked over the lamp and it ignited the tent. Probably burned it to clinkers," Edwin's voice lost its bluster. He felt he'd not done the right thing now, going into the strangers' tent. But it was their stream and he'd be damned if some outsiders were going to fish their spot.

"So you accidentally burned down some strangers' tent that was full of gold, silver, old mining equipment and some smelly crate you couldn't open? Was there anything else?"

The boys looked at each other. A brotherly look. A secret in the woods, don't tell the old man look.

"What else?" Godwin demanded.

They were scared.

"Look son, the damage is done. If there's a gang of people heading up our mountain with plans to invade our ranch I need to know now." Godwin pounded his fist on the table, "What else?" he said.

"There was a gunshot," Elwin said. "But it sounded like it was still down by the stream. We were rushing up the mountain and heard the shot echo up from down there."

"I don't think they saw us or came after us. They might see the tracks soon enough but they didn't see us exactly," Edwin said.

The sigh sucked the air out of the room. Godwin pushed his hands through his thick, gray hair. He went to the pantry, Edwin thought, to get a drink of ale. But Godwin returned with a double barrel sawed off shotgun. He laid it on the counter. "Get the shells from the great room, Elwin. Edwin, get your revolvers and get them loaded for Christ's sake."

It was the first time he'd even said the word for a decade, maybe more, Edwin assumed. He'd known Godwin was on a personal mission to forget the entirety of the religion he'd been raised in. When he said Christ, Edwin thought lightning would strike him dead. It was palpable. The hairs stood up on his neck and the chill ran down his spine. Edwin obeyed and got his guns and got them loaded. He returned to the base, to the kitchen, where the planning of defense was underway.

The shotgun was standing up against the door. Obviously it had been loaded. Elwin was downstairs in the basement now, with the baby. It was a shallow cellar built of stone and a tunnel had been built into it that led to the outbuilding. He didn't need to run to her. But he wanted to. He stayed put at the bottom of the stairs. Godwin hollered down to him, "Stay down there, son. Me and Edwin are going to take a good look outside. If you hear anything but an all clear get to the tunnel."

"Okay. Pa?"

"Yes."

"Be careful."

"I love you, Elwin," Godwin shut the door.

They were armed to the hilt. They walked the porch at first. If the riders were approaching, they might be able to play it cool for a bit on the porch. Out in the open the riders would know the boys had been the ones at the camp. They looked slowly over the expanse. They listened through the light wind.

Godwin knew they'd have to leave the porch and meet the problem head on. He didn't want to. But there were a lot of things happening on his ranch these days he'd prefer weren't. They put one foot in front of the other and marched into the great white open.

Chapter 18.

Irvin sat outside the café on the west end of town where the Sheriff had been eating breakfast with his wife. They parted ways at the door. "Well, Irvin?" he said. His lips barely perceptible under a thick moustache that made him look to Irvin like the pack of walrus' he'd seen off the coast during his time with the reinvigorated naval company that had been brought up to speed after the Civil War.

"Do we have a place we can talk around here?"

"Here's where we can talk. The only thing with ears for a hundred yards is me and you." The bull walrus of a man struck a match on the sole of his boot and lit his cigarette.

"Okay, boss. There was an accident on the mountain. The other two didn't survive. I don't know who but they were shot and killed and I came damn near myself to catching one of the bullets that came down on our campsite."

"You're the only one survived?" Sheriff Smith said.

"Yes, sir."

"So, the Merritt's are all deceased as well?"

"No, sir."

The sheriff's cigarette sailed across the ruts driven into the snow by wagon wheels and horses in the street. "What the hell do you mean? Get back up yonder mountain and don't come down 'til 'n they are. Hear me?"

"Sir, they got help. I ain't coming down alive if I run up there on my own. And I don't mean to get killed for no man."

Sheriff Smith put his palm on his sidearm. He made sure Irvin knew it too. "You have an agreement with a certain board of people who don't mean for any of this to get out. Their payment to your posse is their promise of good faith. You have one job. Now look at it this way. With your two confederates rotting on the side of the mountain in a pile of snow, your cut has grown to the full amount. You know what a man can secure for himself these days with 20,000 dollars?"

There was silence. The blood was rushing to Irvin's face. His fists clenched. He could feel the tension all down his arms.

"A lotta goddamn peace of mind, son," Sheriff Smith said. "Now get up that mountain, dammit, and don't come down 'til the job's done."

"I need more time," Irvin pled.

Sheriff Smith looked up the range at the darkening clouds. Another blizzard was about to pound the region. Rumor was; these blizzards were five hundred year storms. At least, that's how the local tribesman liked to tell it. Sheriff Smith never trusted them though. "You might get more time. That storm might dump so much goddamn snow on the Merritt Ranch that they'll never get down. But if you don't get started back up that hill, you might never reach your reward." Sheriff Smith walked away from him. He spit so hard he could've cracked the earth. "Time's a wasting," he said over his shoulder.

"We'll see," Irvin said to himself.

Irvin went to a few shops and rounded up the provisions he would need for the journey back up the mountain. He got some dried beef. He bought more powder, shells, and a little can of gun oil. He picked up a couple of liters of bourbon. He took it all to a little motel room above a saloon on the secondary road in Butte where nobody bothered him except the red haired waitress who liked to keep him company when she couldn't sleep. That night, she helped him secure his bed to the wooden floor with all the pounding it could endure. She was gone before the sun came up; down the makeshift stairs made of short boards nailed to the side of the building making a permanent ladder on the back of the building. She hustled off into the waning night. He woke up parched. He woke up weak legged and greasy. Irvin bundled up his things and headed out the door.

He started the long ride around the other side of the range just after sunrise. It was going to be slow going and take him all day to come down from the east. He'd not be able to take the same path up as they'd tried the first time. He was going to run all the way around and come down into the setting sun on Echo Cliff.

When he got to the east side of the range and knew himself to be on the neighboring property of Hershel Perzan, a retired but not yet elderly rail baron, Irvin made a little fire; nothing big, just atop a mass of granite rounding a ledge out from under a forest of wild evergreen and spruce.

He drank his bourbon beside the fire. He ate some of the dried beef and when he'd set for quite a while in the dull afternoon light that filtered through the growing clouds he wandered into the woods to take a shit. He'd eaten something not quite right over the past twenty four hours and when he pissed he felt a sharp burn and he cursed his pain and the hell he'd got himself in. He moaned and grunted like some game struck down by an arrow or shot but not killed. His shit steamed in the thin snow that the wind swept under the canopy of trees. He noticed other droppings from larger animals. He said a prayer that he'd be left untouched by the hordes of wild animals that roamed the region. He saw four great owls dozing on a limb about two grown men's height up. They were kingly with puffed chests and crowned heads of silvery feathers. He remembered an owl he'd eaten once when he was younger. It was a dare and he didn't hesitate. He shot that owl out of the tree and cooked it on a spit less than an hour later. It actually tasted good. But he couldn't convince the other guys. They were superstitious and said bad things would happen to anyone who ate an owl. It was funny at the time. Now that he found himself where he was; taking painful shits on the side of a mountain, heading into a growing blizzard, and breaching the Merritt Ranch on an apparent suicide mission, well, he had to wonder if the other guys weren't on to something that day—the day of the roasted owl.

Irvin returned to his fire, unable to sit down. He lounged on his hip and sipped bourbon while smoking his pipe. He could ill afford to fall asleep and chance finishing his journey in the dark or worse a whipping snowstorm. Thunder pealed from the clouds above him.

A pair of eyes watched him.

He got up and chatted with his horse to get his blood moving; walking around the mustang, patting him, talking, and confiding.

The eyes moved low in the canopy. Padded feet stepped lightly in the snow. Made nary a sound. Drew closer, yet patient.

Irvin chewed a dry beef chunk and looked down the canyon from the ledge where his little stop had brought him.

The eyes that had been watching him narrowed. They lowered to the ground just above the snow. Irvin barely heard the steps rushing through his fire before he fired at the wolf. He wounded it. It came at him, through the pain. It had his arm in its jaw when Irvin put the barrel to its head and fired its brains out over the gray canyon. The splatter on the granite ledge, the crimson mist upon the wind. He pried the wolf off his arm and shot the carcass three more times. Then he looked around to see if there were others. The lone wolf was a rare predator, he knew, but not impossible. After all, who out here was he, himself, hunting with?

Chapter 19.

Godwin and Edwin reached the stream about four hundred yards downstream from where the campsite was. If the riders were still there they'd do well to keep their distance. If they happened upon them now they could pass themselves off as idle hunters—the Merritt men, out for food. What a tragedy that your camp was burned down. The wind can do strange things down here at the banks.

They heard the wolves howl from the other side of the stream and probably a few feet up the mountains on Lt. Smith's Ranch. There was a man always kicking himself for buying land up on the wrong side of the stream. Might as well have bought a big pile of cow shit to be stuck standing on the other side of the lucrative Cut Creek Pass, a mine so fertile many remarked they couldn't believe the silver wasn't just rolling out of the mountain. Yep, you still have to get in there, get dirty, and dig it out.

But the Merritt Men had uncaught fish to fry. They smelled the smoldering remains of the camp as they slowly pressed on up the bank of the stream.

"Howdy."

Godwin looked up and there in a tree was a big beard wearing man with a rifle pointed right at him.

"Howdy. I'm Godwin Merritt."

"So?" the big beard-wearing son of a bitch said.

"This is my land."

"You reckon?"

"I can show you the deed." Godwin said. He spat. "That is, if you can read. What are you doing up in my tree, then?"

"Oh, well, I was camped upstream a few paces, pardon, not knowed I was on Merritt land. We had what you might call a little snafu and found our camp a roaring up in flames."

The second man came out from behind them and leveled his pistol at the Merritt men.

"Well, you're on my property and I came out here to hunt up some supper so what the hell you say you put those guns down and we talk about finding out just what exactly happened to your camp. And when we settle that we can settle up on what kind of rent you're going to pay me for staying unknown on my land."

"You drive a hard bargain, Mr. Merritt. I'll be down in a moment." The man in the tree struggled to get down with his rifle on his back and the tree wet from snow. The man behind them had yet to lower his pistol and they stared at each other for a long moment.

For his part, Edwin stayed perfectly silent lest he give himself away.

"Why don't we walk on up to your camp and take a look around," Godwin said.

"I'd like that," the talker from the tree, formerly known as Thing 1, said.

They pushed through the mess of snow and Edwin was a little relieved to see that the entire tent had burned to the ground. He also noticed how the tracks he and his brother had planted all over had been destroyed in a mess of tracks that belonged to the men and their horses.

It drove Edwin crazy about the third man, formerly known as Thing 2, and his whereabouts. There were three men. Where's the third man, he worried. His eyes scanned about so hungry for visual information. Some sign of the third man. Even his horse was gone. Surely he was still around.

"You alright, son?" the tree talker said. "You look frazzled. Look like you're looking for something real hard."

"Leave my boy out of this. He came with me to hunt. You got troubles, ain't no concern of his. Boy's Ma just passed away in the blizzard. You talk, you talk to me." And Godwin showed him the gun he'd brought to hunt. The sawed off

Edwin's heart raced faster than his thoughts. Where's the third man? Did he run off? Did he go on up the mountain ahead of these two? And then he remembered; the single gunshot that he and Elwin heard as they ran up the mountain. The third man. Was he a dead man?

"Alright, fair enough, Mr. Merritt. My apologies. You're young man here, looks stressed to the maximum." The tree talker turned to Edwin and said, "I'm sorry about your mother, boy. Always hard to lose a parent," he shot a look to Godwin, "needlessly." The gauntlet had been thrown down. There wasn't an innocent man around this stream. The trouble was trying to figure out who was going to shoot first.

"I don't want to rush you men, but the sun ain't up too much longer. What's your plan with your demolished camp? Do you have a place to go with what's left? If there is anything to salvage, I mean to say," Godwin said.

"We probably gotta pick up our scraps here and slide on down to that town a piece down the range," the tree talker said.

"Well, do you know what happened? I mean, it's clear the place burnt down. But why exactly?"

"I suppose while we was out on a hunt ourselves our little fire jumped up and lit the tent full ablaze."

"So, you left camp with your fire burning and it got picked up on the wind and caught your tent?"

"Suppose so."

"Then what are you doing holed up in my tree and your partner under a rock waiting to ambush someone?"

"What you saying, Mr. Merritt?"

"Oh nothing, just that something don't smell right around here."

The hands went on their guns. They were silent. Each man wondering what the play was. Finally, Godwin spoke. "Look, I don't care what your business is. I just think your time on my land is up. So move along with your things and we'll call it square."

"Yeah. Yeah. Maybe that's a good deal," the tree talker said.

A gunshot broke the tension. The tree talker fell dead to the ground. Another gunshot before the echo of the first one had even faded. The second guy ran. He took off through the woods along the stream. No one chased him.

Godwin raised his shotgun; Edwin raised his pistols into the woods up the mountain where the shot came from. The shadow slowly moved down toward them. "Don't shoot, God. Don't shoot."

"You've got to be fucking kidding me," Godwin said.

"I come in peace. Well, except for that dead dog," Jack said.

"Uncle Jack."

Godwin looked at Edwin and shook his head.

Edwin said, "Well, he kinda saved our lives."

"You're welcome, boy," Jack said and ruffled Edwin's hair.

"You didn't save anything, Jack," Godwin said. "That son of a bitch took off like a jack rabbit to go tell whoever else he knows that his men are deader than the confederacy." He turned to Jack, "So thanks. But, no thanks."

"What were these boys up to, camping on your stream as they were?" Jack asked.

"That's what I came down here to find out. We were just about to talk them into lowering the guns and then yours went off and well, here we stand, over a dead man."

"What I don't see, Pa, is where the third man and his horse were. There were three of them when Elwin and I saw them earlier."

"Check yonder stream, God," Jack nodded toward the water.

"No? Really. They shot their own man,"

"I was sitting up in a tree when I saw your boys come through here, God. They were quiet as mouses when the three of these assholes lit out for some reason. Probably the limb I rigged to fall down from the dead tree that pokes up over the canopy. It caused a bit of noise and set them off that way," Jack said and pointed up to where they'd taken their horses.

"You were here the whole time?"

"Yep. Didn't want to get involved. You seemed like you had everything under control," Jack said to Edwin. "Reminded me of your old man, back in the fun old days."

"Watch your tongue, Jack," Godwin said.

"Anyway, that tent went up faster than a match. When they rode back into their camp they started swearing all to hell. The dumb one, the one they got belly up in the stream, took the heat for leaving the fire going and probably a mess of other shit. They got on him real strong and he bucked his horse to the water's edge. The horse reared up and then lowered a big buck on the poor guy. Threw him clean off his horse's ass. The guy hit the rocks in the stream and I could tell from my tree up there that he wasn't getting back up. So this dead guy over here just rode up and shot him once in the head. Nothing more you could do. Don't know if they've got a pensioner's plan for bandits and outlaws. Might be something to look into. Could be a big money maker for you someday, boy."

"You saw my boys in trouble and you stayed up a tree?" Godwin spat.

"No. No, no, no. They were never in any danger. These guys never saw them. I heard the two talking after that rotten fish over there got shot. They put the blame square on him for setting the camp alight."

"That's not what they were saying to us. They were looking for someone," Edwin said. He was shivering and his nose was dripping like a sieve.

"Godwin, your boy looks positively frozen."

Godwin agreed, "Why don't we head on up and get some hot tea."

"Capital idea. Thank you for the invite, God," Jack said.

They were walking up the mountain when Jack broke the silence. "How's Mrs. Merritt and the little baby? Bet he's big as an ox by now."

No one said a word. Jack shrugged and started to get ideas; ideas that maybe all was not right on the Godwin Merritt Ranch. The Merritt men moved stiffly up ahead of him and he followed like a good dog. "Still making that ale of yours, God?" He tried some lighter fare to get back on a less stressful topic.

Godwin only grunted an affirmative.

They reached the ranch just as sweaty and out of breath as the two boys had only hours before. Edwin said, "I'll let Elwin know we're back okay." He looked at Jack with broken eyes. Jack knew the news was heavy. These Merritt men looked to be carrying a load and a half on their shoulders.

"Godwin, what's going on? I know it's serious," Jack said.

They went into the great room and Godwin rebuilt the dimming fire. As he stoked and worked the bellows he told Jack Hanshaw what had happened to Freda, Jack's sister. And how she died, in the end, in the very room they were now sitting in.

"I want to see her," he said.

Godwin only motioned with a thumb over his shoulder toward the outbuilding.

Elwin watched from the kitchen window as Uncle Jack plowed through to the outbuilding. The scream that shattered the sky was unexpected as far as Godwin was concerned. The boys didn't know what to expect and the scream triggered trembling sobs in Elwin. He ran out to the body of his mother and Jack threw his arms around the boy. Elwin felt Jack's tears hit his hair as fast as spring showers.

"I'm so sorry, Elwin. I'm sorry. She was a great mother for you boys." His voice gurgled like the stream.

Elwin continued to sob, his chest heaving as his lungs tried for breath that was hampered by his choking throat. Freda's body lay as motionless as the snow. And as silent as her god. Jack knelt down, right there in front of her and blessed himself with the sign of the cross. He bowed his head and began to pray, silently.

Elwin knelt down too.

Godwin sat by the fire drinking whisky. He stared through the wall where no window hung. He looked deep and searched blind with outstretched hands for some truth and reason for his current existence. The wealth of Cut Creek Pass must have come with some curse due before death. Does a man who does not believe in an afterlife have his hell delivered before he sleeps eternal? It was dark in the great room. It would only get darker in Godwin.

Jack and Elwin returned finally to the kitchen, red eyed and freezing. The sun had set about a half hour earlier. Edwin had fed and returned Erwin to his crib upstairs. The meal he made for the men was ham and potatoes. A bowl of biscuits steamed on the farm table. The corn was still firm but ready to eat and they sat without Godwin. Edwin brought a stein of ale for Jack. "Thank you, Ed," Jack said.

"There's plenty in there, Uncle Jack," Edwin said. It was good to hear his name called just Ed. That's how she called for him. He hadn't heard it for a couple of days and as the days went on the boys would begin dropping the "win" and just calling each other by the beginning as they had always, strangely, done for Godwin.

"Did you see the men? At the campsite?" Elwin finally asked.

Edwin deferred to Uncle Jack.

"They did. Well, we did, I suppose."

"Uncle Jack was there the whole time we were there, when I was in the tent," Edwin said.

Elwin couldn't hold back the shock. He nearly pushed his chair across the room in a spasm of anxiety.

"It's okay, El," Uncle Jack said. "I was up in a tree and saw you two approach. I would have jumped in on a moment's notice if I got even a whiff that you two were in danger."

"Two of 'em are dead," Edwin said.

Elwin's eyes were stuck open. "How?"

"Well, one of the guys shot one of the other's that they blamed for starting the tent on fire. Then I had to shoot one myself when God and Ed got themselves jammed up in a standoff. I was still up in the tree and could only go by what I was seeing. The third one tore off in the opposite direction of the ranch."

"Incredible," Elwin said. It was all he could say. He'd never experienced anything like it. He had no points of reference to form a structure in which to house this singular experience.

"Uncle Jack?" Edwin said.

"Ed?" Jack said.

"What do we do about the third man, the one that got away?" Edwin said.

"Ed, nobody "got away". We weren't trying to capture anyone and we didn't do anything wrong. Not about this situation. These men were wrongly camping; trespassing on Godwin's ranch. You and your father were in a situation where your property had been abused and you were then threatened with death. No possible charge could be applied to your actions. That man, the one that "got away" is getting away with murder or conspiracy to commit murder as related to the dead partner of theirs in the stream." Uncle Jack chuckled acutely.

"What's so funny, Uncle Jack?" Elwin said.

"Hell, I'd charge the one on the run with pollution for leaving two dead bodies on the ranch. Not to mention the burnt up campsite."

Elwin smiled and felt righteous about his family's actions this day.

Godwin came into the kitchen. "Thank you for making the supper, son. I'm going to sleep for the night. I need some rest. Jack, can you mind the boys for me?"

"Of course, God. If you're up before me in the morning would you wake me? I'd like to get out and start digging a grave for my sister."

"Aye."

Chapter 20.

They caught themselves laughing hysterically at the table in the kitchen. They refilled their steins for the seventh time. Edwin and Jack were hitting it hard and having what Jack told Edwin was an Irish wake. Elwin had passed out on the couch in the great room at about twenty two hundred hours, as noted by Jack.

"Uncle Jack, have you ever been to Sawyerskill? Back where Pa was from?" Edwin asked.

Jack sat there and leveled his chair to the floor again. He'd been tipping his chair back and rocking as they laughed about the mess they'd left behind down by the stream. After all the handwringing and reassurances Edwin seemed to come to terms with the basic premise of Darwin's theory of evolution as presented by his sometimes-well-read Uncle Jack.

"You have, haven't you?" Edwin pressed.

"Yeah. But don't get too excited. There ain't much going on back there in Sawyerskill. The town was corrupt from its birth. Getting away from there was the best thing for Godwin and Freda; rest her soul."

"Corrupt how?" Edwin asked.

"Don't worry about it. There's no need to go into all the dirty laundry piled up in Sawyerskill," Jack said and went to refill his stein in the pantry. He stood in front of the barrel and sighed quiet and deep.

He could see that Edwin was not going to let it go when he got back to the table and the silence was awkward.

"What do you call a flamingo in the middle of a hurricane?" Jack said.

Edwin stared through him. No smile. No blinks.

"Any guesses?"

"I don't want to hear any more jokes. I want to hear some truth. All my life God and Ma kept the world they grew up in and came from a secret. I want to know who I am. I can't move forward if I don't know that." Edwin was on the edge of tears; drunk, grief-stricken, ashamed.

"I'm sorry. Edwin, I'd love to tell you what I know but if Godwin has kept some things from you he must have very good reasons. It's not my place to betray those interests he wishes to protect," Jack said.

"I just want to know where she came from. Who she was. Who they were before they were out here on this god forsaken ranch," he clinched his fists. White knuckled and lip biting; he fought the instinct to breakdown and cry.

"I know it's horrible that she died. I feel it too. But it's nothing that your parents did. And moving out here and making this life was a big step and will give you and Elwin and Erwin some very big advantages over what might've been had they stayed back in Cut Creek. You're blessed. Despite what you're suffering right now."

Edwin stared at him, "We're doomed."

"No. You can't say that. Nobody can."

"We're out here on our own now. We can't work this out."

"Stop. You should stop and go to bed now. Staying up and drinking isn't going to help you see what you got. Go get to sleep and tomorrow we can talk some more. I need to get to bed anyway, myself."

"How do we bury her?" Edwin said.

"I'm going to take care of that tomorrow. You can help me if you like. But I can handle it on my own."

Jack stayed up too late. His pocket watch read three in the morning when he finally put the whisky down. He lurched up to bed and felt the invisible ocean of drunkenness sway his raft side to side.

The fist on his door jerked him from the worst sleep of his life; up to that point. "Wake up, little brother," Godwin shouted. "You smell like piss and whisky."

"Yeah. Well." Jack swung out of bed, "I had some shit on my mind I was trying to forget in case your son, Edwin, tries to torture the information out of me."

"He ask about Cut Creek?"

"Yeah. I don't know why you just don't tell him about it."

"I will. When the time is right."

"Is that time ever going to come?" Jack said.

"We can start digging after some food. And a trough of coffee; which I can see you might be needing."

"He's worried you won't make it up here on the ranch without her."

"There was a time that might've been so. Things change. Fortunes change."

"Yeah, that's what I told Edwin last night. Or this morning, I suppose it was."

"Come on. We can talk about it over coffee and breakfast," Godwin said.

"Let me splash some water on my face," Jack said.

* * *

On the mountain under pale, moonlit clouds Irvin caught his breath. He was trying to decide if the men he worked for were actually going to pay him for the crimes he'd already committed and for the crimes he was about to commit.

The light in the little building off the main house had flickered dimly on the windows. He watched from the edge of the trees behind it. He'd seen the boy walk out of the house and he appeared to be unarmed.

Irvin sat on a fallen tree at the edge of the line and watched the house a little while longer. He dipped in and out of his tobacco pouch hardly letting the taste of the chew dull before spitting the whole wad and putting a fresh pinch in its place between his teeth and gums. He considered his job as he watched the outbuilding. He knew the boy was in there but not if he were alone or not. He didn't mind killing the boy because he knew what the boy's father had done years ago, letting blood spill all over Sawyerskill and the Mantabawa river. He knew as sure as the big circular saw at the mill ripped apart that Mattocks boy that however Godwin protested in public against his inherited feud that once he got a taste of that killing he took to it like a drunkard to his bottle and anyone else's bottle within arm's reach. Irvin knew the viciousness that Godwin exhibited in cutting down his rivals. What's more, he wouldn't be surprised to find out that Godwin had murdered and lied his way into ownership of Cut Creek Pass. Irvin considered it all sitting on the fallen timber. Once he decided the boy was alone in the outbuilding he moved in the silver night toward the makeshift funeral parlor.

* * *

The water was cold. The washbasin skidded across the marble-topped oak dresser with a horrendous racket. Jack cupped the water in his hands, hands hot from a long night of drinking and poor sleep; the bad blood pressure of poor habits. He remembered thinking the water was too cold; should've have had a skin of ice on its surface. The window was still dark from the night that would soon be bleached in sunlight. His hands pressed against his face when he heard the gunshot. It came from a distance but not very far. He just knew it wasn't in the house. Jack ran downstairs soaked at the edges of his beard and long hair.

The door out of the kitchen was wide open and he caught a glimpse of Godwin running toward the outbuilding and then past it. He chased a shadow toward the tree line. Jack grabbed his pistol from the shelf and after him. He roared in his darkest moment when he was only halfway in the door of the outbuilding. He dropped his chin and almost threw up. He didn't know it was going to be horror on such a level. Godwin knew the moan and yell that blew from Jack's gut came from deeper than his heart.

He skidded into the door of the outbuilding and saw her body still wrapped on the table and then God, Godwin, fell on his knees seeing Jack holding Elwin's head in his arms. On his lap. Under his tears. His boy was dead with a hole in his body where it shouldn't have been. Godwin threw up furiously and voluminously against the door and against the wall of the outbuilding. He crawled on his hands and knees to his son. He pulled him from Jack's arms. Jack ran and followed the footprints in the snow as far as he could, across the tilted mesa and into the timber until his lungs burned so hard that he doubled over and dry heaved with his face nearly in the deep snow.

Jack fired his pistol into the anonymity of the silver horizon haunted with grotesque silhouettes of pine trees. He trudged back to the outbuilding short of breath and weak in the legs.

He stood and watched his breath fog up the air in front of his face.

Godwin stared and took deep note in shock.

The frost on the wall.

The steam from his vomit.

The water in his beard.

The boy, dead beneath his mother.

There, then, Godwin knelt depleted by the loss of his wife and, now, of his son.

Jack waited outside.

Godwin yelled for a half an hour at Freda's supposed god all the while cradling his son's head in his lap. "He was too young, you worthless bastard. You're no god. You're a joke. A prank. He was better than you in every way. He didn't deserve this, you did. Fuck you, god. You're nothing. You never were and never will be. You're blind to our pain. You're lame to their prayers. You're no god. You're an imbecile. I'm coming for you, you piece of shit. When my time on this giant turd is done, I'm coming for you. You're dead." Godwin finally broke down.

He heard the whap-whapping of the belts slow to a stop. The saw blade was still and the blood ran to the dirt floor below riding gravity into the earth to seal the contract and perfect the feud. In the corner of the mill on Sawyerskill he saw Lieutenant Smith with the black wound in his chest—a borrowed grin beneath his considerable moustache.

Every animal has enough brain to tan its own hide.

Jack returned to the kitchen. He wanted to meet Edwin and stop him from going out to the bodies. He was standing in the kitchen holding baby Erwin. Erwin had been screaming his head off and woke Edwin from his blackout. "Too much to drink last night," Edwin said. And when he saw the concern on his Uncle Jack's face he became weak-kneed. "What happened, Uncle Jack?"

"Can I hold Erwin?"

Edwin handed him the screaming baby. "What happened? Where's God? And Elwin?"

"Your brother was in the outbuilding. He's shot."

Edwin ran for the door, "Is he okay?"

Jack stepped in front of him and blocked the door. "Stay in here. Your father is with him. He's taking care of Elwin."

"Is he okay?"

"He's not. I'm sorry, Ed."

"Get the hell outta my way, Jack!" Edwin pushed him aside and ran out the door. He burst into the building and ran to his father's side. His father put his arm in front of Elwin's bloody head to protect him. Edwin threw his arms around his father. He could barely scream through his crying. "Why, God?"

"I'm sorry. I don't know what happened."

"I don't want him to go. Get him back. Get him back, Dad!"

"I can't, son. I can't help him."

Edwin crumbled at his father's feet.

They were in the outbuilding for another hour. Jack stayed inside with baby Erwin. He didn't know what to do so he kept the baby warm and tried to make a breakfast. He only managed to make a pot of coffee and fry bacon. His focus was lost and he mostly stared at the blur. His thoughts all returned to the same thing; thank god Erwin would be too small to remember any of it. He may make it with his innocence intact. The baby was asleep again. Jack took him to the crib in the great room. He went to the kitchen to pour some whisky in his coffee. He sat at the table with the platter of bacon and waited for them to come back in—without Elwin.

Chapter 21.

Elwin and Freda were laid to rest in the graves that Godwin, Edwin, and Jack carved out and dug for them. When the last of the earth was laid on top of them, the men bowed their heads and said not a word. Godwin was the first to shuffle off from the now hallowed ground. He took his wet boots off in the mudroom and took a bottle of whisky up to his room. He did not come out and was not disturbed for the night or the next night.

In that time, Jack minded the care of God's surviving sons; Edwin and Erwin.

The first night was the longest.

Breaking silence is hard even in the grandest of times. When the thread of a conversation has been clipped and the ball dropped, it takes a creative personality to pick it up, find the tip and begin sewing—a pattern of the mind that Jack possessed but the circumstances he found himself in not only cut the thread but turned out the lights and blindfolded him. He watched the boy drink a stein of ale slowly on the porch. Rocking Erwin beside the fireplace, he kept track of the time. It had been dark for an hour and he feared the boy might catch a chill that could put him on a deathbed as well. Jack put Erwin in the bassinet and joined Edwin on the porch, bringing two shots of whisky. Jack raised his shot to the stars, "That Freda and Elwin may find each other among the stars."

Edwin bumped his shot to Jack's and nodded a jerked, choking appreciation. They shot their whisky.

"He's not coming down tonight is he?" Edwin said. "God? He's not coming down tonight."

"He may be lost for quite a while. He's been through a lot of things in his life but nothing like this. He's strong. He's there for you."

"Just not tonight."

Jack nodded and couldn't lift his eyes from the yard.

"It's alright. The only one who's coming out of this with any kind of normality is Erwin. He'll never know the reality," Edwin said.

"You may be right. But this thing that happened today, it's still life. It's a part of living. Elwin is lost but not to your heart and memory. He did what he had to do. He looked at the facts of his life and chose to leave. And probably not out of hopelessness too much but maybe out of hope that he could see Freda, see your mother again. We'll never know. But I know he was a good, young man. I know he was too young to have enough experience to know that life would carry on. That sadness and loss make us stronger in the end if we use them."

"Sounds like a bunch of shit. The whole shooting match. Sounds like the whole show is just a vapor in a dream. If it's so fleeting and quick and what was walking and talking one second falls down dead the next …what's the point?"

"Nobody knows," Jack said, his eyes still in the yard.

Edwin went back inside and left Jack outside to ponder "…his mother's goddamn Irish doubt," as Godwin put it not so mildly.

"If you're out there, keep an eye on that boy," Jack said to the stars and seeing the constellation of Freda's face one more time. The cold wind rushed his face and he smiled and went back to the pantry.

"Uncle Jack, let's stay up and drink a bit," Edwin said with his stein filling under the barrel. It's cold on the ranch. I think I want to keep talking."

"As you wish, lad." Jack stuck his stein out, "Refill, barman?"

"As you wish, sir." Edwin smiled and felt good pouring beer.

Some time had passed as they recalled the good times Freda had brought them. Jack went into great detail summoning a family tale that found Freda leading an expedition of distant relatives down the Mantabawa River and back up Cut Creek where the Merritt's homestead was. They had a mass of property and a launch right down on Cut Creek for transport or leisure though Darwin Merritt, Jack believed, never knew such a word existed even for children. "For Darwin Merritt, play time ended just about the time a baby stopped sucking its mother's tit," Jack said.

Edwin flinched and then chuckled.

"I actually heard him say that one day when I escorted Freda up Cut Creek to the Merritt property," Jack said. "I assure you, he was not joking. Not given over to funniness in any way. A smile probably would've dropped him where he stood."

"Ma said he was a sober man. Said he only knew how to work and not much else. Expected everyone else to do the same."

"That's a historical truth. Mark it down right next to the Confederate Surrender and the Battle of Bull Run. That was a favorite saying of Darwin's. Though he abided north of the Mason-Dixon, he had a rebel streak coursing through his stern heart."

"What about the Hanshaw's though? Were they as severe as the Merritt clan?" Edwin said.

"Well, don't misunderstand. It seems the serious bone runs squarely in the Merritt men. I found Darwin's wife, Emma, funny and intelligent. He'd taught her to read when they were sweethearts. He taught her to read and she ran with it. I think she said Mark Twain was her favorite. Before Darwin died, he took her to a lecture where Mark Twain spoke. She said Darwin didn't smile once through the entire lecture. I gathered from her that his speaking was quite a thing."

"I don't want to talk about this stuff anymore, Uncle Jack."

"Oh."

Edwin tried hard to ask the thing he wanted to know. The good times were great and all. They'd last a lifetime. He wanted to know who cast the shadow. The timeline since God and Ma left Cut Creek and came out past the plains, where the land shot up and suggested nothing but hid wealth beyond any tillable soil; what had told them to make a new home up here? He couldn't get the words.

"What is it, Edwin? Something's got you all tied up," Jack said.

"What did Pa do back in Cut Creek that made them have to move out here?" Edwin said. He couldn't look at his uncle just then. He'd have to hear some answer or leave the room.

"I'm not sure I'm the man to tell you what you think you need to know." Jack was listening for a sound; a rumpling of rug, an incoherent murmuring, a slamming of chair legs or trinkets and pillows. He listened for signs of life from Godwin upstairs. He watched Edwin stare hard away from him. "Throw some more firewood in the stove."

Edwin did as Jack said. He felt he had him. He could feel the earth moving. He'd get an answer to the evasions Godwin and Freda had always constructed. The truth would come out tonight. Too much blood was in the ground not to speak openly even if the two were unrelated. And Edwin, in his adolescent mind was beginning to understand that the two were never unrelated. That truth followed blood. Where blood seeped into earth is where truth would grow like a tree. The iron door squealed on its hinge when Edwin closed it on the growing fire that would heat the kitchen well into the morning.

"Let's go have a smoke in the back yard," Jack said.

Edwin felt the groundswell. He knew there was a chance. The back yard was on the other side of the house from Godwin's windows. And chances are, Edwin thought, he had drunk himself to sleep upstairs by then anyway. He assumed this was Uncle Jack's intent; to clandestinely explain the early days of his parents' relationship and probably more to the point, his father's business.

Jack set his stein down on the snow. It sunk in a bit, nearly to the rim. "Quite a way to keep this ale cold," he said. He went to the door to close it with both hands so to not make a rousing racket.

"We ought to move the barrels out here," Edwin said.

"Good idea. Now?"

"Probably not. Maybe tomorrow. I don't know if Pa will go for it. He likes his ale warm," Edwin said.

* * *

Upstairs Godwin stared at the ceiling in complete darkness. His eyes burned from dry air. He was beginning to drift. Finally. The whisky bottle he'd taken up sat on his bureau, unopened. He'd seen the truth in the outbuilding. The whisky, he decided, would be for later; when his work was done.

* * *

Outside, the cherry at the end of Jack's hand-rolled cigarette sizzled bright and low as he puffed and begged for time. "I'll tell you a little about Godwin's first business back at Cut Creek. You can't say a word about it. Wouldn't do no good anyway."

Edwin hadn't lit his pipe and didn't think about it until he'd been asked to start making promises he wasn't sure he'd keep. To have a pipe in his mouth and just nod without speaking would create an omission he could live with. He was beginning to find alternative routes to the truth. He was learning the strategies of adults who, even with little to hide, bend and maneuver to get what little they want. His pipe was too late getting to his lips when Jack asked again, "You promise not to bring it up with Godwin?"

"Promise." Just a word he thought, out there in the yard where the night went dead.

*   *   *

Upstairs, Godwin fell asleep and dreamed his wife held Elwin in the rocking chair, reading him a story from a slender volume of Christmas tales. Elwin choked as she read and he struggled for air. She kept reading as if nothing were wrong. Elwin struggled with his fists balled up under his chin trying for air but gathering none. Blood like black tar drooled from his lips and his eyes went wide with panic.

Godwin tossed and turned on the mattress. He moaned and mumbled unable to wake himself.

She put the book down and held Elwin in her arms, rocking him as though he were an infant and not the boy Godwin could see. She sang the ancient German lullaby as he struggled for breath and spit black tar blood like a blown oil derrick. As she sang she stood and walked him to the oversized crib that sat beneath the window. He stood over her and watched her lower their boy into the crib that fell deeper and deeper until it was the grave on the ranch.

Godwin woke up sweating and flushed. He took a shot of whisky from the bottle atop his bureau. In the moonlight through the window he saw his old neighbor had returned to chitter chatter.

"You still owe me some silver, I believe. Now, when are you going to do right by me and pay me what's mine? You can't have the whole mountain free and clear without paying your dues."

I don't owe you anything, Lieutenant Smith.

"The hell you say. I did what you asked and I want my silver and Decatur portraits." The conscripted drunkard paced the bedroom and caught sight of the letter. Godwin stood behind his neighbor so that he could see both of their faces in the window. Danforth Smith looked up in the window. "Now, those Decatur notes aren't as sentimentally valuable as the coin notes bearing the image of Admiral Farragut but they'll do, nonetheless. I'd say, you put them in the barrel beside the fireplace tonight and we have no more business to tend to. You can live out the rest of your days with what family you got and pull all the silver you can handle out of your mine and through the gates that just happen to have been on my land."

You're mad!

"Am I?" Danforth's borrowed grin overlaid Godwin's face in the reflection with such perfection that Godwin could not tell between them.

I'll put the goddamn silver in the barrel. I'll put the silver in the barrel.

Godwin was alone in the room thrashing about trying to fill the satchel Red Eagle made with all of the money he could find. He bundled himself in wool and fur and crept to the back of the house where he snuck off into the night. Jack's horse was stronger than Creasy so he stole off into the woods and tracked toward the trail that would take him down to his neighbor's ghastly house.

He shoved his way into the house without a lantern to see. He tripped on a table leg and heard skittering sounds in the other room. In the dark, he felt for a barrel near to where the fireplace must have been. The lid was stuck on, frozen. The wind whipped snow into the open door and across the dark house. He dropped the satchel and picked up the barrel. He banged it on the ground as hard as he could. Cursed it and kicked it, and finally the lid rolled off. He shoved the satchel down in the barrel as if he were trying to drown somebody. "Here's your goddamn money you crazy old bastard. Now stay the hell away from my family."

Godwin trudged to the door and stopped when he saw the silhouette out in the pristine snow at the edge of the bridge. Danforth Smith bowed his head with a tip of his gray hat. Godwin mounted the horse and took off for home with a loud, "Heeyah! Heeyip!"

* * *

"Further on up Sawyerskill from where your grandfather, Darwin, lived was a family that ran a quarry where they were loading out marble and other stone for trade to take down the Kill and then into the Mantabawa. Along down the Mantabawa was a city where they sold the stone and from there it was further distributed around the region. The family that ran the marble quarry were making money faster than they could print it, so Darwin liked to say."

"So, did father work at the quarry?" Edwin said.

"No, that wouldn't have been an option under Darwin's roof. The trouble started when Darwin decided that as Sawyerskill flowed through his property he had a right to collect a piece of the money that the quarry was making shipping marble and such on down to the Mantabawa. Makes sense, I suppose, if you discard the fact that no one owns a river. But, hey."

"Grandfather Merritt was a hustler?"

"Well, that would have been a tad generous." Jack's cigarette had been smoked to the butt end and he flicked it far and high across the deep blue sky. He didn't see where it landed. "Darwin went back and forth with the owner of the quarry. At first, the quarry men paid the toll that had been levied against them, fearing any physical attack which at that time Darwin was quite capable and at ease to do."

"Not buying it," Edwin said. He smoked his pipe slowly, under a skeptical scowl. He pulled his coat tight over his chest and puffed circles straight up into the night.

"I don't need you to buy it. It is what it is and what it is is the truth. Your grandfather was an amateur explosives aficionado. He'd fill a little drum with his signature blend of black powder and secret catalyst mix which he swore could make a blind man see through walls, and then he'd roll it on down to the banks of Sawyerskill. He'd watch the current carry it out what he deemed a reasonably safe distance but which Emma quietly disagreed with and fire a round from his service rifle. Sometimes they didn't explode and sometimes the boom was so quick you'd swear your mind had left your body."

"So?"

"So, one day after the quarry had stopped paying their "due" to Darwin he rigged Sawyerskill to go off. He filled his barrels, about ten of them in total and strung them on heavy wire from one side of the creek to the other. He'd weighted them precisely to submerge just under the surface and then he waited. A massive shipment of pristine marble was being taken down the creek the morning of May 8. Up a ridge on a log, mossy and wet, Darwin sat with his service rifle. The barge lumbered slowly into sight from around the bend. He readied his gun and fired one shot. We heard the boom back up the Mantabawa that spring morning and thought for sure a war was breaking out. The barge was pushed back a split second before it cracked and sank right where it had run into Darwin's wire."

Edwin's jaw had been hanging open for a few minutes when he said, "No way. Darwin was a madman. What made him think that he could do that?"

"His past, I think. Everyone in the area knew who Darwin Merritt was and his legend never weakened. He'd never been challenged when he went after something. And if he wanted something stopped, he'd make it happen."

"Or not happen."

"Ha, yeah," Jack said.

"But, what does this have to do with Pa, Uncle Jack?"

"The feud with the quarry owners ignited the morning Darwin blew their barge to hell and gone. They went back and forth for months getting all that marble out of that damn creek. No one quite knew how to do it and most of the attempts were scuttled before they got off the ground once the contracted men were apprised that the offended party was Darwin Merritt of Sawyerskill."

"How would they get marble out of the creek?"

"That's not really the point of the story. The feud is the problem."

"Okay. But did they ever get the marble out of the river?"

"I don't think they ever got all of it. Somewhere in the murky waters of Sawyerskill just past the Merritt homestead are a few heavy slabs of marble," Jack said.

"So the feud?"

"Your father inherited a righteous feud with the family upriver from them. After Darwin died, your father was made to suffer the feud with no end in sight. If he didn't keep up Darwin's delusion to tax the river for his own gains, the money Darwin made in the coal mines around Sawyerskill would never see Godwin or his new, young bride, Freda Hanshaw."

"What a jerky move."

"Exactly."

"But what did father do that we couldn't go back?"

"A man lost his life. I can't say more tonight. We need to get to sleep."

"Come on, Uncle Jack. I won't be able to sleep if you leave the story there."

"It's not a story, kid. Remember that."

"Okay. Maybe we can get away from father tomorrow and continue talking. I just want to say thanks for letting me in on this. It's very important. And considering all that's happened up here since the storm—it's nice to hear some truth."

They staggered inside with cold limbs and glassy eyes. Jack hung around the iron stove and said goodnight and see ya in the morning. Edwin stopped and was listening at Godwin's closed door on two wobbly legs. He nearly fell against it but stopped himself softly and made his way to his room and fell into his bed. He was asleep before he knew he was in bed.

At the stove Jack began to think of the woman he left back in town. Before he made his way back to the silver mine he'd met her in the office of Mr. Jefferson. Pretending to be someone he wasn't in order to get something he wasn't sure he wanted; he'd hired himself out to the enemy. "Jamie," he whispered.

Chapter 22.

After hours, Mr. Jefferson found that he was alone on the floor. He blew out some lamps and made his way to the basement, to the boiler, and then to the hidden door that opened into the tunnel that led to Wichita's.

He sat in the underground where Madame V. had a makeshift lobby lit up gold and white like some champagne starburst and appointed with not too shabby accommodation; a chaise with only slightly frayed upholstery and hardly noticeable scuffs on the wood claw legs where rats had gnawed until other food was found and a small bar with mirrored trays that held cloudy glasses which the barmaid upstairs refused to retrieve for wash and so it was up to Luthor to wipe them out with a dingy rag giving it a good old fashioned Jimtown spitshine. Upstairs was the main hall of Wichita's. It was upstairs that the general mass of men could, for a price, have their way about a woman with no other obligation than a cash transaction. Downstairs the men who ran the city got away unseen.

He met the woman in a room almost at the end of the long hall. There was little light as he made his way past a half dozen doors and he kicked over a small wooden chair and cursed in the darkness.

In the room she was barely wearing her gown and the heels on the floor near the foot of the bed looked like they'd been cast off many clients ago or placed there as a prop to complete the seduction.

They started slow. He'd take a full hour to get his money's worth. As she did her job, he laid back and confessed his sins to her in mumbles and jerks. She climbed on top of him and closed her eyes until he told her to keep her eyes on him. Not much to look at but all the ego in the world. His thin greasy hair pressed to his balding skull, and the warty neck it sat upon. His money made him tolerable and she would do what he asked to get it.

In the corner of the room as usual was the young man he also paid to sit quietly and watch.

Once, the boy spoke and the woman Mr. Jefferson had thrown on the floor said, "Hush, Luthor. This man is a paying customer."

Tonight Luthor was silent.

After Mr. Jefferson got what he came for, he left the basement the same way he'd entered but with a lighter load.

The tunnel was darker. A light was out. They were unreliable and given to extinguish. It smelled of sulfur and he assumed it had burnt out. He felt his way in the dark back to his building under the streets of town.

One nail. A little nail on the heel of a boot broke the silence in the dark hall upstairs near Bernard Jefferson's office. The silence made the darkness blinding. Bernard reached for his pistol and turned. Three shots hit him in his chest. His own gun fell to the floor without a single shot.

Bernard heard the footsteps slowly walk to him and the hallway stretched out forever. The shooter leaned over to make sure he didn't recover. Bernard spit blood pucks like an ulcerous geyser. He coughed out, "Smith."

The sheriff's boot nudged Bernard's ribs. "Dead as Judas. One less rat in this sinking ship."

Sheriff Smith calmly walked to the basement. He made his way through the tunnel and into the basement of Wichita's. The boy was standing there, somber and dim. "I'm going up to see Madame V."

The boy stepped aside and pointed to the spiral stairs that led up to the office where Madame V. did all of Wichita's record keeping. The stairs on the other side of the basement went up to the public lobby on McCormick.

Chapter 23.

They were the Black Rock Runners. They were the premier moonshiners up the Mantabawa from the confluence with Sawyerskill. Once upon a shine, old Darwin Merritt had been a true friend to them. When he strung his powder line across the river and tossed the marble barge to kingdom come, well, that burned more than one bridge.

Godwin recalled the men vividly as he dressed himself early in the morning. He had hoped the blood spilled back decades ago would be left to soak in the ground and be put to rest. He'd not expected it to follow him. Not expected it to open new wounds. His children knew nothing of the time back home in Sawyerskill.

He couldn't see the tracks in the snow from the outbuilding to the tree line in the dark from his window upstairs. In the window he saw the reflection. *Lieutenant Smith.*

"Your enemies know no limits. They've taken your boy. They will destroy you."

He knew then that the fatal shot that killed Elwin was not from his own gun. He knew suicide was a ridiculous notion. He'd not seen the truth until then. He knew it was the third man; the one who got away down by the stream and the burned down campsite.

Godwin didn't see the resemblance right away. But he knew when he was down with Edwin talking to the campers on the stream that they'd looked familiar. In the distance, through a mist, under the influence of so much stress he'd not recognized the undeniable resemblance to the original Black

Rock Runners. They had such sharp, angular faces stretched over high cheekbones and narrow eyes under bushy brows and foreheads that tilted back so strangely they'd not seemed human to him as a young man. But they were in and out of the Merritt homestead more frequently than some of his own relatives.

This problem would not be over until the third man was found. A journey back to Sawyerskill he thought would be a quiet homecoming, would inevitably lead to more bloodshed and his oldest son would come to know the full weight of the Merritt history in Doris County. Godwin left the ranch by himself as the sun rose the day after Elwin's burial.

Godwin went first down to the stream. It was a tough trip through the new snow that fell in the night. The sky darkened with the approaching blizzard and shortly after sunrise it looked like the sun was already going down. It was going to be a hard couple of days if the new storm was anything like the last one. He knew Jack would keep his boys safe up on the ranch and that an explanation would be expected should he return.

Beside the stream he found the burned camp and the bodies.

He dragged the bodies from their current resting places; one still in the roil, in the stream and the other beside the ashes of the tent.

The ax holstered on his hip had a wide blade for felling trees on one end. The other end was a blunt face used for hammering. It was a Mantabawa style ax forged in the smith shop on the Black Rock Runners' land. BRR was burned into the handle. A full circle forged into the blade head was the symbol of their brand of moonshine. They'd made a killing in their field of expertise. They'd made a killing on his ranch.

Godwin took a moment and recalled Red Eagle's words, "Every animal has enough brain to tan its own hide."

He threw the blunt end of the ax down in a crushing blow to the head of the one who'd been in the stream. The top half of his head was now gone. Another swing and the corpse was unrecognizable. Unhuman; just as Godwin had assumed all those years ago. These Black Rock Runners were mutant killers. Not human, not in any recognizable way.

He set himself to swinging, erasing the men from the face of the earth.

He swung with the mechanical efficiency of the circular blade of the sawmill on Sawyerskill, the one he worked as teenager when he would spend summers away from Darwin's trying to make money in a more honest fashion much to the chagrin of his dear father.

That last summer he was yanked off the job by the foreman at the request of Darwin. Godwin returned blinded by anger and a frustrated will that had plenty of time to boil over on the three hour horse ride home.

He swung the ax with a firm grip that married his flesh to the wooden handle. A violent windmill of precision chipped the rocks beneath the bodies and pulled hunks of unidentifiable organs into the frost of the evening air.

* * *

Godwin dismounted his horse after slowing its gallop to merciful lope after the hard ride from the lumber mill. The seventeen year old Godwin Merritt charged into his father's home. His entrance was grand to say the least as he stiffened his arm and swept all of the ornaments and bric-a-brac of his father's fondest memories of his United States Army service, awards and commendations signed off on by President Franklin Pierce himself, had the stationary to prove it once upon a time. He rounded the corner to the sitting area and Darwin sucker punched him in his abdomen. Godwin doubled over swaying in staggered steps until he came to rest using a chair as a crutch. The steam saw spun in Godwin's head—belts and pulleys whap-whapped and screeched unholy noise between his ears. "I'll forgive you this one time, boy," Darwin said.

"You're the one who punched me and I'm being forgiven?"

"It's your own damn fault, done gone and killt Mattock's nephew."

"Where's Gunther Mattocks now?"

"No sight of him for four days and I don't think there will be."

"This has to stop. All of it. I'm tired of the retribution and vengeance between us all. You have to see it won't end until we're all of us dead, father."

"My hands are tied, son. If I could go back and make it all never happen then I'd have done it. It's what we're stuck with now. You've got to stand up now and fight."

"No. The only way to end this fighting is to not fight back. I want to live to be older than twenty. I want a family and a future."

Darwin smacked him on the back of his head, "Dammit boy. Those no good, second rate hooch shilling, backstabbing, half-mad sons a bitches don't deserve the air we breathe.

*   *   *

Covered in the blood of his enemies as the waters of Cut Creek descended into the snow packed gorge, Godwin's boots shifted the icy stream beside the body, bits of body now. The blood swirled deep red over his boots and around the chunks of the man he'd identified as a relative so near to the Mattocks that had spat at the mention of his dead brother years back that he deliriously thought he had seen a ghost until his killing ax had erased the man's face from the present.

In the blizzard, oblivious to the danger of frostbite, hallucination, amnesia Godwin cleaved sinew from bone and fed the bodies bit by bleeding bit to the burbling stream. Until nothing was left but a puddle of blood and a few scraps of meat. Certainly, some lost predator would wander by and lap up what remains he left behind. Already the spattered snow was being covered and made pristine by the unforgiving snow slipping from the silver and comfortless vault.

He smoked a cigarillo and bemoaned the misplacement of his bone-handled pipe. His arms were tightened ropes from all the swinging and he felt good. The red stream reflected his righteousness in the dull light of the hidden sun. The smell of tobacco was acute in his nose and as if he'd only just smelled it for the first time. Everything felt new, sharpened and vibrant. A brilliant dimension unfolded around Godwin. He could hold a tree trunk and bend its crown to the soil and pluck the fullest fruit. He could push the mountain aside with the tip of his index finger and walk unimpeded through the heart of town. He sat and smoked a moment. In that moment the things he could not do; bring his son back to life, or resuscitate his wife, those things sucked the air from his lungs. He put his head between his legs and screamed. He pulled his pant legs at his shins just shy of pulling his legs out from under himself and threw his face to the rolling clouds of ceaseless snow—and understood the surest thing; that things would fall all around the Godwin Merritt Ranch east of Echo Cliff.

He stood beside his ensanguined stream where pieces of men were lost downstream. He began the hopeless investigation of the burned camp. In a trance he felt through ashes of objects that once existed whole and purposeful. He sifted his flattened hand through the dust and charcoal embers; a powdery down intermingled with boney fragments. His casual movements swept the same spot a few times before his mind clicked and his focus sharpened upon what it was beneath his hand.

Godwin brushed the ashes aside and saw the face in a mask of dust, gray as the sky, looking up at him with a beggar's lament. Godwin scanned his surroundings quickly; up the mountain, toward the stream, ahead and behind. What grotesque treasure had been kept inside their tent? A body-less head? No mere curiosity; he knew. This head served a purpose. Revenge? Blackmail? Terror? Two of the men who might know what purpose this head had were gone. The third, if he could be found, might know. Or worse, he might not. Godwin stood and went to his horse. He charged back up the mountain pass. What could he do on his own with no indication of these camper's employers. They were on his ranch for some reason and under the supervision of someone.

Best to get back in the ranch and take up a defensive posture.

He arrived at the house as the snow began to fall; thick, heavy, silent flakes.

Jack met him at the door.

"Where the hell did you go?" Jack said.

"I went down to the stream," Godwin said.

"Shit, God, what happened?" Jack asked when he saw the blood on his pants and the ax holstered on his hip. "I mean, did you run into someone?"

"No. Yes. No one living."

Jack looked at him sideways and concerned. There was a sharpness in Godwin's eyes he hadn't seen since he arrived on the ranch. A menace traced in the furrows of his forehead. "Do you need a drink?"

"No time for that. From here on out the spigot stays shut. No one gets a drink until this is all over."

"What's over?" Edwin asked when he rounded the corner with Erwin in his arms.

For a split ghost of a second, Godwin saw Elwin round the corner after his brothers. He winced and pinched a tear from his eye. He stretched his eyelids and unholstered the chopping ax from his hip, upending it against the firebox. He put his foot on the hearth and stretched his legs. He didn't say a thing and neither did they. When he turned around Edwin and Erwin were not in the room anymore. What he was looking for was an explanation. He wanted to figure out how to say to Jack that he just chopped up two dead men into little bits and sent them floating down the stream that he and his sons used as their favorite fishing spot and gold prospecting hangout. What he couldn't say was what drove him to it other than rage. Jack would probably think he was drunk or completely mad but Godwin didn't worry too much about that given Jack's own predisposition to drunken madness on certain days when 'just for the hell of it' was a good enough reason. What he said instead was nothing about it. The bodies, should Jack or anyone go looking for them would be gone, with nary a trace. The snow with blood and raw meat would likely be gone in less than a day, buried under new snow the turbulent skies were fixing to dump on the Godwin Merritt Ranch and mountainous environs. What Godwin began to explain ran this way:

"I have a head in a gunnysack outside. It's sitting out on the porch. It is burned a bit and dusted with ash from the campsite. It was in the tent."

And Jack fell into a chair.

"I don't know how to explain it," Godwin said. "It was just a head in a pile of ashes. It looks like a person. I mean, I think if somebody knew the person they would be able to say so."

"You have a head in a bag on your porch?" Jack said. "A head? In a bag?"

"Yes."

"Godwin, I have a serious question to ask you right now."

"What, Jack?"

"Can I have a drink of whisky?"

They both walked to the kitchen and Godwin poured two small glasses of whisky. He drank them both. Then he poured one for Jack. "Sorry."

"Understand," Jack said. He drank his drink in a gulp. "What uh, what about the body?"

"What body?"

"No body?"

"No body."

"There was just a head in a pile of ashes?" Jack said.

"That's what I'm saying. I want you to take a look at him."

"Him? You can tell?"

Godwin said, "I am saying, it's a head that has a face."

"I don't think I want to see," Jack wrinkled his mouth, "him."

"My boy is dead, Jack. I need a little help here. Someone came up here and shot Elwin in the head. Shot him because of our old trouble at Cut Creek. Because of what happened with the Black Rock Runners."

Jack stiffened and choked. "How do you know that?"

"Cause I just chopped up two of them down by the stream. I knew they looked familiar but I couldn't put my finger on it. When I saw the tracks in the snow leading to the woods from the outbuilding last night from my bedroom window, I knew."

"He was murdered?"

"Sure as it's snowing outside."

Jack looked out the window at the whiteout blizzard. "Let me see the face."

They wrapped their faces so only their eyes were exposed and wore goggles over them. Godwin brushed the snow that had already covered the gunnysack since he'd come back. He set it near the wall of the house so that if Edwin happened to be looking out a window he'd not see the severed head. Slowly, he began to peel back the rim of the bag. He peeled it back as though he thought it might be filled with snakes, and that would have been more reassuring than what he knew was in there, waiting to see again and look into his eyes.

Jack jumped back against the railing when he saw the head. He fell on his rear in the snow that drifted onto the porch. He sat up to his belly in snow.

Godwin turned loose the bag. He crunched the snow under his boots and bent down to grasp the forearms and hands of his comrade. Without grunts but only breath shooting out through their thin scarves wrapped snug around their faces, they righted themselves on their feet. Jack was shaking his head the whole way into the house. He removed his bundled clothing in a feverish spasm of zipping limbs and flying garments. His hat landed on the fence that guarded the fire and Godwin calmly removed it.

"It's Jefferson. It's Mr. Jefferson's head. Can't miss the pig head."

"Who's Mr. Jefferson? I mean, who was he?"

"I'm getting a drink," Jack said.

"Slow down. We have to keep control. The third man is still out there somewhere."

"The third man? Who the hell is the third man? There's a lawyer's head in a bag on your porch. You got bigger problems than the third man."

"I'm sure I do. That's why you need. That's why I need you to stay under control of your emotions."

"I'm not getting drunk. I just need a drink."

"One more and then we tuck it all away until the war is over," Godwin said.

Edwin came down the stairs in the back of the house that stood behind the pantry. "Erwin's asleep. But he won't be for very long if the doors keep slamming shut down here."

"Son, I need you to go back upstairs and stay awhile. There's something your Uncle Jack and I have to discuss," Godwin said.

"Uncle Jack?" Edwin said.

"Upstairs," Godwin said.

"Sir." Edwin turned on his heels and went upstairs without a huff. He undressed himself and crawled under the three blankets on his bed. He closed his eyes and thought of his girlfriend and wondered if they'd see each other again before the end of the year. The weight of the blizzard and all it had wrought made it hard for him to breathe. He thought of her; face, hair, fingers. He thought of her and closed his eyes.

Down in the kitchen Godwin and Jack put their guns on the table. They checked them over completely. Godwin said again, "Who is Mr. Jefferson?"

"He's a lawyer from down in the town."

"Tied up with the Black Rock Runners?"

"Apparently so, if they had his goddamn head in their tent."

"Well, what else do you know about Mr. Jefferson?"

"He's tied up with Sheriff Smith too. Was. I guess," Jack said.

"What else?"

"God?"

"What?"

"Edwin was in the tent. Before it burned down. He ran out of there in a big hurry."

"He might have seen Mr. Jefferson," Godwin said.

"Exactly."

Godwin chewed on that. Chewed on it; grinding his teeth to powder. He thought he'd moved far enough. He thought he'd settled upon a high enough mountain from which to see any trouble that might come his way. Was certain Freda would be there to rock him gently beside the fire as they napped in their silver hair. His arms were not long enough to protect Elwin and his mountain was not high enough to see the return of the Black Rock Runners.

Chapter 24.

"Edwin, when the day comes, you'll be the inheritor of the entire operation down Cut Creek Pass," Godwin said. Godwin was building powder kegs with the gallon barrels Freda had purchased years ago for making house wine. They'd sat under a veil of dust in the cellar for more than eight years, maybe even ten as far as Godwin could remember.

"Sure, God. But that's still a long way in the future. And I've got a lot to learn before I can just grab the reins from you," Edwin said.

"It's closer than you think, son. There's things in motion as we speak that are gonna demand of you an earlier trip into manhood than most of the people your age," Godwin assured.

"I don't want to talk about it now. With all that's happened on the ranch. I don't think it's good to consider the future just now."

"That's the trouble. You're thinking right now without being able to know more that would create the picture complete."

They were standing beside the low sweep of snow that was building on the recently dug graves. They had gone out each morning no matter what the weather to speak to Freda and Elwin. Already Godwin was tiring of the notion. He assumed the afterlife was a fairy tale meant to soothe humanity's childlike fear of the dark.

They didn't speak aloud. With their heads bowed to the north they quite resembled prayerful monks. The breath rolled out of their nostrils in thin white ribbons. Edwin sniffled his runny nose but made clear he was not crying by refraining from rubbing his eyes. The early morning freeze wrapped around their chests like a compressed sleeve of ice. Godwin lit his pipe which he'd stuffed with the cannabis he'd been prescribed by Doctor Spuss. He smoked at the head of their graves. Edwin smelled the pungent cannabis and wondered what type of tobacco smelled so strange.

"Can I try your tobacco, God?" He asked.

"Best not fiddle with this. I know it helps but it has a bit of the devil about it," Godwin said.

Edwin smoked his own pipe then. "What happens to the mine if I refuse it? Can Jack take over?"

"Absolutely not. It's not up for discussion. The mine will stay in operation and you will be responsible for it. It's what your mother would have wanted; for you to be prosperous. And that mine out there, Cut Creek, will spit out millions long after I'm dead and buried."

"Who looks after it when we go back to Darwin's old homestead? Will the men be honest left on their own?"

"No. You can be sure of that. No man without observation would be so silly in the face of such immediate fortune. We have other employees planted in their midst who are paid not so much to mine as to mind the mine and make sure its contents are not taken clandestinely or conspiratorially."

"How do you mean, God?" Edwin said.

"There's men down there I pay ten times as much to go in and keep their eyes open for thieves. Anyone's caught stealing or planning to steal from my mine and we deal with it," Godwin said.

"And he doesn't mean calling in the sheriff," Jack said as he walked out behind them. "Elwin's awake but playing in his crib."

"You mean you, Uncle Jack?" Edwin said.

Jack nodded. The satisfied grin on his face made it quite clear he enjoyed his duties down at Cut Creek Pass. Something moaned out in the woods, a deep warbling peal in the quiet snow that was falling gracefully to the ground like ashes—ashes.

"Elk?" Jack asked.

"No," Edwin said.

"Mountain lion. Probably starving," Godwin said.

A shot rang out, the echo tumbling across the ranch, over and over itself, put Godwin on his feet. "Get your guns. Get them loaded."

They rushed through the house getting pistols and rifles, the shotgun, and his ax. They were armed and ready to charge down the mountain to meet the bastards head on. "You stay, Edwin."

He took the baby to the pantry in the bassinet. He shut the door on the pantry and stood watch out the kitchen windows and back door.

Godwin and Jack moved under the limited cover of the barn and outbuildings toward the woods. They walked through the deep snow—thrush and sliff. They didn't know what to expect. Jack saw a movement through the static of falling snow down in the distance. He quietly motioned for Godwin to follow him. They stalked the man who couldn't see them. As they drew nearer with their pistols ready; close enough to see the man's breath rise over his hunting cap, Godwin soon recognized his neighbor. He was kneeling over the mountain lion. "Crunnel, what the hell are you doing shooting mountain lion on my ranch?"

"Merritt, I'm regretfully poaching this lion for eating Friedrich. A thousand apologies, neighbor. But I finally caught this big, dumb son of a bitch."

Jack looked confused and looked to Godwin for an answer.

"His dog," Godwin said.

"Oh." He doffed his own hat to Crunnel, "Sorry about your mutt, Crunnel."

"Kiss my ass, Hanshaw," Crunnel said with no provocation.

"Easy, Crunnel. You know your dog was more doofus than brains."

"Yeah, well, I'm sorry I overstepped my bounds but I had to do the right thing by Friedrich and my youngest has been crying for days about the big, dumb dog."

"Well, you'd do well not to stay on my ranch too long. We're having a bit of a company problem and I don't want no one getting hurt needlessly."

"Got a thief you're running down again?" Crunnel said.

"Like I said; company problem," Godwin said.

Jack nodded at Crunnel.

"Well, what do you want me to do with the lion?" Crunnel said.

"Just leave it be. I'm sure something will be along with a pang in their belly looking for a rare treat. When my schedule clears up I'll travel your way and clear the air. 'Til then, mind the fence line."

Crunnel walked off after a short wave. He muttered, "You mean the stream where you chopped them bodies up and fed them to the fish? That fence line? You godless heathen."

Godwin and Jack looked the lion over. "We could eat her."

"You ever eat lion?" Godwin said.

"No. You?"

"Not yet. Let's see if we can get this cat up to the ranch. Grab her hind paws."

"Sure she's dead?" Jack said.

"Pretty sure."

"Good enough for me," Jack said.

They walked sideways for a while. Each step slow and jerky. The lion's back dragged the snow like a plow. They struggled to persist. Their arms burned and their noses ran. They stuck one foot in front of the other planting their legs in the deep snow like pilings being driven in a swamp.

Finally the beast fell with a crush into the incline of snow and brush. "Should we go to the house and grab a tarpaulin or cart?" Jack asked.

"The horses and a tarp; should do the trick." Godwin huffed and stuck the butt of his shotgun in the snow. He looked down at the lion. "Hell, Jack, I don't even know if she's worth the trouble."

"If you don't want her, I understand. It might be a good project for Edwin though. Get him to clean her and butcher her. Might get his mind off the whole trouble we're dealing with here." Jack looked off toward the canyon behind them and waited for a judgment from Godwin.

"And all there saw just breath and cries, that all there was just death and lies," Godwin said. He rocked the shotgun by the end of the barrel and stared at the top of some high evergreen in the basket of white that was the sky.

Jack didn't look at him. He knew the task of holding it together was a strain no ordinary man could bear. He wondered if any man would be ordinary anymore under the same circumstances.

Godwin walked toward home in the vacuum.

He went upstairs and slept.

By the stove in the kitchen that was warm and smelled of rising biscuits and brewed coffee, Edwin sat with a pistol on the table.

"There was a mountain lion. Your neighbor shot it."

"Where? It sounded so close," Edwin said.

"Between here and the stream. God told him to shuffle off and keep out 'til further notice."

"I'm sure Cunnel took it well, the old fool."

Jack shook his head. "He means well. He said the lion killed his dog."

"Friedrich?" Edwin scoffed. "That was no dog. That was a weasel dressed in dog's clothes."

Jack laughed.

"Biscuits are baking. I'll fry some pork in a minute."

Jack asked, "Where's Erwin?"

Edwin pointed to the pantry, "I was letting him sleep. I could use some too."

"Go sleep in the great room. I'll make the meal and get you up when it's ready," Jack said.

Edwin left the room and slept on the floor in the great room in front of the dying fire and the closed curtains. It was dark as a funeral parlor in the great room.

Upstairs Godwin began to wake and in the haze of his short nap's end he unscrewed the cap on his whisky, the whisky he'd made last spring in the same manner and recipe as he'd been taught all those years ago on the banks of the Mantabawa by the Black Rock Runners. He sipped. After each small sip he pinched his lips together tightly against his teeth. The smell of the whisky, of the moonshine, technically, took him back to the summer of his and Freda's first days together.

She had long black hair wrapped up under a hat with such a wide brim that he could only get so close to her. But she laughed so gently when he feigned an injury from bumping her hat with his head. She dabbed his head with her scarf. The early summer was still cool and breezy as they rowed up and down Cut Creek, the river low from a short drought that really worried no one of his relation but had cast such a worry on her folks that even she commented on the height of the banks.

He told her of his father's business and how he wanted him to go up the Mantabawa that summer to learn the whisky business with the Black Rock Runners. It intrigued her, he believed. It made him masculine in his mind. He'd learn an outlaw's trade yet still become a well-mannered businessman. He'd provide a life for his lucky wife in a future of his making by his determination and intelligence. He set about convincing her that she would be that lucky wife he held in a glass house in his mind. Never did he envision the mountain he now found himself upon.

Chapter 25.

Irvin sat upon the ledge ready to move. He wanted to move on. He wanted to move out. It was not the right time to take on the Godwin Merritt Ranch. Not alone. One day, he decided, he would return and fulfill the terms of his contract with the cartel he'd gotten himself tied to. In the blinding snow, he pushed down the range. He followed the route through the Cunnell land that bordered the old Smith property, and back to town. The stress of approaching his benefactors with his decision to delay the fulfillment of his obligations got the better of him.

Irvin found himself dazed on the stool in the saloon where the sheriff frequently went to sit in the corner, drink his Farrar, and take the paper. He waited for Sheriff Smith who never showed. Stumbling through the streets he rang the bell at Wichita's and followed a woman into a sitting room. He leaned against a wall and waited some more. The woman was talking in a room just on the other side of the sitting room. She was talking to Madame V. "He's really drunk. Stinking."

Madame V. watched him through the large two-way mirror. It was the office where she managed the entire building. It was the office where she personally attended to the prurient needs and wants of the sheriff. And he happened to be sitting on the couch beneath the mirror. Madame V. said, "He looks like he has money. A little, at least."

"What should I do?" the girl said.

"Take him to a room and see if he can get it up," Madame V. decided. "Thank you, Sal."

"Sure thing, V." Sal left the room without acknowledging Sheriff Smith.

Madame V. watched her enter the sitting room and speak to the leaning drunkard. After a short talk they walked out of the room and Sheriff Smith stood up and looked through the mirror just in time to catch a glimpse of Irvin.

"I don't believe it," he said. "That son of a bitch. That skunk-fucking son of a bitch."

"Ahem," Madame V. coughed. "You know this gentleman, our leaning drunk?"

"Excuse the outburst. He's doing some work for me out in the county. I didn't expect him to be in town or drunk."

"I see. I could check in on Sal after a bit and see if he's sobered up."

"I think that might be a good idea. I would appreciate that very much."

"Deputy Morrison's widow taking it hard?" Madame V. asked. "I know there was some distance growing between them before Yeats gunned him down."

"I don't think she'll be okay for a long time. I know there was more going on there than meets the eye."

"Between you and me; he was not entirely faithful to their marriage. He was in here from time to time. Took advantage of a special girl we have here." Madame V. didn't come out and say that her son dressed up as a lady and got paid to give Deputy Morrison a full V as it were.

"Did Morrison come in here alone usually?"

She looked at him to see if he knew already. "Not usually. He and Doctor Spuss would come together and take Sal or one of the other girls back."

He said, "They would go together? On the same girl?"

"Yes. But she'd just sit there while they were together. Never included."

"That's what I suspected."

"How did you find out?"

"There was an incident just after he was shot. The doctor came to Yeats' shop and I'll just say his affections for the deputy were a little more than casual."

She nodded. "Well, I'll go back and peek in."

Sal was in the hallway gently closing the door though she assumed an angry grizzly bear would be hard pressed to startle the drunken man passed out on the floor inside Suite Rouge. She heard the door latch finally and stood slowly upward against the knot in her lower back. It was not all fun and games this business of prostitution; not at all what she considered pleasure in the least. It had become hard work, a grind. Though there were no money back guarantees the way the traveling snake oil salesmen would profess to entertain, there were those cold customers who failing to make their mark, as it were, through no fault of the paid companion's, would refuse to make full payment or hold up the joint with the only hard barrel they could raise. Thus the two way mirror and the pea shooters Madame V. demanded all her girls keep on or near them. The law was a shaky thing in Butte and everyone knew it and everyone stretched it. The envelope had been so pushed and bent the whole town seemed to have become origami experts.

Sal turned around and Madame V. was looking right over her. She stood about a foot taller than Sal, about thirty pounds heavier, all in the bosom it would seem. "He done?" Madame V. asked.

"He never had a chance to get started," Sal whispered. "He was leanin' on the doorway and I motioned him to come in. I leaned over the dresser and looked over my shoulder and started to remove my boots with my feet."

"He was too drunk then. The anchor of whisky dick drops the ship before it ever reaches port," Madame V. said.

"He took two steps in the room and fell on the floor. His eyes rolled back in his head. He might as well be dead."

Madame V. looked her over in the hallway. She'd been fond of Sal ever since she got hired on. That simple encounter in the interview and modeling had driven V. mad. She always promised herself she'd never take advantage of her employees whom she considered protégés. Always said if she wanted a girl she'd go down the road to Syracuse, the only other quality stable in town; upper class gals from big cities east of the plains between here and there. But Sal's demeanor, strong but shy, and sad girl eyes drew her in.

"Do you want me to go back in there?" Sal asked. She knew it wasn't mandatory but that if the customer woke and the girl wasn't in the room, it would spread faster than paid legs. The reputation would tarnish faster than a cuckold's silver and Wichita's would fold.

Madame V. put her fingers to Sal's curly hair. She twisted them round soft and delicate in an expression of love. She smiled only slightly and tilted her head. "Oh Sal, I do. I really do. I want to take you in there and show all that I have learned over the years here in this den of iniquity. I want to put you on a horse and ride you hard across the desert to the coast and play on the shore in the sunshine and surf and know every secret you harbor deep down. But I cannot." She dropped her fingers from Sal's hair to her arm and gripped her bicep. "I have an obligation to Sheriff Smith and he appears to have some unfinished business with our booze victim lying on the floor in there."

Sal halfway nodded her head making it clear she was unsure of how to respond to Madame V.'s confession.

"I'm sorry, dear. I've said more than I should have. I just find it harder every day to let you slip through my grasp."

"It's alright Madame V. I just don't know how to tell you I'm okay with your confession. When this episode is over and you find you still want to pursue your desire I would be more than happy to oblige," Sal said with a faint smile.

Madame V. said, "Oh." She was wary of the acceptance. She'd been trapped and blackmailed before in her line of work. She didn't intend to be burned twice by her need for beautiful women. "You may retire to my office if you like.

The sheriff will take Suite Rouge soon and likely remove our dead fish from the premises. When I know the business in there is done I will speak to you if you choose."

Sal walked away. She turned back and saw Madame V. watching her, "And, thank you, Madame," Sal said and smiled her strongest coquettish smile. She almost bounced the rest of the way to the office.

Madame V. hugged herself with one arm and felt the fluttering of her stomach. It probably wouldn't be love, but it might be close enough, she thought.

Sheriff Smith rounded the corner into the hallway after Sal passed him in the main foyer under the crystal chandelier he'd heard had cost Madame V. about ten thousand dollars. "Well, V.?" he said.

"Sal said he's in there and passed out on the floor. She said he fell flat on his face once he stepped in from the doorway. Alcohol never has been a very useful crutch. For standing purposes anyhow."

"Thank you, V. I'll try not to disturb the other patrons. Hopefully we can figure this out and be on our way."

"Just be careful. We've got a reputation to uphold."
She quietly laughed.

Sheriff Smith smiled. "Did he pay already? I don't want to tie up one of your rooms without getting you your due."

"I can't say for sure that I know." She waved him off. "Don't worry about it, Sheriff. Tuesday's are slow around here." Madame V. headed directly to Sal.

Sheriff Smith put his hand on the doorknob to Suite Rouge and turned the brass fixture slowly to dull the creaking. It smelled smoky in the hall and he could make out the murky notes of cannabis coming from one of the rooms along the hall. It was becoming an issue in town recently. But it was an issue at the present that he did not have time to confront. He felt the latch release and the door began to ease open. The light was dim in the suite. Bands of gold frames and blocks of red walls opened to him. He heard the clicking cock of a pistol and knew Irvin had been roused to waking. He couldn't see him yet in the half open doorway. "It's Smith," he announced.

"I know. Come in," Irvin said and spit a wad of tobacco on the matted bearskin rug.

"You look tired."

"No, I'm fine. Ripped off. But fine," Irvin said.

"I told your girl to give me a minute."

"Uh-huh. I see. I didn't know you had a managing stake in this operation. I'm sure the fine people of this town would be just so tickled if they knew their friendly heroin smoking Sheriff also had a controlling interest in Wichita's horizontal happy gals." He motioned him to close the door with the flick of his pistol. He stood up then and used his pistol to direct the sheriff to sit a piece. "But then, I guess you don't really give a shit about what the people of this soon-to-be-ghost-town think of you. Yep, I can see by the glaze on your eyes that you're not even sure we're the only two people in this room." Irvin backed up to the wall opposite the door and patted his palm on the wall just above the chair rail. "Careful, Sheriff, the walls see more than you think. Never know who's enjoying the show when you're paying Madame V."

"You about done then, Irv?" Sheriff Smith drew his own pistol real slow and leveled the barrel at Irvin. "Now, if I was to shoot you down here and now there ain't a grubby mouth in this shithole town that would say I wasn't in the right. After all, I'm the law." Sheriff Smith stood up and moved a bit toward Irvin. "And you're a dog. A drifter who stumbled out of the saloon and into a whorehouse and wound up shot down by the law. Open and shut just like the pine box they'd throw you in. Dash of rouge around the cheekbones, a bit of paint on the lips, and a two bit prayer over a shallow hole on the edge of town. Now, how do you want to play this, friend?"

"I come to sleep with a whore. I wind up talking to one instead."

"Spare me the sanctimony, killer. How's Mr. Jefferson these days? That's right...headless as a horseman, Sleepy Hollow."

"We're losing our focus, law man. I came back to town to tell you I'll not be infiltrating the Godwin Merritt Ranch alone. The contract was for the three of us, me and my two business partners, to collect Mr. Merritt's dues. Now that the paradigm has shifted I say the contract is nullified. So if you can provide me with two men I'll be more than happy to resume our arrangement. If not, I'll be on my way."

"Shut up. You don't have a leg to stand on. You can't take this matter to the courthouse and tell the judge to lash us with his belt. You'll either hold up your end, return all the money, or wind up like your partners. Your call, chief." Sheriff Smith holstered his gun and walked to the door. "And just for the sake of edification, I don't have a stake in Madame V. Not yet anyway. We were just getting around to that when I saw you stumble out of the sitting room. You make a poor drunk. So, sober up and finish the job you've been paid to do."

"You'll have to clean up the Merritt mess yourself. Just a heads up; he's got a dead son in the ground beside his dead wife. I'll take credit for the son. The wife was already dead when I stumbled into the outbuilding she was laid out in. Looked to have been dead couple of days. Like they's preparing her for burial. Probably waiting for a thaw to start digging. And there's another grown man up there helping him or being helped."

"Which boy did you kill? The oldest?"

"Nope, no, sir. The oldest has it coming though. One day he'll get his repayment for getting my two men killed."

"Freda was already dead?"

"That the wife?"

"Yeah, his wife."

"Then yes. Freda's dead as dead." Irvin spit another wad of tobacco at the rug. "Deader than dead, I suppose." He grinned and chuckled and the spit and tobacco drooled down into the pillow of wild beard beneath his lip.

"Well, make up your mind. If it's not closed up a week from now, we will take an alternate course of action. Either way; Godwin will pay what he owes." Sheriff Smith shut the door without a sound and rejoined Madame V. in her office where Sal and her had been talking for some time.

Chapter 26.

Every day the danger of flash flooding lapped vigorously along the stony banks of the streams. Godwin learned long ago not to gamble with the wily waters that crashed the slopes after heavy thaws.

Years ago, shortly after he opened the mine to operation, he lost half a dozen men and two large hauls of silver at the end of an early spring snow. Knowing this he shuttered the mine and directed it to be kept shuttered until the streams eventually lowered.

The way was clearing but treacherous with muddy paths, the threat of rockslides, even avalanche. Godwin rode down slow at a walking pace. It kept Creasy soothed. He patted him gently on the shoulders. Talked in a low, conversational way. "Doing good there, Creasy. One in front of the other. We get back up to the ranch and the feast is yours. You're a brave one, Creasy." Godwin sat upon Creasy with the pinhole focus his pot of coffee could scarce fail to provide. He had a blunderbuss holstered in an old boot strapped to the front of his saddle. He wore two pistols on his hips. He knew the third man hadn't abandoned his men. He didn't know what turn might reveal the inevitable confrontation. The timeline of the conclusion of this war he was engaged in was hidden deep behind the scrim of so many agendas.

* * *

"We're going back to Sawyerskill," Godwin announced at the table. They sat in the brightened kitchen filled with the sunlight that had finally melted away the worst of the snow. They were about a week out from the last snow of the blizzard.

"To uh…?" Jack said pointing his thumb over his shoulder and struggling with a mouthful of pancake and coffee.

"You got it," Godwin said.

Edwin looked at them both. "To Darwin's?"

"Yes, Edwin." The snow melted at quite a clip the last week and Godwin was tied up like a ball of twine. "So pack bags, pack gear, pack guns, and pack the baby. We're going home; or at least to what's left of it. I want you to see it, Edwin, before it's completely lost to the hands of fate."

"Is there anybody left on Darwin's homestead?" Edwin said.

"Can't say. Haven't heard a word in years. Jack might know something more than me."

"Might know what more than you?" Jack asked.

"Is there anybody left taking up residence on my land?" Godwin said.

"On Darwin's old land? Gayle and her husband, Gunther."

"Is he useful?" Godwin asked.

"Useful to a point. I'm not certain what use you intend to put him to but he is a Merritt man, if not by blood then by a desire to be one. Gunther was born into a lower family in the Viggot Valley. He fought in the war on the losing side but came across the line and learned to get along. Went to the city university on the coast and learned to talk like a gentleman instead of a back country ijit."

"Quite a high opinion you hold for Gunther," Godwin said.

"Well. I think it's a high opinion of your sister, Gayle, that I hold and it extends over onto the man she found to provide for her. You'll find him agreeable. I'm certain," Jack said.

"I guess we'll find out," Godwin said. "Okay, so I'd like to set out in four hours. Can you all be packed up and ready to go by then?"

"I can be ready in two, God," Edwin said.

"Me too, Godwin," Jack said.

"Well, we have to tend the animals before we go. I think four hours will be a good stretch to get all the chores lined up and all the fires put out. It's going to be a cold trip too at least until we get a little south of here but even that's no guarantee. I've been as far south as the national line and seen ice on the ground."

"We'll keep our fingers crossed," Edwin said.

A little over four hours passed when the Merritt's took to their wagon and horses. They began their journey off the ranch, and down the mountain.

They made it down with only a little slip of the hoof by Edwin's mare. She recovered easily and they entered the town through which they would need to pass on their way overland to the depot up in Laramie. The sun warmed their shoulders and necks as they traveled north in the most direct route possible. At Laramie they'd board the Flyer and take it east to Omaha.

Chapter 27.

The journey was hard and not done in so quick a fashion as Edwin assumed upon departure. They experienced no major hiccups along the way back to Cut Creek but the mood changed once they came within about fifty miles of the southern stretch of the Mantabawa. From there they would follow it on along north to where it made the confluence with Cut Creek and then it'd only be a matter of an hour or so before they got to the Darwin Merritt homestead; a place Edwin had never seen and only rarely heard about.

"What are the people called that live in the shacks by the river back there? The ones with hardly anything for coats in this cold?"

"They'd be the Bog Bay Devils," Jack said.

"The…" Edwin started.

"You heard me," Jack said. "Don't talk to them. Don't trust them. Hell, don't even look at them. They're walking leaches, Ed. Suck you dry once they get hold of you."

"What do you mean, Uncle Jack?" Edwin said.

"He means, don't mess with them. They're devils, like he said," Godwin said. "Bog Bay Devils."

"Sorry, God. It's all so different back here," Edwin said.

"Once we get to your grandfather's homestead things will start to feel normal again," Jack said. "There's just a different breed of people back here. They were born under a bad sign into the least acceptable circumstances. Anyone who's tried to lend them a hand ended up losing that hand for good."

Godwin nodded to reinforce Jack's thesis.

"What was Darwin like, God?" Edwin said.

"I could answer that but I think his home would give you a better first impression of the man I called Father," Godwin said.

Edwin blushed. Godwin, himself, frowned upon any of his own children calling him Father. Had it been too much to live up to? Was his own father so strong willed and terrible that the name made him sick? Or was he the strong willed, obstinate terror who preferred his own children call him God under the simple explanation that it was short for Godwin? Edwin puzzled over this in a soft abstraction the remainder of the trip and truly for the rest of his life.

From Omaha, Jack and the Merritt men switched routes and boarded the train that would carry them into Chicago. The bustle of the terminal in Chicago was something that very nearly derailed their entire journey if only due to Godwin's intolerance for crowded cities. They pushed through to the platform where they boarded the Lansing Line that finally carried them into the state of Michigan where the Mantabawa, Cut Creek, and the Darwin Merritt homestead lay unseen by Godwin Merritt for decades.

They approached the confluence where Cut Creek lazily washed into the swirl of the Mantabawa. A grove of medium height monkey trees bowed over the two rivers in the narrow island that sat off the shared bank.

The sound of axes chopping wood hammered through the brush and the diffused light of dusk as they made their way up the path freshly cleared and smoothed likely, by Gunther. Erwin began to rouse in the nest of blankets that Edwin had made in the reed basket Freda crafted when she lived back on the Mantabawa. A lot of things were coming home that evening. If Godwin were thrilled about his overdue return to Darwin's homestead he didn't let a corner of a grin slip and

Edwin's anxiety about the whole trip was approaching a shaky crescendo.

They rounded a wide u-shaped bend in the pass and then came upon a wide driveway cut through a dense line of woods still bare from the winter cold yet leaving Darwin Merritt's homestead well hid. The trees stopped in a well maintained line about a hundred yards past the main road they'd just got off.

"Is this Darwin's?" Edwin asked?

Jack nodded. They rode quietly through the land. A half dozen deer stood in the middle ground between the trees that hedged the road and the thin seedlings that spotted the yard before they came upon the house and the two men chopping wood whose axes they'd heard from the road.

"Which one's Gunther?" Godwin asked.

They looked identical in their red flannel shirts and black heavy pants. They chopped ferociously but precisely as well. They appeared to be shaping a log, a beam maybe, hewn from a felled fir.

"It's hard to tell from here," Jack said.

The men stopped working when they saw them. Now that they were right in front of them Godwin was even more perplexed. "It's hard to tell from here, Jack. And I'm standing right in front of them.

The man on the left stuck out his hand, "I'm Gunther. Nice to meet you, Godwin. This is my brother, Helmut. He's helping me reinforce the shed. We had a wild wind this autumn that nearly knocked it over entirely."

"God, they look exactly the same," Edwin said. His mouth was a little open and his eyes looked at each brother in turn to analyze and find some difference that would make it easier to identify them. None could be discerned except for the other, Helmut, had different shoe laces on his boots than Gunther, but the boots were the same color and style.

"Quite a thing, Edwin," Jack said. He turned to the brothers and said, "I believe my nephew has never seen twins in person before."

Helmut said, "We get that look often when we travel. People don't often see folks seven feet tall and identical."

Gunther added, "We almost joined a traveling sideshow when we were young and started to realize we were going to be seeing a lot of hushed and nervous people huddling at a distance from us. But, Helmut joined the army shortly after the war began and I followed him, just to make sure he came out the other side of peace time."

"Almost like looking up at the twin pines on my ranch out west," Godwin said with his head tilted upward just like Jack and Edwin. "Don't mean any offense by it."

"We've heard it all, don't bother us any," Helmut said.

A female voice came shrieking out of the front door of Darwin's house, "I live and breathe, it's Godwin." She ran up and hugged him hard and kissed his cheek. "Been too long, brother. Welcome back home."

"Thank you, sister." He stepped back from her embrace and introduced Edwin. "This is my oldest son, Edwin."

Edwin said, "This is his youngest son, Erwin." She took the baby up in her arms before he finished his sentence.

"He's a doll. Both of them, Godwin," she said.

"Before we get too far," Godwin choked up a little. "Freda passed away, about a fortnight ago. She collapsed in the kitchen, held on for a while, day at most. She drifted off and died. It may have been a stroke or exhaustion from nursing Erwin out of wretched fever over a week's time. But we buried her on the ranch once the blizzards passed and the ground yielded a little.

"Oh my!" she gasped. "That is so awful. I'm so sorry, Edwin. And dear, dear Erwin." She sobbed immensely. She'd been fond of Freda in a natural sibling way as if they'd grown up in the same house and were natural sisters.

"Let me take, Erwin," Edwin said and he too was crying quietly. His aunt's tears had become contagious. Jack's eyes were welled up also.

Godwin steeled his nerve and started to speak but double over. He turned and vomited on the dirt. The full weight of the tragedy he'd suffered on his ranch over a few days' time had finally hit him. It blasted him right in the gut. He heaved and no more came out. The brothers cast an identical look of shock not for the vomit but for the obvious pain this man they'd just met had been dealing with for only a few days. Gunther looked to Helmut and nodded for him to go inside and fetch some water. Helmut would return with a glass of whisky instead.

Jack put his arm around her and held her. He was bracing her against his side when Godwin rose slowly from his knee.

"Elwin has died also." Godwin's lips quivered, his voice collapsed, and his tears streamed in continuous rivulets off of his face.

Her knees buckled and Jack tried to hold her upright but he was only able to let her go down slow enough not to fall. She tripped on her own breath nearly hyperventilating. Her husband, Gunther, went to her side and put his arms around her. He couldn't think of anything to say in the eternity of her sorrow. He clawed and scratched and kicked his way through the memories in his mind but none of them offered a blueprint or manual of what to say. She put one arm around him and wept. Through his tears a memory surfaced in Godwin's mind and he saw the spot where she was now weeping was near to if not the exact same spot where Darwin had taken his last breath. He memorized it and was able to mark it like a treasure map. "X" marked the spot.

Long minutes passed like steam from bull shit. The wind pushed dark and cold tree limbs and in the swaying inches they creaked and moaned like stairs beneath the lost widow walking her worries to and fro. The motionless humans in still life preserved the solemn expression of the news that a child had been lost to violence. Godwin still could not bring himself to allow Edwin to know that his brother was murdered. Maybe he didn't want him to experience fear of wondering if the man with the gun would return to the ranch; for he surely would; as sure as Cut Creek would spill its secrets into the waiting Mantabawa.

"Let's go inside and get something to drink for these men," Gunther said to his wife, trying to get her on her feet again; even for something as simple as a glass of water. "They've come a long way. Let's get them some refreshment." Gunther nodded toward the house.

Godwin, Edwin, Erwin, and Jack headed into the house. They'd been inside for a time and had removed their coats and boots and taken glasses of water followed by whisky for the three grown men and a bottle of milk for the baby. Godwin was rocking Erwin in the rocker that Darwin had built as a teenager even further east than they'd traveled to get to Cut Creek from Godwin's ranch. It was gorgeous maple with Darwin's full name emblazoned on the bottom side of the seat. As he sat in it, Godwin could still see the signature his father had written with a hot iron pen and sealed over for the years to never wear through.

She came through the front door with Gunther leading her by the hand. She sat on a couch beside Godwin and leaned to him. "I'm sorry I lost my nerve out there. I can't imagine what you've gone through."

"Don't worry about it, dear. Nothing can be done about it all now. We have to find the strength to keep moving. But with all that had happened, all the horror of burying them young. I wanted Edwin to see where he came from before it got to be too late. So, I'm sorry for showing up entirely unannounced."

"You are welcome here any second you need to come home. I know you had to move away. It sounds like you'd built a nice spread out west. I'm just sorry that you won't have

Freda to share the rest with. God, I don't know what to even say right now."

"Don't say anything, sister. It's over now. Can we stay in the house overnight? Tomorrow we can get the cabin on the river set up if it's not already and stay out there for the duration of our visit."

"You can stay in the house as long as you want. I don't know what the cabin looks like. We don't go down there much after the first frost."

"You don't still think he's there do you?" Godwin said.

She just looked at him. Didn't know how to answer. Godwin laughed a little.

"What?" Edwin said.

"Your aunt is silly sometimes," Godwin said.

"Why?" Edwin pressed.

"She has a superstition. Or a fear, I guess, that Darwin haunts the cabin after the first frost," Godwin said.

"That was his favorite time to go down to the river and fish and 'play' with his toys," she said.

"What toys?" Edwin said.

Jack made a hand gesture that looked like a blooming flower and a sound from his mouth of an explosion.

"You told him about the explosives Darwin used to make?" Godwin said.

Jack didn't say anything.

"It's my fault, God. I asked him to tell me about grandfather. I asked when we were on the ranch, drinking and smoking out back. I was too down about Ma and had drunk too much ale. I needed to hear something about this place. And you and Ma never talked about it," Edwin said.

Gunther and Helmut took themselves to the cabin without mentioning it. They spent the evening cleaning it up and clearing out a mass of things that had accumulated over the years. They checked the windows every so often to see if anyone was walking toward it. There were things in the cabin that might make it uncomfortable to say the least should the wrong person happen upon them.

Chapter 28.

They were out there all evening. Just before sunset, Gunther had gone back to the house to let his wife know he'd be out helping Helmut clean up the cabin. He intended to stay out there all night and into the morning if that's what it took because more than likely their visitors would request a look around. And then the shit would be in the open. So they worked through dim light and cold wind beside the river. They'd put out the fires finally and would begin dismantling the rather elaborate set up they had built within the cabin walls deep in the property on the hallowed Darwin Merritt homestead.

"We don't have the band wrench. We can't separate the fucking bands and get the copper pot up off the floor if we don't have it," Gunther said.

Helmut ransacked the pile of materials they'd already sorted and loaded into some crates.

"What are you doing, Hel?" Gunther said.

"I'm looking for the band wrench, Gun," he said.

"Well if it was in that pile of shit don't you think we'd have remembered that? It's gotta be back at your house."

"Well, I guess I'll have to go get it then," Helmut said.

"Don't be stupid. You know we don't have time for that. By the time you get back it'll be daylight and they could ramble down here any time."

"Well, what the hell do you want to do? If we take it apart without the band wrench we'll have to build a whole new one from scratch."

"If we don't take it apart, we're going to blow the whole operation," Gunther said.

"Maybe it's meant to be. Maybe things are supposed to come to a head here and now," Helmut shrugged.

"You're tired. You don't know what you're saying. If we screw this up, it's not an oops. It's death and graves for us. You heard what he did. He chopped them up and shoveled the pieces into the stream on his ranch. You heard what the man from Black Rock said the last time he delivered the rye." Gunther was sweating. The fires had been extinguished under the stills but the heat in the cabin was intense. Paint on the window frames had blistered and coagulated more than a few times since they installed the stills in the cabin.

"Maybe they won't come down here. Maybe they got more important business to do," Helmut said.

"No. Not a gamble I'm screwing around with. Get the hammer and get the crowbar and let's get these bands off the damn pots," Gunther said.

Everyone in the house had gone to sleep hours before and it was only Edwin who sat up in the front of the house. Unable to even close his eyes for fear of nightmares that had been following him into his sleep ever since he saw Elwin's body; he'd settled into some nascent insomnia that surprisingly to him had not been quite so agitating. He had reached Zen equilibrium. What he did at night almost became a ritual. He would smoke from his wooden handle pipe. He would recite a prayer his mother taught him to say at night when he was a child. He would smoke until his throat became dry and hoarse. And then he would drink a half cup of whisky until he could think no more and the dark images his memory projected just turned off.

After midnight he was on the porch having a whisky from a bottle he found in the cupboard. It had a hand-painted label on it. The color was clear but had a glint to it that suggested it was not quite what it seemed. He smelled it and tasted it before deciding it was good enough to drink not in a man-of-taste kind of way but simply in a life-or-death, is this shit gonna be the death of me tonight kind of way.

On the porch he drank his whisky slowly and felt the cold that seemed to start from the inside out in this country wood they called the Beril Flats. He felt drunk quicker off this whisky it seemed or maybe, he thought, it was just due to an abysmal lack of sleep. He put his head down on his arm on the railing of the porch and inspected the curves of his wooden pipe that stood upright with a faint ribbon of smoke rising toward the stars that danced like spinning plates in the periphery of his sight. "This is some strong whisky," he grumbled through mostly closed lips. "That pipe looks like a little house with a chimney letting out smoke," he continued to grumble. He closed one eye and then the other trying to play games with illusion. Then he picked his head upright quickly. He saw the smoke he thought he'd been looking at. It was coming from farther down through the leafless trees. There was something down there with a fire going. "If you go wandering around the woods at night you had better take your gun," he grumbled over lips that were moving to keep warm.

And that's when one of his feet threw itself way out in front of the other and the other did the same and he found himself marching like a bewildered giraffe through dark country woods he'd never been through before. Though he assumed he had his pistol on his hip when he got close to the cabin and put his hand to where the butt of his gun should be, it wasn't quite there.

He backed off a bit. Then he got scared. He saw them moving. He saw their silhouettes move fast, back and forth on the other side of the drawn shades in the windows. He crouched and steadied himself with a hand on the frozen ground. He was in over his head and he panicked. If they came outside he'd be busted for sure. But he didn't even know who was in there. Sure it could've been Gunther and Helmut just cleaning out the cabin as Gunther had said when he came back to the house earlier that evening. Or it could be much worse.

The door on the other side of the cabin opened and was slammed shut. Edwin squatted paralyzed. He tried not to even breathe in case whoever it was that came out caught a glimpse of his breath in the bright moonlight. He was dead in the water if they caught him. Then a thought occurred to him. What if they were just hanging out? What if they just invited him in for a drink while they cleaned up the cabin? Why had he been so paranoid and certain they were up to something sinister? "Must be the whisky and no sleep," he grumbled and quickly went to the cabin door to announce himself.

Gunther answered the door, "Edwin," his shock written large across his face.

"Sorry, Gunther, I saw the lights through the trees from the porch while I was smoking. Do you guys need any help? Or..." he trailed off in a slur when he saw the big stills behind Gunther.

"Better come in then, Ed," Gunther said.

Helmut was frozen with a hammer and a crowbar in his hands.

"I...wow...WOW."

"We need you to have a seat, Ed, okay," Gunther said.

"Sure. Wow. This is a whisky factory," Edwin said and fell into a chair.

"Was. Now it needs to be cleaned out," Helmut said.

"I think I just had some of your product," Edwin said. "It was in the cupboard. I usually need some to help me sleep."

"You probably should've gone off to sleep then. We need you to promise not to breathe a word of this to your father or Uncle Jack," Gunther said.

"Why? What's the problem?" Edwin said.

Helmut was a shot nerve away from pulling out his pistol on the kid. He started to pace the room and that's when he bumped some barrels off the table and they rolled around the floor. One stopped just right so that Edwin could make out the logo, BRR, under a winding stream and two oak trees.

"Black Rock Runners," he sighed.

"Exactly. But it must be in the past. The trouble your old man and grandfather had with them must be forgot. The trouble is history. Now, BRR is a new group. We're a company really. The old feuds must be left in the past. Can we trust you to keep this mess quiet until we can ease Godwin into the news about BRR?" Gunther explained.

"I'm not sure what I can do," Edwin said. He was terrified and gripped the fabric arms of the chair he sat in as if it were a cliff he was about to fall away from.

"If you don't feel well, I'd suggest you go up to the house and try to get some sleep. If you feel okay, we could use your hands down here dismantling and hiding the still," Gunther said.

"Just until we have a strategy for explaining the situation to Godwin," Helmut said. "If he were to see this on his father's land and under the stress you and him have so obviously been forced to endure, well who's to say how he might react," Helmut said and checked the butt of his gun with the heel of his hand.

"And there's absolutely no reason this cannot be something made to be prosperous for us all," Gunther said.

"It's proven to be profitable. We just need the time and situation to map it out for your Pa," Helmut said.

Edwin stood up slowly. And just as slowly Gunther eased his hand to his side near to where his gun lay on the table behind a pile of tools and materials; springs, funnels, screwdrivers, wrenches, and the like.

Edwin leaned on the chair, "I get what you're asking. But you're asking me to put you ahead of my family. A family I'm losing at a rate that's making my head spin. I guess I don't have an option but to play along or risk losing more of my family. But how did you get my aunt to go along?"

Helmut and Gunther looked at each other.

"She doesn't know?" Edwin sat back down. "So she hasn't been down here in a long time, then." A puzzle began to put itself together in Edwin's mind. Except it was a puzzle that had no picture on it; only blank white pieces with grey jig saw joints.

"So are you going to help us ease your father into the reality of Darwin's homestead? It's a profitable future where only a bitter residue of a futile feud once thrived." Gunther waited for an answer. He could see Edwin was still drunk and his ability to make a sound decision was questionable.

Gently, intently, as if a gun were to his head, Edwin started putting tubes and valves into a crate atop a cabinet near the big copper pots.

Helmut gripped his shoulder approvingly, "Thank you, Ed. If we can manage this right, you Merritt men will become wealthier than you already are with your silver operation out west."

"Helmut," Gunther stopped him. "Help me outside with the smokestack."

"Right now?"

"Right now."

They went outside and Edwin kept packing loose items into the crate. He worked slowly not knowing what he should be doing and being drunk still he was nearly spinning. He wished so badly that he had remembered to bring his pistol before he got all the way down to the cabin.

"You're letting on too much in front of the boy," Gunther said.

"I'm just trying to make him see the positive side of doing business instead of the bad blood," Helmut said.

"Yes, but he doesn't know who he's talking to. We shouldn't know that his father runs a silver mine in Colorado. It's going to make him suspicious."

"Suspicious hell. He's plastered. He won't remember any of what we talked about come morning. He smells like he got into the good stuff," Helmut said.

They didn't break a decibel above a whisper but there was a quick and deep tension in their palaver that could erupt with just the wrong comment.

"We'll keep him down here a couple of hours and then send him back up to the house to sleep off the 'shine. We're just going to have to hope to hell that he sees the light and lets us bring in Godwin at our own pace," Gunther said.

"You didn't know they were coming to visit at all?" Helmut asked.

"How could I? I thought they'd all be taken care of. That's what I was told. That soon this would all be sewed up and we'd have a mine under our belts too."

"Somebody screwed up," Helmut huffed.

"Big time. And when we find out which one, they're gonna be wishing they hadn't made it back to the Mantabawa," Gunther said and held the door open for Helmut to follow him inside.

Chapter 29.

All plans that Godwin had made as he laid awake in bed in the late evening before were cast aside when Gunther and Helmut came rushing inside. They were out of breath and Helmut hid his head in his hands after he fell into a chair at the kitchen table where the rest of the house had just sat down to eat breakfast. Gunther relayed the news in quick bursts, "They came in the dawn and held us at gun point. They tossed the cabin and stole a few things but mostly just destroyed the inside of it."

"Who?" Godwin shouted.

"I can't say a hundred percent but looked like some of the vermin that gather down Bog Bay. I don't know how they thought coming on the Darwin Merritt homestead was a good idea. Don't make any sense. But they had us cornered when we was coming out of the cabin," Gunther said.

Helmut added, "We'd fallen asleep for a half hour, maybe after staying up all night trying to get the cabin cleaned up for you all. They had caught us unaware."

Edwin felt sick to his stomach and the pinching headache made it hard to think; hard to recall the true events of the night as he spent it in the cabin helping these twin interlopers clear out their moonshine operation. He tried to recall what they said and what little he knew of the history between the Merritt's and the Black Rock Runners. And what did Jack say about Bog Bay? It was all too much. A slight jarring of the table when Helmut jumped to his feet sent him overboard and he ran to the sink to vomit.

"Get upstairs, Edwin!" Godwin was in no mood to deal with a drunken boy.

Edwin held onto the walls for support and went out of the room in agony and shame.

Jack said, "Why would they sack the cabin?"

"Don't know. All kinds of rumors been swirling about Bog Bay getting up on a 'shine move. They had enough of being low life's I hear and want to cash in on the trade. The laws all around this part of the country are still trying to keep us all dry and the majority of the folks around here are fit to be tied. Tired of being told how they can relax and unwind, party and get down," Gunther said. He poured himself a cup of coffee from the steel pot on the iron stove. The fire inside was just glowing coals but it'd been burning all night.

Gayle had stayed up with Erwin who slept most of the night but was fidgety and whimpering every hour or so. She was glad to hold the baby in her arms as long as she could hold out and set him down every so often to reload the stove and keep the kitchen warm at least. Now, as they all sat on edge with nervous eyes, Erwin slept peacefully in the old crib that Godwin and Gayle had slept in as babies.

"You couldn't identify any of them though?" Jack said.

"I just know they aren't from anywhere up in these banks; not Cut Creek, not Mantabawa," Gunther said.

"Definitely Bog Bay scum," Helmut said.

Godwin held his breath. Kept his judgment checked. Things weren't what they seemed he'd felt the minute he set foot back on Darwin's land. He thought maybe it was to do with all the hell burning back west. Thought the smoke from so many fires had clouded his ability. But these men, twins; "the devil working double time," Darwin used to tell him whenever they'd seen twins. And hadn't there been twins on the Black Rock land when they were associated? Hadn't there been two grown Mattocks' boys that grew up looking like one was walking around hugging a mirror? And then he leveled his eyes at Helmut. And Gunther. And Jack. He held his breath and listened to the story that was being woven. He saw the yarn, and the pattern it was making.

"What do you want to do, God?" Jack asked.

Godwin only pursed his lips and shook his head a millimeter or two.

"We gotta do something. But I don't know where these men came from. They could've have gone anywhere by now," Gunther said.

"You said they were Bog Bay. You sound pretty sure of that. The only thing Bog Bay Devil's know how to do is go back and rot in that Bog Bay rat nest," Godwin stood up from his untouched breakfast. "So, I'm heading down to make a call on the devils."

"What if it's not them?" Jack said. "Then you got a big mess that we might not be able to handle just yet."

"I can handle those shit eaters fine. There *was* two of you," Godwin said to Gunther. "So, how many of *them* were there?"

"We saw three. They said there were more on the river," Helmut said.

Godwin stared at Gunther, "Bog Bay don't travel the river. Not while I've been living. That some new development?"

"Can't say for sure," Gunther stammered.

"That isn't necessarily true no more," Helmut said. "And you haven't been round home in so long there's no telling what's changed since you been gone."

Godwin stood and looked at Gunther and Helmut. He could smell the rats. He knew they could see his righteous anger. "I'll have a look around my cabin now," he left his plate untouched and put on a coat, hat and pigskin gloves. He had been sitting at the breakfast table with two pistols on his hip. He hadn't trusted anything since being back home. "You coming?" he said to Jack.

"Of course," Jack said.

Helmut looked at Gunther for direction. Gunther just walked out behind Jack and worked on playing dumb but not too dumb. He put the shovel to work in his mind and dug deep for a truth that would be believable but keep them from going to war on Bog Bay; a step toward mutual destruction for Black Rock Runners and Bog Bay Devils. Caught in the middle was a man sometimes called God.

Godwin walked around the cabin slowly, not letting on that he was looking at anything in particular. It was not going to be hard to put these lies on the table that he was being told by fourth generation Black Rock Runners. He had them pegged. Either sons of Erik or Oleg Mattocks, it didn't matter. They had no currency anymore in Godwin's world. However it played out, his sister's heart would be broken. But he intended to tell her himself that she'd fallen in with the wrong family. He was almost as upset about the clean mud and snow around the cabin, the undisturbed land beside the landing on the river, the nascent signs of any real cavalry of plunderers as he was about being absent from the affairs of his family for so long. But he thought he'd made the right move sheltering his own family from the past of this poisoned confluence.

Destruction definitely had been done inside the cabin and the boys had done their best to remove any sign of what they'd been using it for. But a bracket here, a brass valve ring there, and some flecks of blackened copper on tables that he'd never seen before all testified that these two poison brewing weasels were using Darwin's property to further the Black Rock fortune. His stomach turned but he didn't show it. In his absence and his sister's aloof ignorance a bloody enemy had set up camp in the heart of Darwin's property. The smell of distilled spirits clung to the room, haunting the very air with its harsh sting in the flu of his nostrils. Godwin drew two pistols from his hips. He told the twins to sit. He was still trying to figure out what Jack's part in all this was when Helmut made a move for his own gun. Godwin shot him damn near point blank in the forehead. The scream from Gunther's mouth was hard and sharp and could've shattered the windows if they'd not been boarded up, judging from the water stains, some years ago. How long they'd soiled Darwin's land with their dirty booze was hard to know. But Godwin aimed to find out. "If you've got a brain you want to keep you'll spit some truth into this here barrel," Godwin said; the barrel of his pistol less than six inches from Gunther's forehead.

"Monster," Gunther yelled, the word scraping like hooks all the way up his throat.

"This morning you find yourself a changed man, Gunther," Godwin began. "What you've done in this cabin, on my land; what you see beside your feet—that's the penalty. But you've got a few more minutes to live. That you could stretch into hours but like as not no more than a day. After that and I would fail to live up to my name. It was a bold move. And I commend you on having at least balls but they were no more connected to your brain than Helmut's head to his neck."

"God," Jack tried to calm him.

"Now I'm sorry you put me in a position where I have to cut short your time on this land. And I'm sorry you made me shoot your brother dead away in front of you. And you certainly know that all of the blood that is about to be spilled because of your little conniving to get a still on Cut Creek is nobody's fault but your own. But I bet somewhere under that coonskin hat you think you can talk your way out of this end that I'm helping you along to. Bet you came up with some conspiracy that puts you down on the bottom of it just trying to do right until you could send word out west to the Godwin goddamn Merritt Ranch that you was only trying to find out all you could to get things right and keep this whisky war from blowing up the whole confluence," Godwin put the barrel of his pistol on Gunther's forehead, "Now tell me, am I right?"

Gunther nodded yes.

Godwin laughed a very small laugh. "You don't want to do that. You nod your head hard enough and my finger is liable to drop a hammer on a blast cap you'd rather not see ignite. No, son. What you want to be doing right now in this type of interview is use the tongue your ma gave you cause that little liar's tongue that sprouts out of the devil's ass like a blown sphincter isn't going to get you very far today. What you learned from big daddy Mattocks and his papa before him is going to be damn useless to you today. Ain't no fight you can bring except that against bearing false witness will help you through the next few minutes."

"God?" Jack said. Again trying to calm Godwin. Again falling on deaf ears. The gunshot had been loud enough that the three living men all heard the echo of a ping for a long while.

Up at the house, Edwin pulled himself together enough to grab his guns—pistol and shotgun. He ran past her, "I'm going down to the cabin. Did you hear the shot?" He was out the door before he could hear an answer from her.

As he skidded to a stop at the bottom of the hill he checked his pistol. Checked the shotgun. He wouldn't be empty handed this time. The only trouble was figuring out how to go in without getting shot up. He edged to the cabin and got up under the boarded window to the main room on the side. He could hear murmuring. He couldn't define the words but he knew God was speaking.

Inside, Godwin took a seat in a chair and held his audience captive with his tongue and barrel.

"Did you…" Godwin trailed off. "I'll save that one for last." (did you marry my sister for love or this game?)

"Did I what?" Gunther said.

"Shhh. Not now. We'll get to that later. Maybe. It's up to you, Gunther Mattocks."

"God? Can I speak to you outside?"

"Yeah." Godwin turned to him, "I'll follow you." He got up and followed him to the door. Once Jack stepped out Godwin slammed the door shut and locked it. "There. Now we talk openly."

"Just shoot me," Gunther commanded.

"Sorry. I know it hurts. I've lost family recently too. But I bet you already knew that." Godwin was on a roll now and really felt at home. The reignited feud and the righteous killing and the knowledge that he was in the right defending Darwin's homestead from these moonshining terrorists. It all made him sharp as an eagle talon.

Gunther stared at him. No blinked eyes. No quivering lips. Just cold eyes to match the cold blood in Godwin's icy veins.

"But I bet you already knew that. Even before we showed up here," Godwin said.

Nothing.

Outside Jack saw a shadow stretching from the side of the cabin. He pulled his gun silently. Cocked the hammer and was ready to pull the trigger. He jerked the gun up. "Shit, Ed. You got to be careful out here just now. God's inside. You should go up to the house and look out for anything."

"I heard a shot," Edwin said.

"Helmut is dead. There's trouble with them. They're Black Rock Runners. Remember what I told you about them?" Jack said.

Edwin nodded and put his gun in his holster. He leaned the shotgun against the railing on the porch. They kept their eyes on the open panorama. The river looked silver on its surface for the pale sky that cold morning.

* * *

Inside on the blood splattered floor Helmut was face down and legs twisted. Gunther tried to keep from looking at him. But his eyes would dart back against his better judgment. Gunther's hands were on fire. He was beyond angry. He'd heard Godwin Merritt was vicious and cold. His old man told him tales he thought were more made up than true. But there and then with his dead brother in front of him; he knew his father hadn't made up a stitch of the gruesome things Godwin had done.

"I only know what came over the telegraph," Gunther said. "I haven't been able to leave her side all week. She'd had an infection and fever. The doctor said she wouldn't make it if I weren't there to clean the gash."

"What gash?" Godwin asked.

"On her right thigh. We'd been riding and her horse bucked her. She rolled off of a stone and her thigh opened up like a picador gored in the ring by a raging bull. Didn't you notice her limping?"

"Who sent the telegraph?"

"I don't know. I only know the gist of what it read."

"And?"

"It said your wife and son were dead. Said the third man reneged on his contract." Gunther spat toward Godwin's shoes. "He's a dead man walking. Just like you."

Godwin chocked him on the clavicle with the butt of his pistol. The sound was dull, a blunt thud. The pain in his neck dropped Gunther to the floor; damn near face to face with his brother. "You son of a bitch," he moaned.

"I'll shoot you dead right here for talking about my mother. You should know better than to insult your wife's mother. Makes you sound more like an idiot Bog Bay dum-dum. But then, you Black Rock boys were never much in the way of manners or courtesy," Godwin said.

Struggling to his feet and then to sit in the chair he'd rolled out of, Gunther said, "From what my pa tells, you don't have much room to talk, *God damned Merritt.*"

"You don't stack up to your father one bit. He was standing where I'm at he'd waste you in a heartbeat. Bury you in a shallow grave on the bank of the Mantabawa and never speak of you for shame."

"Like I told you. Don't matter what happens here. You're a dead man walking."

"Tell me one thing," Godwin said. He walked to the door that went outside. "What does the Black Rock Runners gain from setting up shop on Darwin's land?"

"We control the confluence. No distiller gets access; we skirt the sheriffs and get into dock down at the mouth of the Mantabawa. Then, boy, we live like kings; selling to every café and restaurant in the dry city down there."

"Bullshit," Godwin said. "Whoever told you that knew you were a simple idiot."

"Look out world, dead man coming thr" the shot stopped his tongue or drowned it out.

Outside, Edwin made to rush the door to go to his father's aid if he needed it. Jack stuck out his arm and had to hug him and dance him around to stop him from opening the door. "You'll get your head blown off rushing into a room like that," Jack said. "God's alright."

The door opened and Godwin walked out. Didn't say a word. He went down to Cut Creek about seventy yards from the porch. He washed his hands and face in the icy waters that ran smooth and fast toward the confluence. Edwin raced down to his father. He stood behind him. He stared and felt dumb not knowing how to speak to a man he knew had just murdered two men.

"It's okay, son." Godwin said looking at his reflection in the water above his own head. "It had to be done. They'd have killed us if we didn't do it."

Edwin immediately thought to himself that the word "we" did not apply there in that situation. That he had not killed anyone, didn't intend to kill anyone, and would prefer if his murdering father would just as well leave him out of any future accounting of this tale should the law go looking for the man who put down a pair of twins on the banks of Cut Creek.

"Have a seat, son." Godwin rocked back from his haunches to sit on the snowy, muddy riverside.

Edwin hesitated and watched his father just stare across the water. Finally, Edwin sat beside his father. Jack went up to the house. He was already polishing the lie they would have to tell her. That her husband and his brother were up to something heinous and were afraid Godwin and Jack would hand them over to the sheriff. That they drew on Godwin and he had to shoot them or be killed himself. Distilling spirits and distributing them were bad enough crimes but Jack and Godwin would have to embellish that a little further to make sure that she would come to peace with the resulting body count.

"There's a place not far from here where all of this trouble began, before you or I were born. Darwin told me he was just a baby when the war between the Merritt's and the Mattocks family began. There was a period of atonement and peace when I was younger. Darwin tried his damnedest to put the fighting to rest and work together. It was his belief that we could all get stronger if we worked together. They put on a good face and said the same and for a time we did get a hold of all the big business up and down the Mantabawa and our own Cut Creek."

"It doesn't look like things were ever peaceful here," Edwin said very quietly.

"No. I think you're right, son. The Mattocks' were always in it for themselves," Godwin said.

"But what business did Darwin do with them?"

"He helped them with transport from the quarry upriver from here. He helped them with the stills, nearly invented the recipe they used that made them famous. The paranoia got to him, and religion. Mother had got wound up in the local Catholic parish, working side by side with the other women, trying to change the way rough men lived and worked. They got caught up in temperance and the evils of drunkenness. Darwin saw the way things were going with the outlaw booze business and made up his mind not to do it anymore."

"But why would Black Rock Runners care what he did?" Edwin said.

"From what Gunther said before he died, they wanted control of the river. When I was younger, Darwin blew up a transport boat of theirs as it came down Cut Creek from the stills set up around the quarry. He rigged the bridge that used to cross on down a mile or two. He loaded some small kegs with black powder and blew the bridge on top of them. The high alcohol booze on board the boat intensified the explosion. Old Man Mattocks said he could hear the explosion from his house out off the east bank of the Mantabawa. Which is a pretty dubious claim."

"What can we do now?"

"We have to fight. It's a war. Not like the last one America went through. It's a blood war. They don't make the papers like the state wars but it's still war. I want to tell you what it means; why it's blood war now. Back home, the three men camping on the stream, you remember them?"

Edwin nodded. "They were part of this?" he asked.

"Yes. The third man who got away from Jack's shooting, he sent word back here over to Black Rock Runners. Gunther knew about your Ma and brother. He knew they were dead."

"God?"

"Yes, son."

Edwin started to cry. Godwin pulled him into his arms. He held him hard and they didn't move except for Edwin's deep, shaking breathing. Edwin pulled away all covered in tears and snot. "They killed Elwin? They shot him in the outbuilding while he was talking to Ma in heaven?"

"I'm sorry, Ed. The third man. I saw his tracks in the snow from my bedroom window that night. I knew there was no way Elwin shot himself. I'm sorry I couldn't tell you 'til now."

Edwin wailed and screamed no words; just the hard anger of raw chords in the cold air that stung his face. Godwin tried to get up and wrap his son in his arms again to calm him. The screaming would do no good right then. Godwin's mind was paranoid and defensive and he had been scanning the woods and river ever since he stepped out of the cabin.

Jack and Godwin dug the graves for the brothers Mattocks on the other side of the water. It was Jack's suggestion. "Let's not desecrate your father's land with the likes of these two," his tone flat as a rail. After the bodies were fully buried and curses spit in turn the men crossed back to Darwin's homestead. The sun was low and the shadows' long fingers stretched into every thought as Godwin sat beside Sawyerskill on a rocking chair his grandfather had built. The action was smooth and without creaking. Godwin was smoothing out the shaft of the new pipe he was carving. A meditation in the slow whittles and smooth sanding down as he rocked beside the water. The graves across the Kill were silent as he made a notch on the shaft of his pipe. The murder of Helmut played across his mind as he slowly dug the notch. He marked the graves with his tired eyes. He returned to his pipe and made a second notch and the bullet went once more into Gunther's head midsentence. He rocked and contemplated his newly finished pipe as he packed a wad of tobacco inside. The smoke rose in a thin prayer from it, Godwin closed his eyes, and almost allowed a sense of relief to overcome him. All at once, the creek was silent. He opened his eyes. On the opposite bank of the creek he saw the silhouette come closer out of the woods. Rough boots splashed water as the man walked across Sawyerskill.

Now, I paid you your silver. I left it right where you told me, in the barrel by the fireplace. Go on, now. Get!

"Is that any way to talk to a soldier? I've got something you need. The keys to the mine?"

I paid you your silver. Go.

The Confederate rags blew away in the breeze.

Chapter 30.

Jack walked into the Regal Hotel in Sawyerskill just after sunrise. The winter morning was too cold for his liking. After he checked in for his overnight stay, he took a long, hot bath; steamed up the bathroom and main quarter with a low lying vapor, as a cloud sits on a mountain road. He crawled to his bed, exhausted by the steam and the whiskey he'd poured down his guts while he languished in the tub. He laid face down and felt the bed or the room or himself spinning. Gently his eyes shut and he slept.

He woke up at sunset and wasn't sure he hadn't slept through the night and was now waking up in the dawn. He didn't care until he remembered he had a rendezvous. He scrambled the sheets of the little narrow bed looking for his pocket watch. A thud down on the floor. He looked and there it was at his feet, face up. There was still an hour to go before he needed to get to the office where Bernard Jefferson "practiced" law.

He was unpacking his shave kit and wishing for hot water in the pot on the table instead of the cold water. A polite knock on the door and he furrowed his brow. Not expecting a soul, he picked up his pistol on the desk, tucked it in his waist, and pulled his denim coat on. "Who's there?"

"Mr. Jefferson sent me. Carter Hemm, here," the voice beyond the door said.

"Why did he send you? How did you know I'd be here?"

"I picked you up at the depot. Followed you. Mr. Jefferson's request. Can I talk inside? It's no small affair."

Silence.

Jack thumbed the hammer on his pistol.

The door unlatched.

The big moose that was Carter Hemm marched into the room until the window turned him back. He was preoccupied with his errand and began pacing a disorganized circuit. At one point he bumped an unlit oil lamp from the table and disregarded it's breaking upon impact with the hardwood. By this time, Jack had a secure handle on his firearm. His guest, of a very loose definition, had unnerved him more than a little.

"So, you cannot go to Mr. Jefferson's office. Under any circumstance. Understood?"

"No, not understood. You're marching and pacing and destroying Regal property is a little distracting," Jack said. "Bernard and I made plans to meet at his office. Now, I assume you really are his messenger but, all due respect, I've never met you before. I intend to go to his office as planned unless you can persuade me with a little more than your word."

"Understood." Carter Hemm stopped his frantic pacing and walked to the table. Only then did Jack see the briefcase Hemm had been holding onto, white knuckled, the whole time. He turned a small key in the lock and popped open the brass latch. From his spot by the door, Jack only saw an empty briefcase. He didn't want to go near the imposing moose, Hemm. Didn't want to go near him any more than a little girl in a Sunday dress wants to pick up the fresh kill in the mousetrap on the kitchen floor. Hemm swept his thick arm and invited Jack to get a closer look.

Jack said, "Looks like an empty briefcase from here. So what?"

Hemm pointed his finger down at it in a repeated stabbing demand.

Jack walked over and saw the severed hand.

"Bernard Jefferson, deceased. The authorities have yet to discover his body," Hemm said.

Jack went for the door. "In over your head," flashed through his mind before attempting to flee. Hemm stomped his foot down on Jack's calf. "Please, don't go just yet. Mr. Hanshaw. Our friend, Frank Miller…of the Copperhead Saloon, has a better proposition for you. Much better than our dear friend," Carter Hemm patted the severed hand the way a mortician reassuring a widow might in the cold eve of a funeral. "Yes, sir. He desires, rightly I believe, that you kill Godwin Merritt and in return after the estate is carved up among the interested parties your due will come."

"Pig sticking son of a bitch," Jack said.

"That's right, Mr. Hanshaw. It's a small world up here in the mountains. New face come into town is damn near front page news. Now, you cut Godwin Merritt down and in return a percentage of the output of Cut Creek Pass shall go directly to the vault of your choosing."

Jack rubbed his calf deep and hard and said, "Just a simple betrayal for a few pieces of silver."

"Oh, come down off that horse. Don't be simple. This is more than a single payday. This is a payday in perpetuity. Think about your future, your kids' and their grandkids'. All set for the rest of their days," Carter said.

"So it's true. There is nothing left to chance."

"Chance doesn't cut the mustard at this elevation, Jack," Carter said.

"No. I suppose you're right."

Carter Hemm opened the door to the hall. A bigger man stepped inside. This man was silent. He was the kind of silent that made others rearrange their thoughts, their preferences, what if anything they would be having for supper. To the end, he was the means.

"I misled you earlier when I said I was here on Mr. Jefferson's behalf,"

"You don't say," Jack said.

"I come with the message Gunther Mattocks paid me to deliver, in person, to you."

Carter could see Jack's chest deflate.

"You forgot about them all, didn't you? Thought all that was just a mess somebody else would be cleaning up in time. Suppose, in a way, you're correct."

"That make you the maid then? Or just a bitch to the big, dumb Swedes back on the Mantabawa?"

Carter's fist hit him hard and with such a force downward, Jack's chin bounced off his shoulder.

Jack spit blood on the floor. "All due respect, of course."

The big guy with the dumb demeanor smacked him in the back of the head. He shook his head to scold him.

"Going to be quite a honeymoon tonight, then," Jack said to the big guy.

"You may want to limit your conversation with my friend. He takes offense to the word, 'please'," Carter said.

"Duly noted," Jack said. He spit more blood onto the wood floor. In the dim room his blood was just a black pool.

"Now, I want you to stay in for the evening. Write a letter to your mum or something. Bigman, here, will keep you company."

"Now why the hell would Gunther Mattocks want me to stay here? And who the hell is Frank Miller to get into this business?"

"That's it. You nailed it, Jack. It's just business and you and I both know that Godwin owes a great deal to his old neighbors. Frank Miller helped your brother in law start that hole in the side of the mountain that's spewed out so much silver he could fund his own economy. Godwin forced him out shortly after the money started piling up. Quite a few stars are lining up to get Godwin Merritt what's owed to him."

"You guys got it all figured out. You're just gonna go up there and lay waste to him and take everything that's his? Well, that's brilliant," Jack said.

Carter looked at his muscle. The big guy's fist hit Jack on the back of his head and he fell to the floor. Knock out.

The door shut behind Carter Hemm and the prisoner and the guard were left to their night.

Chapter 31.

Irvin walked the hall in the kitchen car on the train to the east coast. He walked askew to the walls for the hall was hardly wide enough for a full grown man to walk straight through. The wall that blocked the kitchen was warm and opposite from the windowless wall on the outside. As he stepped across the gap between cars he saw the rail ties and snow in a small gap in the floor which rocked like a boat on the sea. He felt drunk but had sobered before he left town. The run in with Sheriff Smith had not gone his way and he knew it wouldn't have but still did what he had to do. The sheriff could play his end however he wanted but Irvin would walk up to him and tell him the terms had changed given the altered circumstances of his company of lost men.

He sat in a chair in the lounge car. Smoking a cigarette and thumbing a found book, something by a man whose name he could not pronounce and decided it sounded made up or French. It was an interesting catalogue of days and inventories of a man who lived on his own in a wood. It gave him the idea. He could do that. He could disappear as it were. The train was carrying him back to a world he was well entrenched in; knew all sorts of men in society and under it, was able to call a whore or a taken woman with the same ease. He could drink on credit in hotel lounges where presidents and senators stayed. About the only thing he couldn't do was take a shit in the street with the rest of the animals.

He read the book with focused thinking and meditative understanding. He was redirecting his life and it would be for enlightenment or evolution as well as survival. Sheriff Smith had reach. He used to be a federal man but settled out west to run the territory and take his tribute really without restraint. He could send word and Irvin would be found and disappear with no further notice. No one would really look for him in his absence, he assumed. This drove him to seek shelter in isolation. He would become the monk described by the Henry Thoreau he was reading between long thoughts that drew his eyes to the night passing the long windows on the train.

And it's not that he didn't notice the lady sitting behind him on the other side of the lounge car. He saw her plainly in the golden light reflecting the cabin in the window in front of him. He saw her watching him. He saw the man beside her that seemed to not be with her. But a woman riding a train alone was not a common occurrence.

He read his book. He pictured the cabin he would build in which to live simply without drawing interest from locals or passersby. He saw her dress rest above her heels. He saw the curls of her blond hair beneath a bonnet or ribbon, some type of hood undefined in the shadows the light manufactured in the window.

The man beside her left the car without acknowledging her. Irvin pondered the future, the immediate future. Could he become the isolated survivor of this blood war? Could he get that girl behind him and still move on away from her? Would the man be notified if he tried anything whatsoever? Life happens to those who dare, he remembered Sheriff Smith saying once upon a time; long before he shot his deputy and Yeats. And long before he became a professional criminal in the employ of the law.

He watched her in the reflection. He was dizzied by the streaking snow that fell too fast outside the windows of the speeding train. He watched her stand up. She pressed her dress down in front of her legs. She was smiling, but at what, he could not say. He closed the book he'd found and was gently tucking it into the cushion of the chair when he saw the man who'd left her side standing at the door of the car. Irvin had nearly stood to approach her when he saw the man and her walking toward the door. She followed the man out of the car. Irvin's lungs fell flat and he gathered his nerves from the tangle on the floor they'd become anticipating some encounter with this mystery woman whom he was certain had been watching him from behind.

He retrieved the book from the cushion and settled in to read. Page after page, his eyes began to glaze and his mind pulled him out of his chair and took him like a rag doll through the train cars' dim corridors that finally led to his own room in the back, right side of the sleeper car. Irvin laid down in the stiff bed, a bunchy mattress made of bricks and glass for all he could tell. But he was tired beyond care.

The rocking of the train car kept him deep within his sleeping mind and he dreamed of a woman in a dress in the back of the train.

The man outside his door was on bended knee using tools of his own design to work the lock on Irvin's compartment. There was a tiny click of the mechanism. A silent turning of the knob and the hinge creaking like a clockwork. He'd snuffed the light in the hall and no light escaped from the sleeper compartment. A boot struck him in the face before he even rose from his position on his knee. Hands on his throat took him by surprise and Irvin began to yell at him in a slurry of spit and vowels. "What are you looking for? Why are you breaking down my door?"

The man had no idea who Irvin was. He was looking for someone else. He tried to speak, "I didn't..."

Irvin threw fists at the guy. A few shots to his ribs. A couple of good blows to the mouth and a shattering stomp on the man's leg.

"What are you breaking down my door for?"

"I I I I..." the burglar couldn't talk. His jaw might have been broken for all Irvin could tell and he cared even less.

Some doors began to open up the hallway from his room. A man poked his fat head into the hall, "What's the trouble out here? Why are you waking the whole car?"

"Go back to bed, this doesn't concern you," Irvin said.

"You woke us up, I'd say it does, mister," the fat head said.

"This man broke into my cabin. Call the porter and tell him to take him to the lock up."

"Jesus, did you beat him to death?"

"He's still alive. Just get the porter if you want to stick your fat nose into somebody else's business," Irvin said.

The fat head went off toward the other car in his robe and slippers hollering, "Porter! Porter! We have a thief in the sleeper cars." He exited into the next car and Irvin could hear his screaming waking up the whole train as he ran for the porter.

Irvin bent down and spoke quietly to the busted up man in the hallway. "What are you looking for, thief?"

"A woman on board, her purse. I thought she was with you," the man said.

"Are you the man who was sitting beside her in the lounge?" Irvin said.

"Yes, yes. I thought I pegged you two together in some kind of act," he said.

"I thought you were together with her," Irvin said.

"No, I'm a hired man. She has something that doesn't belong to her."

"What?"

"None of your business."

"It is now, thief. You came to my door," Irvin said. "We leave this train together now."

They told a handful of lies to dust off the porter and get to the next stop, a hundred miles away, where they would follow the woman through a maze of clandestine activities. Irvin would be lost to the wind. His isolated cabin in the woods would have to wait. He wanted her more than money.

Chapter 32.

The wrought iron arched over the lane that curved off from the mountain road. Painted white letters framed in the arch read Edwin Merritt Ranch. Edwin was proud of what was his and figured old God would have posted such an arch on this land long ago if he'd only thought of it himself. As it stood, the ranch was now Edwin's to do with as he pleased. And, as the prime operator of the newly flush mine he could spare a grand here and there to spruce up the ranch a little. He pulled on up the road in his truck that chugged along, bounced over knuckled gravel, and he wondered what the modern era would become.

Inside the house he could tell that Godwin had not heard his truck drive up to the front where a new oval lane of ornamental obsidian stone laid on the front lawn. A raised fountain with limestone rim was embellished with antiquated scribbles as Edwin saw it, but the truth of the ages from ancient Greece as Erwin preferred to call them when, infrequently, he was able to return to the Merritt ranch, stood splashing in the center of the oval lane.

"Did you see the paper today?" Edwin said.

His father shook his head no. Godwin's long white beard was stuck to the fleece coat he wore. The soft green coat was worn down to a vestigial rag. The lining had hardened and flaked off at the edges. Stitches hung like dead men's hair all up and down the seams. It smelled of stale fires and carried bad dreams inside like the pocket of a cyclone.

"President McKinley has died. He was shot a couple of days ago, remember?" Edwin said.

Godwin nodded.

"That poor man. I suppose we'll never know what he was assassinated for," Edwin said.

Godwin was sitting in the wheelchair that Doctor Spuss had imported special from an artisan in Nova Scotia. It was a beautiful oak with a light varnish that looked to glow when he was in sunlight or beside a roaring fire. Doctor Spuss had become a regular visitor to the ranch due to Godwin's deteriorated state.

*   *   *

One night, the first year Erwin had gone to college in the east, Dr. Spuss had come to perform his regular examination of Godwin's vision and pulmonary condition. They always had Dr. Spuss stay for dinner and a glass of ale after. Godwin was still fully ambulatory at that time, not so now. After they had gone to the porch to drink their pints in the crisp autumn dusk in the shadow of Echo Cliff, Edwin and Godwin had found themselves unsettled by the absence of Dr. Spuss and Erwin. Godwin hobbled along into the house to investigate and there did find his youngest son and the good doctor in the most intimate embrace he'd ever observed two men not father and son engaged in. He hammered his cane upon the planks underfoot. The doctor sputtered apologies and Erwin protested eloquently. Godwin hastily scurried to the porch and said not a word to the doctor for the few short minutes he remained upon the ranch before forcibly excusing himself toward his own bed to sleep off what he called, "the foul arrogance of hand of Old Scratch," he said, bowing off the porch. "Now excuse me to my own home, where I may rightfully sleep off these inebriated appetites."

Erwin, for his part, chose to stay in the east for over two years before his next visit home. Many letters were sent between the ranch and the Atlantic coast. None of them doing anyone any good but Godwin's stroke and wheelchair bound recovery distilled a tincture of sympathy in the boy who Godwin said had more of his mother about him than his father. A sentiment Erwin never really knew how to digest. Nevertheless, Erwin returned the summer of the stroke that ruined his father. He sat beside his father and explained his love for man while Godwin sat, his mouth appearing to be wired shut just enough to let a small sliver of black show between his lips and two eyes that bugged and shook in fixed orbits above his nose that hung with dense black hairs.

* * *

Edwin dropped the paper that he refolded neat and proper so Godwin could feel as if he were the first one to see the day's news. A long time ago, Godwin taught Edwin how to read a newspaper. He'd said, "It doesn't matter that you read the newspaper, Ed. It matters that you fold the paper up properly when you're done with it so that the next fella that comes along knows you at least have respect for him." Edwin never forgot it.

"God, I've got to go soon. Cut Creek Pass seems to be providing more silver now than it ever has. We're following a new vein and it's yielding big weight."

Through his bent mouth, permanently twisted by what Dr. Spuss said was a stroke, Godwin said, "Good, son. I'm happy for you." He put his hand up and Edwin shook it on his shoulder. The hands he knew had done whatever it took to keep them alive. The hands that buried their own wife and son on his ranch, were then reduced to papery wrinkles over soft bruised meat and bones nearly too weak to hold a glass of water or a fork and knife to cut a steak.

"Tonight the woman I introduced you to last month is coming up here with me to have dinner. After that, we will be going down to town to the theater; some opera she wants to show me. I may take a room in the hotel if we stay out too late. Will you be alright 'til morning if I do?"

"Yes, son," he said through his hanging lips.

He left the ranch, his ranch, the Edwin Merritt Ranch east of Echo Cliff, in his truck. Black paint shined along its creases and curves, gleamed under the darkening sky that held its storm for now. His was the first private automobile in Butte. He rode slowly down the hill, to the road. He went to Cut Creek Pass to oversee the mining of the new vein in a corridor they'd christened just the other day after a celebratory toast at the company party in the bar of the hotel. "To Black Rock Run," his partner had said with his glass of champagne in the air.

The assembled crowd of miners all rejoined, "To Black Rock Run!"

He met her there at the party to celebrate the good fortune of Cut Creek Pass. Thirty-five years and running the mine was still producing revenue and growth. He feared the day when the stats would go the other way and start their decline to the last speck of silver, when they'd have to slap a blockade on the entrance and dissolve the company.

The noise was tremendous. The mountain itself grumbled and shook like a waking beast. It spewed smoke and dust from its mouth. He watched the plume rise and drift and hang in the air. A man walked through the column of smoke toward Edwin. "Ed, this beast can't be stopped. The more we take the more she seems to want to give way," Jack said.

"Uncle Jack, I'm tempted to sell it off and live off the residuals for the rest of my days."

"No, boy, you want to squeeze this thing for every last flake of silver she'll give you. How's God doing today?" Jack said.

"He's up and reading the paper. I think he's glad to have me out of the house most days. I hover like he's an infant but he's lost the strength and some nerve."

"Don't judge him too harshly, Ed. He did every hard thing that had to be done to make sure that you never had to worry about the Mattocks'."

"I don't want to talk about all that. Are the men all doing good? No broken bones?" Edwin said.

"Everyone's alive and whole. We had a close call with the glycerin in Hell Tunnel but it worked out, finally."

"Spillover?"

"Possible. I think they just got ahead of themselves and packed dynamite too close to the powder in the gig holes," Jack said.

Back on the Edwin Merritt Ranch, Godwin was working an old boot, trying to get a sole reinforced with some double twine.

His fingers were gnarled and stiffness in the settling bones made him hurt. The settling fall was pulling leaves again all around the ranch from the grove that Edwin had planted. The orchard had become Edwin's obsession in the intervening years. All day he was tending business with the mine, talking about the old Cut Creek Pass days with Godwin or trimming, touching and talking to his trees. A wide plank on a short post had weathered but a fresh coat of painted letters read, "Freda Elwin Orchard".

Godwin wheeled himself to the great room where Edwin had installed a massive window in the front wall whose roof had been raised ten feet to a gabled facade. The room eliminated in the alteration was Elwin's.

It upset Godwin to no end when the renovation was under way but Edwin casually would remind him, "This is the Edwin Merritt Ranch now, God. I've inherited more than a fortune of silver from you. I also have the bones of my mother and brother in the Edwin Merritt Ranch environs."

The words haunted Godwin's mind just as the lives those bones once carried. But he inherited a blood feud from his father and his father before him. The only satisfaction was that he'd seen it through. The war was over. The journey he'd taken Edwin and Erwin on back to Darwin's homestead decades ago had ended with the defense of Merritt property and principle and what's more, defended Merritt blood.

The trouble with the law was fleeting. During a shootout on Black Rock Runners' still outside the Mattocks house, two deputies were shot dead. The sheriff retreated and called in the federal men. Upon their return they found the remaining Mattocks men hanging upside down in a line of trees. The old man had been decapitated under Godwin's knife as his son watched with Jack's pistol pressed into the back of his head. They made him watch. They'd tried to negotiate. But old man Mattocks was the most obstinate of old timers. He wanted blood. That's what he got. In the great room on the Edwin Merritt ranch Godwin wondered if the old man ever thought it would be his own blood that ended the war.

* * *

The headstone in the cemetery read, "George Arthur Smith." The cemetery was once on the edge of town but now was well inside the town's limits. Irvin found it after asking around. He finally went into the new Sheriff office and said he was an old friend of Smith's. The clerk at the desk said, "I suppose it doesn't break any policy of disclosing residency if he's dead."

"No kidding?" Irvin said.

"About ten years ago. He was shot in his home. A botched burglary was the final legal word on the matter."

"I see. Do you know where he was buried?" Irvin said.

So there he stood, looking at the final resting place of the man who once ran that town. It swallowed him up and left nothing but a bunch of whispered gossip of the truth of how the town was built up.

Irvin thought of his own history in the years since he'd last seen Sheriff George Arthur Smith in the Rouge Suite at Madame V.'s which was now a posh cantina with silver service and black tie wait staff.

All those years ago, the train ride through the winter panorama had turned violent in an instant. But he followed the mysterious lady who'd caught his attention with her incandescent reflection in the lounge car. He and the thief who mistook him for her accomplice followed her through ashen streets in a town just along Lake Eerie.

Along the way, the thief confided he'd been obsessed with her for years; tracking her whereabouts for some jilted husband who'd lost track of her. He said he had been sniffing out the reason; whom she was living with or working for, he knew little. There was some talk of trade in a black market of wayward girls. The rumors outweighed that investigator's facts and soon Irvin began to suspect the thief to be a liar too. When he began to speak of bodies pulled from their graves and carved up in experiments in underground societies, Irvin decided the thief had lost all touch with reality. In an alley behind a building the mystery woman entered they had waited for her to exit. Irvin deceived the thief into turning his back on him. He slid his knife under his ribcage and up toward the heart. He made quick and deep work with his blade and buried the thief under a pile of garbage after looting all identification. Irvin found her exiting the front of the building shortly after, making quick work of a courtship. It was a dark affair that bloomed into a love uncannily true and deep. They found the cabin in a wood that he would build onto, making room for the children she would bear for him.

Along a summer day as Irvin fished the pond around the mountain from where his cabin and family stood, a man came knocking on Irvin's cabin door. The children were found beside the stable. The mysterious woman had all of her secrets laid open and then released from her mortal coil in a gruesome reenactment of Godwin Merritt's actions beside the stream on his ranch one day many years before.

Irvin returned home with many fish, whistling all the way and sure that he'd be happy around his table with the feast he was bringing home that afternoon. They'd eat, wash and sing songs while she played a fiddle on the front porch steps as the summer sun lazily set on the green hills their side of the range.

He came home to a massacre. The rage blinded him. The sorrow folded him. The loss broke him. It was true after all, what the investigator said years ago. The woman they pursued was Worrell Mattocks' daughter. She had run off to escape the violence of her family. Now, it swallowed her up.

They didn't need to leave a calling card that said "Black Rock Runners". They didn't need to telegram him and say, "Hey, pal, did you get our message?"

He would plan his revenge and execute more swiftly than them. They'd waited years to catch up to him. And just maybe that's how long it ultimately took to find him. They may have lost him at any point along the journey from Madame V.'s to the little town along Lake Eerie. He didn't know and it would never matter.

So that outside of the cemetery where Sheriff George Arthur Smith lay rotting beneath the soil, he knew there was only one more left to kill. He may not have gotten to this point on his revenge list had the bulk of the work not been done for him on the Mattocks' land back east from here.

Irvin stopped into a studio on McCormick and asked the photographer there to make a black and white portrait of him. "There's a second part to this deal."

"What's that mister?" The photographer was writing out the ticket number so Irvin could come and pick it up.

"I won't be needing that. This envelope has a letter in it. I want it to remain sealed and I want it delivered along with my photograph to The Rocky. This money here should make it easy for you to oblige me."

"Well, mister, I don't know if I can…"

"If you don't, one of my men will stop by here in a week and make sure you never take another risqué photograph again."

The photographer bit his lip.

"There's nothing to worry about if you just do as I ask."

The photographer nodded.

Irvin left the studio and headed out of town to Cut Creek Pass.

Chapter 33.

They closed the mine for two weeks. A collapse in an old shaft killed nineteen men and the local sheriff had a hell of a time keeping the peace in the county. The survivors wanted Edwin Merritt's head on a platter for not ensuring their safety. They wanted his head for not paying any compensation to the widows and children the men left behind. They wanted his head because he was a bastard. "He sure as hell ain't no Godwin Merritt," Samuel Cluskie told the reporter out of Chicago when asked what the miners were rioting for. "Edwin'll leave you out in the cold and take the socks off your feet if he thinks it'll save him ten cents." The quote enraged Edwin when he saw it in the local paper, The Rocky.

Edwin was in the mine on the last day of the strike to check the new safety measures he'd had put into place. He hired out the job to some out of town men who didn't mind living on the edge. Edwin walked in the mine. He was leaving and climbed toward the entrance of the main shaft. A shuffle of steps behind him made his heart race.

Irvin swung the pick ax through the air, chest high and sunk it clean through Edwin's ribcage exposing the tissue of his heart on the ax head. He couldn't remove it and let the body fall with the ax sticking out Edwin's chest and back. He pulled his wide brim cowboy hat down over his face, which he'd blacked with soot and dirt inside the mine. He passed himself off as a laborer and made his way out of Cut Creek Pass. Irvin headed up the mountain. Decades slipped through his grasp but he was on his way to finish the job he promised.

He walked the way to Godwin's ranch as if someone were guiding his every step.

* * *

Godwin sat in his wheelchair and slept by the fire that burned lower than before. His face was young in the reflection of the window to the foreman's office. The office was dark. It was getting on to five in the morning on a Sunday. Nobody scheduled to work that day. The sawmill operated six days a week. "One for the Lord," the owner always said. Godwin went in that morning to pick up a bag of tools he forgot to take home the night before. Saturday he worked for seventeen straight hours, was too tired, and left his personal tools behind. He walked through the dark mill with a lantern and the silence of the mill put the hairs on his neck out. He couldn't say why at the time but he knew he wasn't alone. As the light from his lantern filled the open area ahead of the main saw a hand tugged the lantern from him and he was struck at the back of the knees.

He tumbled to the hard dirt floor.

"Godwin Merritt, you son of a bitch. God's own ambassador of peace on earth and good will towards men," the voice said. Godwin knew in a moment it was Mattocks. He didn't want this. Wished he'd not journeyed out to fetch his tools. But, his pa had told him they were adding onto the barn so he snuck out and tried to get them before they'd start the work that Sunday morning. Here he was, alone with a Mattocks hell-bent on doing who knows what.

"I don't have no fight with you, Mattocks," he said crawling away to get up.

"You better fight, Merritt," he said and kicked his boot heel down on Godwin's calf. "You fight or you're gonna die and no one's ever gonna see your face again."

Godwin hustled to his feet and turned to fight. He threw wild punches that barely grazed the boy's abdomen. He was Mattocks for sure but he was a younger kid than Godwin. Younger, but bigger. The boy had fists like bricks and when they connected with Godwin's cheek the first time he heard a hell of a loud crack in his jaw.

Godwin picked up a lumber handle in the tussle and hit the boy in the ribs, another loud crack. The boy wrenched the handle out of Godwin's hands and swung towards his head but lost his grip and the thing went flying across the big platform that the steam saw stuck out of the middle of like a jagged fin.

They rumbled around the open area like drunks fighting to lead in a spastic waltz. In their wild fight one of them hit the switch that fired up the sawblade on the platform.

Godwin gained the upper hand and put the boy into a chokehold. He dragged him and his kicking feet to the platform and twisted his body over it. The legs tumbled over themselves and the saw made easy work of the limbs lopping them off at the shins. The boots tumbled across the platform and fell to the floor with his feet still in them. Blood flew in wild arcs while the boy flailed, his neck squeezed between Godwin's arm and chest.

Godwin pulled the hatchet that hung off the platform. He pushed the boy away and buried the hatchet into his face, split his nose like an oak by a lightning strike. The boy, bigger than Godwin but younger, fell to the ground. The hatchet handle hit the ground before the body and split the head open so far that it exposed the brain. Godwin stared at the spinning blade with its red ring along the jagged edge. He went to the kill switch and cut the power. The saw blade made a hollow whirring sound like a musical whistle as it slowed to a stop. He was seventeen in his dream but the words of Red Eagle came to him there though they'd not meet until decades later. Yet, in the nightmare that haunted him whether he was asleep or awake the words of Red Eagle always found their way to the singing saw. His attacker, full of Mattocks blood and sinew, would look up through the pain as the blade made its way through the meat of his leg and begin to smirk. Finally, when the ax handle stuck up from its blade embedded in the

Mattocks boy's skull the corpse laughed as he reminded Godwin in his madness, "Every animal has enough brain to tan its own hide." The saw blade made its last sharp note and Godwin woke up, just the same as always.

It sat on the armrest of his chair. The bone-handled pipe he'd found under Elwin's mattress. The son laid into his final resting place would have wanted his father, upon his return from the vengeful expedition to the Mantabawa, to the home of his ancestors, to the land soaked in feud blood and curses, to have his precious pipe back in his possession.

Outside, a shadow fell upon the steps of the porch. The rain that had given way to a chill wind had done the work of washing the dirt from his face and he was mostly identifiable.

His boots thumped the planks of the porch.

Godwin sat in the great room in his wheelchair with a blanket over his legs and a pistol under the blanket. He heard a knock on the front door.

As slow as a slug half poisoned by salt he rolled himself around to the door. His hair was long and white. His face ran with deep wrinkles around a mouth twisted by a stroke. Moreover, the wheelchair had made him weak, frail to the point of shattering in a breeze. He struggled to open the door and roll around to see whom it was that knocked on his door.

An older man stood across his threshold. A wide gray hat held in his hand over his belt buckle. A salt and pepper moustache as thick as they come pointed down toward a stubble-shaded chin. *Damn it, I paid you your silver, Lieutenant Smith. I put the satchel in the barrel beside the fireplace just like you said.*

The man spoke. "Are you God?" He drew back the hammer on the pistol behind his hat.

Godwin Merritt handled the pistol under his blanket. "Do you have a gun?"

"They say every animal has enough brain to tan its own hide, Mr. Godwin Merritt."

Two gunshots blew the men away like pheasants out of the October sky.

Irvin's body lay crumpled on the porch.

Godwin's lifeless body remained upright in his wheelchair, mouth agape. Whoever would happen upon the scene, be it the new sheriff, Erwin Merritt, or a straying crow, they would see Godwin locked in stone, eyes widened in his final moment of terror, mouth open wide when Irvin's bullet pushed his soul up into the brisk wind.

From the ashen sky fell a mercifully quiet snow.

It happened on the Godwin Merritt Ranch east of Echo Cliff.

Acknowledgments

The author wishes to thank a few people for their contributions in the making of this book. Readers who helped with the initial read through of the manuscript: Gabriel R. Miller, Michael McCrite, and Anders Urbom. Nicole Tone for editing services.

END NOTES

[i] confluence. Dictionary.com. Dictionary.com Unabridged. Random House, Inc.http://dictionary.reference.com/browse/confluence (accessed: March 07, 2015).

[ii] kill. Dictionary.com. Dictionary.com Unabridged. Random House, Inc.http://dictionary.reference.com/browse/kill (accessed: March 07, 2015).